The
Counsellor Heart

by the same author

The Brandenburg Hotel
Death of an Angel
Gallows Child
The Witch Hill Murder
Copper Gold

The Counsellor Heart

PAULINE GLEN WINSLOW

St. Martin's Press
New York

Library of Congress Cataloging in Publication Data

Winslow, Pauline Glen.
    The counsellor heart.

    I. Title.
PZ4.W78Cq 1980   [PR6073.I553]   823'.9'.14   79-25350
ISBN 0-312-17014-9

In all the world of earth, one man has been born,
one man alone has died.

Jorge Luis Borges
The Gold of the Tigers
(Translated by Alasteir Reid)

With thanks to R.H.T. and L.S.
for technical assistance

PROLOGUE

1 MAY

Just before eight o'clock on a fine morning, Holmwood Road was still quiet. A small street between Belgravia and Kensington, it was out of the main flow of traffic and on either side chestnut trees in candle gave it a pastoral air. Milk bottles stood on the steps and cats hid in bushes, watching the chirping sparrows.

A light blue Austin, going westward, had the road almost to itself. The driver, a woman with an eager look, was smiling. A hundred yards behind her was a silver Mercedes, sparkling in the sun. She had given it an admiring glance and then forgotten it. Suddenly the silver car put on a burst of speed. It was gaining rapidly and had edged into her lane. She could not pull further left, she was already near the kerb – the car would scrape her side.

Just ahead Holmwood Crescent curved off south and east. Spinning the wheel violently, she made the turn as the Mercedes came level. As she pulled up, she found herself in a narrow cul-de-sac where the chestnuts spread to form a tunnel and the morning light was filtered through the dense green leaves. Her heart was thumping and there was sweat on her palms.

The Mercedes swung after her – to apologize, no doubt. Three youthful figures tumbled from the car, two boys and a girl – they wore masks over their faces. Just back from some party – a special party? Today was May Day. One of them poked a thing that looked like a gun. Another pulled at the car door, and two of them grabbed and jerked her out. Her foot twisted and scraped and her shoe came off but before she could cry out she was bundled into the other car.

She looked up and saw one of the youths spraying the windscreen of the Austin with bright red paint. MAYDAY. Students –

'What am I supposed to be?' she said. 'Queen of the May?'

One of the youths laughed. The girl turned swiftly. Something glimmered in her hand. The woman gasped with pain as a needle jabbed into her arm and then the world went dark.

ONE

3 MAY

When Bridey woke the blindfold was slipping a little on the bridge of her nose. Her hands were still tied tightly behind her back; her wrists were sore. The floor beneath her struck damp and chill through her skirt. Yet the weather had been quite warm – The cellar. She remembered the cellar – a blow to her mouth. There was still a taste of blood though her mouth was dry. The wall at her back was chill, too.

Yes, she was still in the cellar: the air was stale and damp at the same time. Her head ached. Somewhere in the room there was a pail that had been used. She thought she remembered having woken before and being taken to that pail – or had she dreamed it? Her mind was fuzzy. Though she couldn't remember eating she certainly wasn't hungry; she felt sick. How many days, she wondered, had she been here?

And where was she? They had given her something in the car – a needle – more than once. The car – it seemed a long time ago, but it could have been yesterday, or last week. She only remembered the car, the door, the cellar steps. If she had been in a plane or a boat, she had no recollection. Water – did she remember a gleam of water, or was it just a jumble in her mind? The blindfold had been put on in the cellar, not before, so perhaps –

For whatever reason, she felt sure she was still in England, or Great Britain anyway – why, she didn't know. She took a breath to try to clear her head – it was the damp, the damp and the smell of disinfectant, Jeyes fluid. Yes, this was a British cellar. Except for that pail it smelled like all the British cellars she ever remembered, even the cellar at Lawdon Court which the housekeeper used to send her to scrub once a week, or mushrooms would grow in the corners. When she had finished scrubbing she would go outside to throw the dirty water down the drain and idle a moment if it was not too cold, smelling the soft air of Somerset, so much like that of home, laden with water, fresh through the year, and she would stare up, blue skies, grey skies, drifting cloud until, very often the housekeeper would call – Don't wander, she told herself sharply with a frightened clutch at her belly. You must think. The words in her head turned into old Miss Leary at the village school; think, think Bridey, you'll never made a scholar like your sisters.

Think! What was wrong with her mind? She concentrated, trying to puzzle out what had happened. It would be easier for them to keep her in the country rather than trying to smuggle her out. Yet she remembered screaming when she came to the first time – she was being dragged into the cellar – and they hadn't bothered to put a gag on her. So there was no one nearby to worry about, if anyone could hear at all.

They. Them. She gave a long shudder. One of them was in the cellar now. A light breathing came from somewhere close – probably the girl. If it was the same one. She felt almost sure that she hadn't been alone since it happened. Not when she was conscious at all.

How long could she have been here? Charlie must be looking for her, but did he know she was kidnapped? She hardly ever stayed a night from home. He must know that. The Yard would be searching for her, but how could they know where to look? If only she'd screamed or done something to attract attention when they first dragged her off, instead of doing what she'd done, making silly jokes.

At first she couldn't really believe it. Eileen, her elder sister, had always said she was a fool. Giggling and playing about when she was supposed to be working; buying a lace-trimmed petticoat instead of saving for a rainy day. All the years she had been puffed up with herself; because she was glad to be Bridey Lawdon and not Eileen, still Collins at fifty, although Eileen was headmistress at her school; as though her silliness were something special. Look where it had got her, Eileen would say. Eileen, with a face like a rock now and her hair carved in it. Always knew what she was doing. If anyone tried to kidnap her they would get as good as they gave.

Stupid Bridey. She had been going to Alma, who had decided not to get rid of the baby after all. Bridey had found a couple who wanted a child, and all the arrangements were made and waiting for the lawyers to have finished. So she was going over because the girl had five months to go and might need cheering up. A silver Mercedes had swung very close, nearly driving her up on the pavement, and she had hastily pulled away into the side street, lined with chestnuts, which was a dead end.

Fool that she was, she had been afraid of scratching the pretty silver car – let alone Cynthia's Austin. Cynthia was always so good about lending it – twice last month the Mini had broken down, and now again. The young people had been out of the silver car in seconds, and even with them dragging and pulling at her, she had not been able to take it seriously. It was the shock – and make-believe. As if she didn't admit it was real, then it wouldn't be. It was a good thing Eileen could never know that.

Sensation, sharp, acrid, jolted up through the queasiness, familiar as though she'd never outgrown it: hot, dumb, shame.

When her parents found out from the teachers that she was a dunce, she couldn't raise her eyes from the ground.

'Well, the girl's good enough with the cows,' her mother had said, not caring at all about the books. And Charlie hadn't cared either. He only laughed at her a little sometimes for reading only the picture papers, but no laughter to make her burn, even when he searched for something in the kitchen drawer and found the paper romances with pictures that she liked to look at when he was out for the night. No one had laughed at Mrs Charles Lawdon, or called her stupid, and she had thought the heat was gone with the growing pains, but it had been there all the while, just hiding, waiting for its time.

The thin boy had taken out a can of spray paint and squirted it all over the windscreen of the Austin. Had they meant to kidnap Cynthia? They would be disappointed. She remembered the thin young arm wielding the spray, and the word MAYDAY. And the girl had pulled out the syringe, and instead of screaming what had Bridey done? Made a foolish joke.

She rubbed her head on the wall behind her. It was cold, damp, and rough. She could get the blindfold down, but what was the use? If they saw, they would tie it on again. Especially the girl. And it was the girl there. Both of the boys breathed harder, and one of them occasionally fell asleep and snored. Memory came in bits, but she could only remember the three of them. Others could have come in, and she not have noticed in her drugged sleep.

It was the snoring one who had given her water and helped with the pail. Her cheeks flamed as she recalled it. She had been as docile as a child – there must have been something in those injections besides sleeping stuff. That hadn't been the girl. As soon as the girl had seen her, her eyes had been angry. Bridey stumbled when she was brought into the cellar and the girl had struck her across the face. Perhaps she had taken the stumble for an attempt at escape. Bridey had tasted blood in her mouth.

  Much better that the girl didn't know Bridey had come to. She had to think, and carefully. If they had meant to kidnap Cynthia – that would explain why the girl was angry when she had a good look at her – it might have been done for money. Gervase and Cynthia weren't rich, but the kidnappers probably wouldn't know that. She and Charlie didn't have any. Not even ordinary savings, let alone enough for kidnappers. That was her fault, she'd never been a good manager. If they wanted ransom money, where would it come from?

Or had they meant to take herself? Even in Cynthia's car, with the scarf on her head, she still was nothing like Cynthia, tall, fair, and well dressed. I still look like the kitchenmaid, she thought, even after all these years. But she had picked up the car at Cynthia's ... She didn't know. If they had really wanted herself it was worse, because then they would want information. And she didn't have any. If they thought she knew Charlie's business they were wrong. He never spoke of his work at home.

Perhaps they would torture her. She shivered. She'd

always been a coward; never able to stand a bit of pain. It was one of the things she'd been ashamed of, even as a child. She used to prick her finger with her sewing needle to try to learn to be brave. Funny, she had forgotten that till now. It never worked. At the sight of blood her insides had gone to water, and she would holler so much at the sight of her own blood that Mam would wrap up her finger in a bit of cloth and give her a biscuit with sugar on it. As a grown-up woman she had tried not taking aspirin when she had a headache, but she gave in, or else would make herself a cup of hot tea and fill it with sugar, like a great baby. Torture? – her insides were water already.

It was no use thinking. If they had meant to take her, then they were terrorists who wanted something from the government. And they were too young – they could be students still – to be criminal extortionists in the ordinary way. Perhaps they thought that as Charlie's wife she was important, although she wasn't. A Chief Superintendent at Scotland Yard wasn't important – Charlie always laughed, and said the great test was the loo, and he still had to walk down the corridor like all the rank and file. He worked so hard she thought he should have some honour, even if it was only a private WC.

Now here she was with a stinking pail for all her pride, and not even a moment alone to use it. It was mad – there was no sense in any of it. To pull her, Bridey Lawdon, from the road, from her life, to put her here – and she who could be of no use to them at all. Her thoughts ground through her head. With all the important people that there were it *was* mad. Her head ached so much she wished she could stop thinking. If only she could have a cup of tea. Suddenly it seemed strange that that had gone with everything else. Tea – always as handy as the nearest kettle and tap, and now that gone to nothing unless these youngsters chose –

Her bottom and back were sore. She moved – she must have bruises, because that hurt worse. She wondered how long she had half-sat, half-lain where she was. The chill of the floor went right through her. It was the blessing of God it was warm outside; the place must be freezing in winter.

A tattoo beat against the wall. The girl was tapping from impatience. Not used to being cooped up. But *she* was free to come and go. If it's just the three of them they must be taking eight-hour shifts. The tattooing stopped, and quick steps sounded; she was pacing up and down. Not a long-suffering one. Perhaps her relief was late.

Bridey felt a longing to move the blindfold and see where she was and look at her captor, masked or not. But perhaps it was still dark. If there was any light in the cellar surely it would penetrate the blindfold, now that it had eased. Oh, God – would they keep her in a place with no light at all? She couldn't bear it, to be buried alive – No, she calmed herself. They wouldn't be willing to sit in darkness, day and night.

The pacing stopped, and then began again. Bridey tried to remember what the girl had looked like. All she had seen were eyes through the masks; the girl's and those of one of the boys had been dark and shining. Clothes ordinary enough not to be remembered. Blue jeans and shirts. The shoes – it was a long time since she'd polished a family's boots and shoes, but to this day she still took notice – the dark ones wore shoes of soft leather that wrapped round their feet with an expensive look. The fair boy wore a workman's half-boot that certainly had never been near a cleaning rag. And the girl, tall and thin, had carried herself like a duchess.

What had she, Bridey Lawdon, fallen into? Alma, what must Alma have thought when she didn't come – but she would know now from the papers and the telly. Would she change her mind? With her friends all telling her it was so much easier to have the 'abo'. No one else from St Anne's would go, because Alma had asked her to say nothing, and she had kept her word. Perhaps that was one life gone already, and a girl with a sin on her conscience.

All at once, though she'd been sitting quite still, Bridey felt dizzy, or something like it. She hardly knew if she were spinning in the cellar or if the cellar was spinning round her. Suddenly a picture of Sister Alphonsus came into her head, gaunt, forbidding, and, just as quickly, faded away.

There was one thing she could do, Bridey thought, and that was say her prayers. No good letting her mind wander. Not seeing anything so long was making *her* mad, hearing this young, doubtless good-looking girl, and seeing the face of Sister Alphonsus. The children had believed she knew everything, to the last hidden little sin. Clump, clump, her heavy tread to the cottage doors, bang, bang with her fist, and when her business was over with the woman of the house she would look down on the nearest child and say, 'Be sure your sins will find you out.' The child, in dreadful fear, would swear to itself to be good and say its prayers, until the days went by and the visit was forgotten. Sister Alphonsus, she must be dead these many years.

Her beads were in her bag, of course, lost as it was so often. Even Charlie, who was so good, would sometimes say, for heaven's sake, can't you find one place for it and keep it there? Then he would laugh and say he spent more time looking for her bag than he did looking for criminals, and she wouldn't worry any more. She would have to pray without her beads. She screwed her eyelids tight as if that way she could shut out the light tread of the girl, and tried to gather herself together and pray to St Anne to rescue her and save the child that was to be born.

When she finished her prayers she noticed the girl's pace had quickened. Definitely not patient. Not many young people were. Bridey remembered the girl's carriage and her hands. She saw her hands clearly. Thin, olive-skinned, strong – she remembered the blow to her mouth, and winced – the nails beautifully manicured. She had noticed more than she realized. The boy, the fair one, he had had hands like a mechanic's, big and square under the fingernails.

Bridey tried to feel her own fingernails, wriggling the rope on her wrists behind her back. Perhaps she could tell how long she had been a prisoner by their length. But although she could feel them she hadn't much idea. What a fool, she couldn't think how long they'd been before. Couldn't remember when she'd last looked. There was that manicure set she had got as a wedding present, still like new, the box lined with silk, the tortoiseshell gleaming. When a nail grew long she used Charlie's clipper.

The rope on her wrists was tight, and chafed as she moved. Her arms ached all the way up – their position was pulling the muscles, and her circulation was probably affected. She moved her arms a little, cautiously. She must move about. In a Red Cross class she had learned the results of slowed circulation: gangrene if it was bad. Her captors might decide to let her have exercise, but they were young, and perhaps they didn't know such things. Or didn't care ...

Of course, they thought her still unconscious. She would have to let them know she had come to, but she was afraid of another needle. What they were giving her she couldn't imagine, but she felt awful, as though her breath smelled. How long could it have been since she'd eaten? She'd made a quick cup of tea in the kitchen that last morning. She'd been alone, Charlie had not come home that night. She'd left the pot unemptied, the dirty cup and saucer in the sink in her haste to be gone: the blue willow-pattern. She hoped nothing had happened to that. Then she'd snatched a slice from a cut loaf as she left, no butter, she'd been trying to lose weight. Very likely she had, now.

A step approached – a heavy tread. Her heart banged. Was this the torture? What could she say? Sometimes, she remembered, Charlie had told her a bit about his day, but not since he was assigned to Special Branch. He was good, Charlie, and naturally he would have thought for her feelings, whatever they were.

A light tread; Miss Impatience. A door opened with a squeak, and then banged. By the sound the door was heavy, but Bridey could hear the voices, faintly, from outside. An old house, the doors were a bad fit. She strained to hear. The girl's voice, high and sharp; a low, grumbling sound – it could be the fair boy.

Bridey was alone. Now was her chance. She wriggled her head against the wall, bending her neck and nodding, in spite of the throb over her eyebrows. Rearing up, she angled the top of her spine flush to the wall, and then, with a heavy scrape to the back of her crown, the blindfold lifted at the back and slipped right down her nose.

She opened her eyes wide: they were sore, and the lids

scraped, as if there were no juice in her. Her sight was blurred, and she had trouble focusing. She blinked, squinted and stared, and realized that there was no lamp on, but the room was in a greyish haze. A dim light was coming from outside; it was late evening, perhaps, or very early morning. She looked round but couldn't make out much. The source of the light was high on the side wall. Her eyes hurt, and she blinked.

The door opened, and she froze, pretending to be still asleep.

'... not eight o'clock,' he was saying. 'Haven't finished my breakfast.'

The voice was West Country Irish – the voice of her own youth. It could be her own brother talking, her father, or her cousin Rory himself. But this boy was fair, square-built, stolid. Not the dark, hot-eyed Irish like Rory. The girl had dark, bright eyes, but passion-cold, not passion-hot. Bridey's mind danced off – Pease-pudding hot, pease-pudding cold, pease-pudding in the pot nine days old. She caught herself up – could this be delirium? Her cold hadn't been that bad, though it had gone to her chest a bit. Charlie had said to see the doctor. But the cellar was real. It wasn't going to go away and she wake up in her own bed. She was there until someone found her – but how could they? She shut her mind to that.

Rory. She had been thinking of Rory. But she didn't want to think of him either. Why had she been surprised that the boy was speaking English? The others had struck her as foreign, she realized. Though why ... the olive skin, the aquiline lift of profile under the mask? The dark boy didn't move like a British boy. He was as graceful as the girl. A pair, they could have been brother and sister, but hers was the greater arrogance – she was the leader. The thought of the girl made her shiver. It was very foreign, that intense, vicious enmity – Rory would laugh at that.

To Rory it was the English who were that vicious – the tales he would tell, and some of them must be true. Yet it was hard for her to believe. In all the years she had known so much kindness and thoughtfulness. And what did the English owe her, a penniless servant who had come to England, willing to work, that was true, but with heaven knows what jumbled loyalties and hopes, let alone the knowledge of Rory and his men? God forgive her, she had never told Charlie about Rory, but perhaps he knew. It would be like him to be silent all the years.

What a world. She had always tried not to think about such things: it's all too deep for me, she had decided. And now she was a prisoner, a prisoner like an English soldier kidnapped over the border, an Irishman in Long Kesh camp, except she was a prisoner of her own. It was just as it would be. The things she had refused to think about had come to think of her.

The door banged shut and a key grated in the lock. But she was not alone. The Irish boy – he breathed heavily, with a slight whistle coming from his nose. He gulped – he brought his tea with him. For a moment she thought she would give all the six counties, if she had them, to anyone in the world for a mug of tea. Then fear struck again; she'd forgotten to crawl her head back under the blindfold, and she tried to wriggle down. But the boy must have seen her head move towards that tea like a dog to its dish, for he strode towards her, and she smelt his sweat as he leaned down. She tensed herself, ready for a blow or another blindfold, or both, but instead the mug was thrust at her parched lips.

The wet and the taste of the tea made her so grateful she nearly cried, and she swallowed in great gulps; the nausea subsided. The boy's smell was strong, and not just from today either – heavy things not washed. He had no woman. His girl partner was not the sort to wash a man's clothes. There was kindness in him to give the tea. As she drank, the blindfold had fallen completely to her chin. No use to pretend any more.

He still wore the mask. Next to him, on the floor, was a tin tray with a meal – water and bread. He drew a piece of cheese from his pocket and put it to her mouth.

She nibbled, but it was hard to eat, and another wave of nausea went over her.

'You can untie me, surely,' she said. 'I'm not the world's

champion boxer to be knocking you out, great lad that you are.'

His light eyes stared out through the mask – she could swear he was embarrassed. He turned his back and walked away, to sit hunched in the corner. She wondered how long he had been one of 'our boys'. Not long. This was his first abduction, she guessed. Nothing like the lads who had gone and shot Molly McClinchy just a year ago and her nursing an infant, all because she had once gone out with an English soldier when she visited her auntie in Belfast. They thought she had to do with two of Rory's men being caught, and not a hair had they turned; she had had it all from Eileen. Eileen, who had seen a lot in her time, but she had been sick at heart.

Did they mean to shoot her, Bridey Lawdon? Her stomach leapt to her throat. The taste of cheese was sickening. She couldn't die. There was Charlie, Alma, the Red Cross – the pile of flowered stuff still in a heap by her sewing machine. She had seen it in a good shop, so bright, so smart, with a touch of silk in the cotton, dear beyond reason. She had yearned for it as a young girl yearns for a lover. Then she had seen the last few yards in the sale and rushed in and snapped it up, using all the week's food money, and carried it off in triumph, treating herself to an éclair for tea to celebrate her new living-room curtains. Don't be a fool, she told herself. What do curtains have to do with anything? The priest would say, if the Lord wants you – But there was nowhere in her she could feel the Lord would want her before her jobs were done. Not even the curtains finished. You're a pagan, Bridey, the priest said, when he gave her a penance for some other foolishness.

She tried to think sensibly, but there was no sensible reason now she was captured why she shouldn't be shot. Thirty-five pounds in the bank – she had given fifty pounds to St Anne's for Easter, Lord knows they needed it, but it had been a bit of showing off, too. Gervase and Cynthia's was family money and tied up in knots. The government would hardly give up anyone of importance in exchange for her. She was only important to Charlie, and even he didn't need her any more. It was a long time since Charlie was a young man at odds with his father, not knowing what to do with himself, glad to hang round a young and willing maid in the kitchen. He had long been established and as steady as could be.

And she remembered Charlie saying – why did she have to remember that, when she remembered so little of policemen's talk? – that the government had decided never to give in to terrorists; it merely spread the plague. Only one exception had been made, for a plane-load of schoolchildren. Charlie said they were right. She could hear his voice clearly and see his face. Charlie, with his serious English face, so sensible, so kind, with a lock of hair that still wanted to fall on his forehead so that he was always having it cut short; a little grey now in the brown, his cheeks not so pink as they had been, but he still made her think of a little boy, middle-aged as he was. His smell that she loved, soap and talcum powder.

Sitting here in the grey half-light she was thinking of Charlie as if he were dead. In the past. But he was outside, looking for her, she knew that. He, and Mr Manning, and her friend Merle most likely. And others. Very clever men.

Those good thoughts put no heart into her. Rory had been in England, many times for all she knew, and they'd never caught him. A nation of schoolboys, Rory called them. They had run the world and never understood it. Not understanding was their great quality, it made life easier, Rory said. And much more, for he was a great talker. He should have been an actor or a priest, but he kept his fine voice for whispering in corners abroad and at home, talk and argue all night long. He had called her a traitor when she married Charlie, and she a young girl puffed up with love and pride. Had she been? She wondered, now.

Time went by, and she had no watch and nothing to tell the time but the breathing of the boy, who had fallen asleep in the corner and was snoring again. Yet it was a little lighter than it had been. Day was coming, and finding its way into the cellar. She could make out green streaks of damp on walls that had once been whitewashed plaster, but now the plaster was flaking off, bit by bit.

An Englishman and a policeman – Rory couldn't believe it. Charlie had only just joined the Force. She had wanted to be married from her own village, the Lawdons would have been pleased to have gone, and how proud she would have been, but her father had decided against it. The Troubles were long since over, and she couldn't understand, and had thought it only Rory, fanatic that he was. She had been married in England, from Lawdon Court itself, where she had first gone as a servant, green as green. And only her father and Eileen on her side of the church, Kathy already in the convent, and none of her old friends and neighbours to wish her well. But she and Charlie were already making friends and it would have been a happy time, but Rory had come from nowhere the night before, appearing and disappearing before the sun rose, his hawk-like profile black against the silver mirror of her window, to put a shadow on her day. For a wedding present he had given her a lashing with his tongue to make her cry.

'I know your kind,' he had said. The words had stayed with her over the years. 'You'd be glad if we dropped dead, every last man of us. Then you could heave a sigh of relief, couldn't you now, and mourn for us once a year in your fine English house, and talk to a few Irish friends when you've all a drop taken about the good old days, and pretend you were all good IRA supporters, safe in the knowledge that nothing could ever happen to disturb your fine English life, by God.'

Was it Rory who had sent these children for her? Was she to die like a dog at the hands of her own? For a moment she flared with anger at her cousin and his ways; Bridey's temper, blazing out of control – she hadn't felt it for more than half her lifetime. She had thought that was gone, too, but she was burning now. Rory – they had played together when she was a child and he only a lad. And when she was older had she not washed and baked for him and run his errands, and all unknowing what he was about? Almost unknowing, she had to amend, as she cooled a little, because in truth she neither understood nor cared much, then.

And wasn't there a time, later – she grew angry again –

when Rory had an eye to her, as a man to a woman? But of course, nothing had mattered to him except his cause, and she had had to go to England because there was no money to keep her at home. After her mother died her father had married again and there was hardly room in the place for two women of different blood.

The boy stirred; his boots scraped the floor and brought her back to the cellar. What was she dreaming of? What was she to Rory now that he would spare her if he could? Anyway, sense told her these were not his people. If he were to kidnap, he would take someone of value. Besides, although the young man snoring there could be one of his, those others – Rory had never liked to work with foreigners, he trusted none of them. And his discipline was harsh. She couldn't imagine the dark-eyed boy and girl taking Rory's orders; the girl looked as though she had never taken an order in her life.

Outside, feet crunched down on gravel. Bridey tensed, opened her mouth to scream, but the scream strangled in her throat. Perhaps it was another one of them – someone come to – The pain in her head banged wildly, and she was sick. Fool, she told herself. What difference does it make, one more? The three of them can kill you if they want – the girl would do it without a thought, Bridey knew that.

She lay back, trembling. Footsteps sounded overhead and then faded, and it was quiet again. Her heartbeat slowed. Soon she looked at the water in the dish. She leaned sideways, almost falling, and dragged her hips along the wall so that she could reach. It was cool; very rusty, but it cleared her foul mouth. When she felt better she looked round again.

Yes, it was an English cellar, she was almost certain. Thank God for his good light. It came from high on the side wall where there was a small barred window. With the stronger light, her spirits rose a little. If she had been kept right underground, with no look at sunlight, that would be the worst. She remembered her friend, Merle Capricorn. Poor Merle, with his claustrophobia that made him ashamed – now she understood. She thought how he must have been, a little boy put to work by his selfish old devil of a father, buried under six feet of earth to enhance his father's act, in all the timeless horror of the world of a child. While she was in darkness she had known a child's fear.

Now she managed to gnaw a piece of bread, snatched up with her teeth, then wriggled back until she was sitting up. A beam of sunshine divided itself through the bars. The scraping of the skin of her wrists sobered her; she couldn't move much, her wrists might be bleeding now. And no one to make her wince with iodine here. Her legs stuck out awkwardly in front, giving her the look of a trussed chicken.

Still, she *wasn't* trussed, she could wriggle – She drew her feet towards her, trying not to drag the heel of her one shoe and wake the boy, tugging on belly muscles she had not used in a long time, and lowered her knees to the right until calf and thigh lay along the floor. With a hard thrust from her fingertips on the wall behind her she pushed herself forward until she was perched on her knees and toes. The ankle-rope was tight, but she could manage to move her toes enough to walk. Each step was no more than an inch, but the shoe scraped on the cellar floor with a noise that was thunderous in her ears.

Her heart pounding, she watched the boy, but he snored away placidly. He was like her brother Jack, she thought in swift relief, Jack who could never rouse himself to do the milking, and had her father's wrath on his head, until, in a fit of temper, he had gone off to America. Cautiously, she dragged herself towards the light. It would take half the day to cross the floor at this rate. Someone might come in – whoever had crunched the gravel. No use to think. She hadn't got far, but her knees flared with pain. Put your mind on something else when you have a hurt, Mam used to say. The dank puddle in the corner, the water had got in a long time ago. The rising damp. Think of Jack in America – they had heard little from him after he arrived there and Bridey always wondered if some poor woman was trying to get Jack up of a morning and being cursed for her pains.

Pains – she must have bruised her kneecap and jarred her

thigh-bones besides. And why she was struggling she didn't know. The window was too high, and it was barred – but bars in an old building could be loose – Fool! Without loosing her hands and reaching up she could never touch them. She moved on, anyway. It was better than sitting like a lump.

When she had crossed half-way she made out a dark shape in the far corner. It was a wooden box. She drew in her breath. Just an old crate that had held bottles, but it was over a foot and a half high. If she could stand on that she would be as high as the window; she could see out; she could look at the bars, she – Veering round, though it was an extra, painful, four or five feet away, she made for the box. She remembered the mermaid whose every step felt as though she walked on knives.

You're getting old, she thought; in her comfortable life she hadn't noticed, and her vanity wouldn't let her admit it. A little stiffness in her fingers only on a cold morning. It meant nothing. Not that she was not due for that time of a woman's life, overdue if she faced the truth. Not that it mattered. Years before the doctors had said she could have no children.

Pain shot up through her hip, and she almost lost her balance. Keep your mind on what you're doing, girl. She scrambled on. When she was a few inches from the box she craned her neck to watch the boy, but he was still breathing steadily. Even with that silly mask he looked like that blessed sleeper Jack.

Twisting her head and neck to the left she got her nose to the side of the crate and pushed sideways, scraping, shoving, using her head like a cat's until the box, not too heavy, thank the Lord, moved a little. As she pushed she struggled into the emptied space, then pushed the box further and wriggled after it. Then it was easier, she just butted it forward with the crown of her head until it was under the window.

Then the hard part came. She used her shoulder to wedge the box flush against the wall. Turning, thankful to get off her knees with her tights ripped away and her skin scraped, she sat on top of the box. If only she were thinner; there was no room for her feet. She wriggled to one side, leaning the other way so that the empty crate wouldn't topple, and swung her feet into place. Her heart pounded against her ribs as she centred her feet on the crate, face to the wall her rear end stuck out for balance. She got a shoulder against the wall, but the crate tottered; she swayed; she was going to fall; the boy would wake; she'd break her back – it settled again, and she rose until she was standing at full height on the box, her head at the window.

Air blew on her face – the glass was long gone, with only dark jagged shards at the base. She touched the bars with her face – rusted and rough. But they were only six inches apart. She butted them fiercely with her crown. Reaching up on tiptoe she pounded till her head sang; the bars rattled, but they held. The concrete base, she could see, was crumbling – but not enough. Never could she get through, even if by some miracle she could haul herself up. Lashed with disappointment, her eyes filled with tears, and she bit her lip so hard that again she tasted blood.

She was crushed by the defeat, even though there had been no chance of victory. Crying, sobbing out loud, she leaned her head against the bars. She stood for what seemed an endless time, with the boy hawking and snoring away in his careless freedom. He, in the cellar like herself, and yet still belonging to the world of ordinary men and women. She knew she must control herself. She closed her eyes and said a prayer for patience and courage.

Trying to blink the tears away, she peered beyond the bars. As her eyes dried she could make out that there was not much of a view; the sill was set at the level of the ground, but at least she could see a patch of grass sprinkled with daisies basking in the warm and golden sun. Slowly, very slowly, her disappointment drained away. She could see the blades of grass quite distinctly now, and a buttercup glowed at the edge of her vision. A bee hovered above it in careful deliberation, and then lowered itself to the sweet centre. Somewhere, not far off, a wood pigeon called, plaintive, sweet. As she gazed and listened, her cheeks still wet, her frantic mind was soothed, and when a butterfly winged down to touch the grass her spirit lifted and for one instant she was close to joy.

TWO

4 MAY

'Very warm for May,' the ticket collector was grumbling.

Chief Superintendent Capricorn emerged from the Underground at his East London destination against the press of passengers going the other way. A woman hurtling by almost pushed him back through the barrier, but his tall body held its ground. A touch of his old, almost forgotten trouble, claustrophobia, had given him a brush in the long tunnels, and he was relieved to be in the street. The relief was forgotten in disgust, for the first thing he saw was a shabby man in his sixties at a magazine stand, furtively buying a copy of *Fawn* magazine.

The blonde, vapid face of Muffy Mirro grinned lasciviously above a large, bare expanse of bosom, apparently oiled to catch the eye. She looked like what she was, Capricorn thought with a sourness unusual in him, a candidate for a sex killing. But he was not his usual self on this bright – too bright – day, with the sun already striking warmly into the street. He had never started a case with such – reluctance hardly described his feelings. Only the discipline of the Metropolitan Police had taken him away from the search in which he had been so vitally interested to handle this sordid killing, which he believed the local men could have handled themselves.

The story of the sex murder had, of course, been spread over the popular press that morning – with pictures. There were plenty of nude photographs of Mirro to gladden an editor's heart. It had certainly pushed the kidnap of Bridey Lawdon, the middle-aged wife of a Scotland Yard Superintendent, to a back page. Not that there was any news in the kidnap case. Since the day Bridey had disappeared and the car she had been driving was found in a cul-de-sac, there had been no word, no ransom note, no demands. The only things the police had to work with were a shoe left by the driver's seat, her handbag in the back of the car where she usually left it, and the word sprayed in bold red letters across the windscreen: MAYDAY.

One school of thought at the Yard believed it to be a political kidnapping because of the connotation of the name, though no one had heard of such a group. Others pointed out there was no way of knowing that it was the kidnappers who had sprayed the car: it could have been anyone with a tin of paint and the impulse to use it – after all, it had been May Day. Capricorn discounted this. It was a quiet area not populated by students, and there were no other painted slogans close by. Some detectives thought it might turn out to be a case of simple extortion; Bridey could have been mistaken for her sister-in-law, Lady Lawdon, whose car she had been driving.

Capricorn had been up all night at the Yard in conference, trying to find some starting point. He did not believe it would turn out to be simple extortion. Lord Lawdon was not very rich. His inheritance from his father, the famous Arabist, had not been a great one, and it was now much reduced by taxation and his own interest, philanthropy. Bridey could have been taken from motives of revenge: her husband, Chief Superintendent Lawdon, had been working for the past year with Special Branch. But if revenge had been the motive, it would be more likely that the family of one of the regular Special Branch men would be the target. They had talked in circles; they had nothing to go on.

Every available man, including Capricorn and Lawdon, had been out for three days, pumping all the informers known to the Yard, but the word had come back plain from the underworld: not our job. Capricorn believed it. Bridey Lawdon was liked on both sides of the law. She was known to be a 'soft touch' for ex-offenders; it was said that the more men her husband put in prison, the poorer the family got. There had been offers of help from unexpected quarters, but so far without result.

When the request came in for assistance in the murder of this Fawn, Capricorn, as the only available super in the Murder Squad, had been given the job. He had protested vigorously that he was not available, but his Commander had said there were over a hundred men of Special Branch and Anti-Terrorist Branch on the Lawdon case, as well as Flying Squad and Regional Crime Squads, and until they got a lead there was little they could do.

The Commander had added, less formally, that he would cut off his own right arm to get Bridey back, alive and well, but it would do no good, and they could only get on with their jobs. He wished he could send Lawdon himself out on another case, but it was no use trying. Capricorn had to consent, but, like any detective, felt that no one else could do exactly what he would do to find his good friend.

They had known each other more than a quarter of a century. He had first met her at her wedding – Charles Lawdon, who had once seemed a useless young playboy, in a little trouble with the law, had been persuaded by the then Sergeant Capricorn to try for a life of service with the police. His career had been as successful as his marriage. Capricorn had thought for many years that much of his own warmth for Bridey Lawdon had come from the help she had given the once-flighty Charles. Certainly Capricorn had never thought of her romantically; she had been part of his normal background – a cheeky, cheerful London sparrow. Yet when he had learned of her abduction it had been a great kick at his heart.

Bridey. She had glowed at her wedding, laughing in the church to a few raised eyebrows as she lost a slipper, bouncing down the aisle. He had thought of that when they found her shoe by the car, not white satin this time, but dark leather, scuffed and worn, trodden down on the outside of the heel. She was not a woman to trouble with her dress.

A thousand memories flooded his mind. Bridey, who had invited the rather solitary Sergeant Capricorn for a home-cooked meal, chatting over a drink as she cooked, with a cigarette somehow perilously poised in the corner of her mouth. Bridey's letters, every Christmas, and on his birthday, which very few people knew. Bridey, rushing over to help his housekeeper when he was laid up with a broken leg. Bridey, who was always there at the end of the telephone to sympathize with him in his troubles, or to rejoice with a vigour he himself would have hesitated to express at any good fortune that came to him. So much a part of his life, the most valued part of his life, without his ever realizing it. Now, to think of her not being there was like stepping on to firm ground, only to have it snatched away and to fall into nothing.

Yet he knew that, special as she was to him, she had many such friends, many of equally long standing, most of the detectives at the Yard included. Of course they were doing their utmost. His comfort was that Manning, the 'grey ghost' of Special Branch, was in charge of the hunt, and in Manning he had complete confidence. Capricorn was thankful that he had dissuaded him from leaving the Force in a moment of depression.

It was an effort to clear his mind as he turned into the street where the Fawn had lived, and the effort did not relieve the childish lump in his throat. But he became a detective again as he approached the murder house, taking note of the surroundings. It was a strange place for this famous Fawn to live. He looked at the long row of nineteenth-century houses, still respectable, drab except where they were graced with front gardens full of spring flowers, and here and there the glory of a chestnut tree in candle.

His chief had shown him an article on Muffy Mirro in the current *Fawn* magazine. In an interview she had expatiated on the immoderate eroticism of her nature, her liking for very masculine men who could be 'real brutes, darling, when I turn them on', and the smartness of her bachelor flat, where she lived surrounded by angora cats and heaps of jewels, gifts from her admirers. Nevertheless, two uniformed men were standing guard outside one of the shabbiest-looking houses in the worst part of the street. Some of the houses were boarded up ready for demolition, and the drabness edged into squalor. A very dirty camper was parked in front.

Inspector Copper, his friend and colleague, drove up to meet him. Copper had come straight from home in a white sports car, and the sun shone on his red hair. He was brown and healthy looking after his holiday in the south of France.

'So long, darling,' Copper said, giving a casual peck on the cheek to the girl at his side, a pretty blonde girl dressed in the uniform of a woman police constable. 'Want to take the car?'

'No,' the girl said, getting out, revealing a pair of elegant legs and an attractive figure. 'It'll be quicker in the Tube.'

She waved goodbye and strode off rapidly, avoiding Capricorn, who knew her as the daughter of the Deputy Commissioner. Capricorn tried to look disapproving, but as Copper hailed him with a smile and 'Hello, guv,' in his exaggerated Cockney speech, the Superintendent couldn't help feeling more cheerful than he had for the last three days.

'Pulled you off the Lawdon case, have they? Those bastards,' Copper went on, perhaps referring to the Yard hierarchy, or more likely to the unknown terrorists. 'We'll clean this up in a hurry, and you can get back on it if poor old Irish hasn't been sprung. Any leads?'

'Nothing at all.'

They were walking into a narrow hallway with faded wallpaper, and worn-out linoleum on the floor. 'Everything in my flat is white,' Muffy had said in her interview. 'White carpet and white velvet walls – and of course, white satin sheets.' Capricorn felt a faint stirring of pity for Muffy Mirro.

'Super's upstairs in the bedroom, sir,' the constable said.

The stairs were uncarpeted, and the policemen's shoes clattered on the wooden treads. The Yard photographer and fingerprint man were waiting for them on the landing. The local superintendent, who introduced himself as William Bly, was a solid, sensible-looking man in his fifties, with a pair of sharp eyes behind his spectacles and a brisk manner.

'It might be simple enough, Capricorn,' he said. 'We're holding her boy-friend.' He nodded to a room down the passage. 'Swears he's innocent, of course, but it doesn't look likely. The only thing is, there might be a problem about the time of death. Sherwood, our surgeon, will tell you about that. The boy claims to have been in a pub until at least half ten. So, since most of her time was spent in the West End –'

True enough. It was quite proper for Bly to have called the Yard, and it was not his fault that a great part of the Force there was in a state of personal anguish.

'Any lead in the Lawdon case?' Bly echoed Copper's question. Capricorn gave the same reply. Plainclothes men had been hunting the area where the car had been found, but nothing had come of their efforts.

'I'd met Mrs Lawdon,' Bly said, polishing his spectacles. 'When my wife was ill, two years ago. She had to be in bed for three months and Mrs Lawdon would drop over when she could and spend time with her. I came in one night and found she'd taken the stove to bits, cleaned it all and put it back together – I'd rather let it go. With me being at work and the children gone now, my wife was alone a lot, you see.'

Capricorn did see. It was amazing how many stories he had heard like that since Bridey disappeared. He had always known her as the kindest of women in a group like the Metropolitan Police where the wives were noted for their helpfulness to each other, their families and friends, but Bridey's acts of kindness, always so quietly done, with no parade, were only now being fully recognized. She had been to so many people just what she had been to him, he recognized with a little added pain, and a sigh for his own vanity.

'Except for the doctor, the body hasn't been touched,' Bly said, preceding them and blocking their view of the bed for the moment.

The room itself was far from Muffy's description to the journalist. Wallpaper, linoleum not much better than that in the hall. A large wardrobe, a smaller one and a chest of drawers, dating from the thirties, with a crazed, soupy brown varnish and veneers that were sprung. A flowering plant in a plastic pot sat in a piece of brown wrapping paper on the chest with a knot of string beside it. By the bed was a small white rug, modern in design and discordant in that room, with a pattern of the Fawn emblem, made famous as a symbol of extremely youthful sex.

Then Bly moved to one side and Capricorn saw the figure on the bed. In the presence of death, the familiar feeling took hold of him. His previous thoughts and impatience died away. Muffy Mirro lay white and stark in a dark pool of her own blood. Her wrists were tied. Her throat had been cut, but the killer had not ended there; he had carved out his own sick erotic fantasies. Her flesh had been slashed in a way roughly resembling the slashes on the Fawn costume, and the knife had carved an F deep into her breast.

Capricorn looked at what the day before had been a living woman and was now a carcass to be carried off for the mortuary and the grave. A foolish girl, vulgar no doubt – but who was he to judge what she was and what she might have been? A life had been taken and confronted with that awfulness his resentment, if not his pain, was dispelled, and he went methodically to work.

The weapon had not been found, and he arranged for a search of the house and the surrounding area. He checked over the notes made by Bly. While the print man was working Capricorn had a few words with Sherwood, the Divisional Surgeon, whom he had met before. Sherwood put the time of death tentatively as between ten and eleven. Although he was a man of long experience, getting on in years and rather frail and thin, he was still sensitive. He saw Capricorn's face as the body was taken away, the bright sweep of hair hanging down from the stretcher, all that was left of the charm of Muffy Mirro.

'Many of those wounds were inflicted after death,' Sherwood told him, trying to abate the horror. 'That first slash was a workmanlike job. She wouldn't have been aware of much more than that.'

His quiet voice relieved some of the tension in the room.

Copper, who had turned white, began to recover. That lover
was always upset by the murder of a woman, and now
Copper must be reminded of the death of his wife not so long
ago.

'What about the landlady and the other tenants?' Capricorn asked Bly.

'The landlady doesn't live on the premises. She rented the
house to Muffy Mirro – we haven't got her real name yet –
and the boy. She lives at Southend; I have her address. The
boy lives here with three friends. They are a rock group, the
Rotten Apples is the last name they used, I think. Three of
them are away on tour; they were offered work with another
outfit that didn't need a guitarist, which is why Hoggett is still
here. Unlucky for him. Claims he went to see his family
yesterday, over by Clapham Common. Came back around
midnight; found what we saw; and called us in. You see it all
in that statement there. No blood on him when we got here.
I took a look at his clothes.' Bly nodded to the smaller
wardrobe. 'Those things are all his. We've put him in one of
the other boys' rooms. He was hysterical this morning, but
he's over it now. He's had breakfast.'

Capricorn had already looked at the male clothing, mostly
blue jeans. Hoggett's hair was long and stringy – unfashion-
ably so now, Capricorn reflected – but his fresh face and
clear grey eyes gave him the look of an ordinary English lad.
He was clutching his electric guitar, whether for a feeling of
security or as a kind of status symbol Capricorn could not
decide.

'Ed Hoggett,' Bly said crisply. 'Chief Superintendent
Capricorn and Inspector Copper.'

'Yard dicks,' Hoggett said, sounding depressed. 'I've
already told 'im –' he pointed a thumb at Bly – 'I didn't do
it. I don't know why I'm being kep' here. Muffy was my girl
and I'm more upset than anybody. The carving was diabolical and you ought to be out finding who done it and not trying
to fit me up.'

'The Superintendent just wants to ask you a few questions,' Bly said patiently. 'Nobody's accused you of anything.'

'Yes, I know all about it,' Hoggett said. 'Not yet, you haven't.'

He certainly didn't look like a young man who had recently committed a fiendish crime. On the other hand he seemed more worried than heartbroken.

'I do want to ask some questions,' Capricorn said pleasantly. 'You've already been advised, I'm sure, that anything you say may be taken down and used in evidence.'

'That's what I mean,' Hoggett said. 'What are you giving me a warning for, if you don't want to lumber me with it?'

'You don't have to be saucy.' Copper was sharp. He had noticed the young man's lack of emotion and he wasn't liking it.

'You've already given a statement to Superintendent Bly,' Capricorn said. 'So we'll just go over a few points. You say you've known Miss Mirro for over a year – was that her real name, by the way?'

Hoggett stared rather vacantly. 'I dunno.' He cast his mind back, frowning. 'Might have took it for the Fawns. They all have fancy monikers.'

'And during that time you lived with her here?'

'We was engaged,' Hoggett said. ''Smatter of fact, we was going to get married this summer.'

Having seen their domestic arrangements Capricorn wondered why the delay, but forbore from inquiring.

'Five of you rented this house?'

'Well, me and the group –' he hesitated but went on, 'we were in here as squatters at first. The landlady lives in Southend and – but it was a rotten lark because when we had to go away, there'd be other kids moving in and mucking the place up.'

Capricorn had already observed the comparative neatness, typical of a working-class household. For a moment, fleetingly, he wondered why it was the richer, better-educated young people who seemed to enjoy squalor.

'So once Muffy came here, and there was someone in the place every night, and she was making good steady money as a Fawn, we took the lease. The landlady knew Muffy

could pay, and she always got the rent on time. We told her
we was getting married and she didn't say nothing.'

'And you say that all went well, and you had no reason to
believe that Miss Mirro was in any danger, until you returned
from a visit to your mother last night, at about twelve
o'clock, when you let yourself in with your key, went straight
up to the room shared by you and Miss Mirro, where you
found her dead. You then telephoned the police from the
instrument in the hall.'

'As God's my judge, that's what happened,' the boy
said.

'How did you come back from Clapham Common?'

'In the camper. It belongs to the group but the others didn't
need it. They've gone out with the Warlock Five and they're
using their stuff.'

'And the front door was locked as usual?'

'Yes,' the boy said. ''Course, anyone could get a key to
fit.'

'Or Miss Mirro could have opened it,' Capricorn said.
'Was it her habit to answer the door when she was alone in
the house?'

Hoggett thought for a moment.

'Not many people come round at night,' he said. 'I dunno.
Sometimes in the day I've seen her go and have a look first
from the front room window, but she mostly just hollers for
someone else to open the door. She never said nothing about
not answering when she was by herself. It's quiet round 'ere,
see. Nothing ever happens.'

He looked blankly up at the policeman.

'So she might have opened the door,' Capricorn said.
'Perhaps, too, the caller was someone she knew.'

'She wasn't expecting anyone. She would have told me,'
he said.

'Or someone might have followed her home from the
club.'

'She didn't go to the club. She was taking a few days off.
If she had been, she'd've come home about three o'clock in
a cab. None of the Fawn Clubs close till two, and the girls
all have to stay to the end.'

'Had she been ill?'

'No. She was all right. She was a bit cheesed off with the management. Thought she should've been getting more money, and she didn't like being treated like the others, since she had all the spreads in *Fawn*. They're really only waitresses, you know,' Hoggett explained. 'In the country they're maids, as well.'

Capricorn knew, but let him explain. The Club Squad had a file on the Fawns in London and Capricorn had looked it up. Unlike the American business that had inspired it, the Fawns had not begun with a magazine – that had come later – but with a London club, which had branched out to buy several good country houses, some in out-of-the-way places of the sort too large for family use any more.

Each house was run as a private club, principally for men, with attendance by extremely young and mostly pretty girls, dressed in ankle boots, caps with fawn's ears and a short – tunic, he supposed it had to be called –' of thin, muslin-like stuff, dappled, and cut in loose patches to look as though it had been torn from the girl's body. Unlike the cheerful sexuality of its American counterpart, there was a strong suggestion of sado-masochism in the get-up of the Fawns, which was strengthened by the pictures in the magazine that was becoming a national favourite. Men of Capricorn's age at the Yard disliked the entire Fawn phenomenon; the younger ones accepted it as part of the times.

The more photogenic of the Fawns appeared in the magazine, nude or erotically done up, with the Fawn on the cover given great prominence. It was suggested in the magazines that Fawns were obvious choices for the casting directors of television and films. So far no director had taken up these suggestions.

Muffy Mirro had been the most successful of the photographed Fawns. Her ample charms – a little too ample, the purists said, but she seemed all the more erotic for that – had increased the circulation of the magazine every time her pictures appeared. The last edition was almost vanished from the stands even before the news of her death had been broadcast. Capricorn could understand why she felt restless in her role as cocktail waitress, even one that got a good deal of lascivious attention. Muffy had been hoping for better things.

'And you last saw her –'

'Yesterday morning. Well, about twelve o'clock. The kids was coming out of school down the street when I went out.'

'Did Miss Mirro say anything to you about her plans for the day?'

'No. She was still in bed. She's used to sleeping late from the club,' he explained. 'I had told her the night before I was going over to Mum's, and Mum likes to have dinner early, but I think she forgot because she was wild when I got up and she said why was I making such a bloody row.'

'Yes, I see. You've given your parents' address. What time did you leave there?'

'I went out for a beer with Dad and my brother and I left at closing time, eleven I think it was.'

'Where was that?'

'The Three Crowns. I've already told 'im.' He glared at Bly as though he were responsible for all of Hoggett's troubles. 'Alf Gorbel's. He was behind the bar and he'll tell you. He knows me well.' Hoggett spoke with a vehemence that carried conviction.

'I see. Now, you've told us that you and Miss Mirro were engaged to be married, and also that you knew of no one who had threatened her or made her uneasy in any way. But in her position it would be natural for her to be admired by many men, and some of them might have wanted to get to know her better. Did she tell you about anyone like that? Did she perhaps go out to lunch or dinner on occasion?'

'No,' Hoggett said, sullen again. 'I told you, Muffy was *my* girl.' 'Course, while she was working a lot of old geezers gave her the big eye. And she used to lead 'em on a bit, that's how she got such big tips. But she never 'ad nothing to do with 'em outside. Laughed at 'em, she did. Used to do imitations.'

He sighed in memory of those pleasant moments.

'She didn't go out. When she wasn't working she was

'ome. She liked to watch the telly. She could sit and watch
for hours, even the kids' programmes. Only time she went
out is if she came where me and the group was playin'.
Wouldn't 'alf stir them up in the pubs, Muffy. Wanted to sing
with the group, at first, but she couldn't sing for toffee. We
was trying to save up, but a lot of her money went on cabs,
coming home. She used to get the all-night bus, but after her
picture was in the book she didn't think it was right. After
all, she *was* somebody. That book.' His face darkened.
Capricorn understood him to mean *Fawn.*

'You don't believe the stuff they put in there, what that
fellow said Muffy told 'im. That's just the stuff they like in
Fawn for the old farts. Ever so upset about that, she was.
Said he made her sound a bit bent. She was straight all right,'
he grumbled. 'Used to live in a caravan with her Mum before
she was a Fawn, and they both worked at Barton's factory,
making toys.'

He seemed to feel that that settled once and for all any
story about Muffy's sexual activities.

Capricorn inquired as to the whereabouts of this mother,
only to learn that she had died the previous year – 'always
ailing, she'd been, Muffy said,' – but Hoggett didn't know
any details. It had happened after Muffy had been living with
him for about a month. She had gone to the funeral and
disposed of the caravan, 'but she didn't get much for it. All
went for the funeral, she said.'

Capricorn made a note of Barton's. He paused.
That seemed all he wanted from Hoggett just now.

'By the way, I noticed a plant on the chest of drawers in
your room,' he added. 'Was that there when you left
yesterday?'

'What plant? We ain't got no plant.'

'You could have a look,' Capricorn suggested. 'You might
remember it.'

'I'm not going in there,' Hoggett said, uneasy.

'It's all right,' Copper, aware of his feelings, explained.
'She's gone.'

Hoggett still looked very reluctant. 'There wasn't no plant
when I left,' he insisted.

'Then possibly Miss Mirro brought it in herself, or her assailant did.'

'Brought a plant?' Hoggett said with disbelief. 'That nutter? And Muffy didn't want no plants either.'

His mouth gaped in bewilderment.

Copper eyed his chief, who recognized behind the apparently expressionless look of the CID man Copper's opinion that Hoggett was, as a witness, worth very little.

Suddenly Capricorn gave the lad a reassuring and engaging smile that reminded Copper once more that his chief had been a performer, Merlin Capricorn, a charmer of audiences, a ladies' delight.

'I'm afraid I'll have to ask you to come down to the station so that you can help us a little more about our inquiries. And we have to make certain investigations. But you're not being placed under arrest. You don't have to be told that this is a very serious crime and I am sure you want to help us get to the bottom of it.'

Hoggett hesitated for a moment, his dislike of going off with the police battling with his desire to get out of that house. He gazed at Capricorn, seemed reassured, and allowed himself to be led away. Capricorn drew Bly to one side and asked that all of Hoggett's garments, including the ones he was wearing, be dispatched to the police lab to check for blood. That much, he thought, he could keep away from Copper, who was still pale under his tan. His new friendship with Meg Hardcastle had not brought him forgetfulness.

'Copper, you'd better get back to the Yard,' he told him. 'Get some Aids and start making a sweep. Bly here has already sent out a call to question the rest of the group. There's the landlady, and we want statements from any Fawn who knew her, especially regarding other love-affairs if any, or someone who might have been giving her trouble. Try the editor and photographer of *Fawn* magazine. Comb through the model agencies in the West End. She was dissatisfied, so it's odds on she was making the rounds. Get on to all the photographers we know in London who go in for girlie work. Inquire round the studio managers in Chelsea, Tottenham Court Road and the Victoria district and the ad agencies. Start sifting.'

Copper nodded and went off gladly, his car a white streak in the sun. Capricorn and Bly went through the house together. Thompson, the fingerprint officer, was leaving and Capricorn stopped him for a moment.

'Did you try that bit of brown paper on the chest? Came off the plant.'

Thompson nodded. 'It was wet in the middle. The dry bit was all smears – no luck there, I'm afraid.'

He plodded off, his round shoulders hunched in a macintosh, despite the blazing sun – a confirmed pessimist. Bly looked at Capricorn inquiringly.

'She probably brought it in herself,' Capricorn explained, 'but that paper had no florist's mark, and the string was tied in a very clumsy way.'

'Present from a neighbour or a friend, most likely,' Bly gave his opinion. 'Probably been sitting there a week, but Hoggett wouldn't notice.'

Capricorn had to agree.

There was nothing in the house to indicate that Muffy Mirro had entertained her caller anywhere except the bedroom. The ashtrays were empty. There was both beer and spirits in the living-room but no dirty glasses, although in the kitchen sink they found a mug and a plate, a knife and a teaspoon. The plate was old and cracked, but the mug looked new, with pictures of animals in bright colours – the kind of thing meant to be a present for a child. Capricorn wondered if Muffy had bought herself this gift, and then tried to estimate how old she was. 'Love Goddess,' *Fawn* had called her. He looked at the rabbit, smilingly cleaning its whiskers, and sighed.

'Except for the stove and the fridge, I'll bet this kitchen hasn't been changed since the house was built,' Bly remarked.

'And yet it looks as though someone has done quite a bit of housekeeping,' Capricorn replied as they looked through cupboards, shelves and drawers.

'Um. Not too many tins, either. A lot of stores. Look at this.'

A large illustrated cookery book was tucked away in a corner.

'The girl, I'll bet. They think they're leading the rich, full life and they end up acting as unpaid housekeepers.'

'And, in this case, a lot worse,' Capricorn said soberly, and they went on with the search for the weapon in silence.

When it became obvious that the search would be a long-drawn-out affair, Capricorn assigned a group of men to continue and walked back to the station with Bly.

'What do you think of Hoggett?' Bly asked.

Capricorn took this to mean what did he think of Hoggett as a possible murderer.

'The barman might remember if he stayed until closing time. I took a look at that camper – it's falling apart. He must have taken at least an hour to get back, even at night. And he called you at twelve.'

Bly nodded, rather regretfully. 'The PM might narrow down the time of death a bit. But we have to show that he left the pub, got back at the latest at half eleven, killed her, got rid of the clothes with blood on them, disposed of the weapon, to call us at twelve.'

'He could have done it,' Capricorn said slowly. 'But it would have been premeditated. Not a matter of coming home, perhaps finding her with someone else and quarrelling. Unless he had an accomplice who took the clothes and the weapon away.'

He looked with disfavour at the boarded-up houses. Not much chance of having a nosy neighbour watch what was going on here.

Bly followed his look.

'Yes, a nuisance – in more ways than one. The council started buying them up because there were plans for a road cutting off through here, a by-pass from the main road. But they don't have the money and it doesn't look as though it's going to come off. Not in my time, anyway.'

'We'll have to go house to house, just the same,' Capricorn said. 'Do you know anything about the boy?'

'Uniform Branch have had complaints of noise since the group moved in. Late parties and that sort of carrying on.

The old-timers in the street are working people, have to get up in the morning, and they are having the devil of a life between the squatters and this lot. But he has no record of ever being in any trouble. Never had a real job, of course, none of them. They live mostly on unemployment pay and Social Security when that runs out. I believe he's peculiarly untalented, even for this day and age.'

'No fighting, no rough stuff?'

Bly shook his head. 'And I got on to Clapham Common last night, just checking. He grew up there, mother, father, older brother. No reputation for violence. Layabouts, the lot, but more inclined to nag Social Security than get into trouble. The father's been done, but just for petty theft.'

Capricorn tried to visualize a young man not accustomed to violence committing such a murder, quickly cleaning himself up, disposing of the evidence, and in a few minutes ringing up the police. He found it difficult. It would have been so much better for everyone if this young man were the murderer. And after all, so many killings were just as simple as that. But this one, he knew, with a sinking of the heart, was not going to work out that way.

'Yet his motive was strong.' Capricorn was trying to persuade himself. 'The girl must have had thoughts beyond an unsuccessful guitar-player, after all her publicity.'

Bly nodded agreement.

'And he seems a callous youngster,' Capricorn went on. 'No real emotion except worry about his own position.'

His effort failed. The facts were against Hoggett's guilt, and unless he was very wrong the boy was not a killer.

'He seemed shocked enough last night,' Bly, a fair-minded man, pointed out. 'And you know, although he talks of an engagement, I don't think he was in love with Mirro. I don't think he's in love with anyone except himself. You know how it is with the youngsters now. Too easy, if you know what I mean. They don't have the chance to get excited over a girl. He got a tart and Mummy at the same time. That's the thing that bothers me.'

He blinked, took off his glasses, and wiped them carefully.

'I think he would have been annoyed if she left him, it would be inconvenient, but –'

The two men gazed at each in unwilling agreement. There might be enough passion here for a black eye, but hardly enough to mean murder.

At the station the first call Capricorn made was to the Three Crowns. Mr Gorbel lived on the premises and took the call at once. Yes, he remembered the Hoggetts being there the night before. And Ed had been there until closing time, half ten – longer, he'd hung about, jawing outside about another quarter-hour, until he'd had to shout at them all to clear off. He was quite sure it was Ed, all right – the boy was pestering him all night to hire his group, although he'd tried them before on a Saturday night, just to oblige, and they'd practically got the raspberry. As a guitar-player, Ed Hoggett should have stuck to being a house-painter like his father. Was he in trouble, Gorbel wanted to know. Wouldn't surprise him if Ed was. It was better when they took young layabouts like that and put them in the army. Gave them a bit of discipline.

Mr Gorbel had not read his morning paper, apparently. Capricorn explained briefly, heard Mr Gorbel's view on young tarts showing themselves off with nothing on, and hung up.

'If it wasn't Hoggett,' Bly said, in his crisp, practical voice '– though I still don't rule him out – it could be anyone. How many men have it in for a girl like that? Well, Super,' he said, recollecting it was now a Yard case, 'I expect you'll sort it out. We'll co-operate as much as we can, of course.'

Capricorn thanked him. The warm morning was stifling in the station; the bright sun streamed through the windows and the myriads of flecks of dust to dazzle his eyes. Bitterly he remembered Copper's words, 'We'll finish this one up quick and you can get back on the Lawdon case.' Now it looked as though they'd have to sift through half the men in the country. The lengthy routine would have to be followed. While Bridey at any time could be killed by her captors. Bridey, locked up in some unknown hole with God knows what kind of maniac.

And nothing he could do. For he was merely a Chief Superintendent, and it was for him to obey orders, not to choose who would work on what. Bitterly he thought of the times he had been offered promotion; he had always refused because one more step in rank would have taken him from active duty to a desk and administrative tasks. Now for the first time he saw the penalty of rejecting responsibility. He could have no part in the search for Bridey and could only get on with the job assigned to him.

After hesitating just a moment, he rang a very busy office at the Yard.

'A call came in,' he was told briefly. 'Man's voice. Too short to trace. Said Bridey was being held by MAYDAY – the Saviours of the Workers of the World. That's all. Could be a hoax, of course.'

There was a babble of sound at the other end, and his informant hung up. Capricorn sat for a moment, listening to the receiver buzzing angrily at his ear. It had been Burke speaking, an old friend, a kind, fatherly man – very sympathetic now. A dozen questions came to Capricorn's mind – but he had no right to interfere. One after another course of action suggested itself; his body strained with the desire to be up and moving. But the file Bly had given him demanded his attention. The Chief Superintendent went on with his task.

THREE

4 MAY

Late that night Capricorn parked his car in the quiet square where he lived, looked up at his house to see if any lights were on hoping that there were not. However hard he had worked in a day, the sight of his home had never failed to refresh him. Except tonight.

Lights were on, upstairs and down – his domestic affairs reflected the discord in his mind. He had lived for many years in happy bachelor solitude in the downstairs flat with only Mrs Dermott, his housekeeper, coming in during the day to take care of his needs. An access of wealth had made it possible for him to buy the whole house, and he had rejoiced in at last being sure of privacy and quiet, with no noisy tenants overhead. Special quarters had been prepared for Mrs Dermott, who now preferred to live in, and he had blissfully expected life at home would mean perfect peace.

The peace had lasted a few days. Then his women friends had pointed out that Mrs Dermott was no longer as young as she had been, and that although she was willing to do the work, the care of Capricorn, with his odd hours and a large house, was too much for her alone, even with occasional help, and Capricorn really should have a younger girl as well.

Capricorn had felt remorse for his thoughtlessness, especially since at that time Mrs Dermott was entering hospital for minor surgery, and he had engaged a daily maid. She had lasted until Mrs Dermott returned. Capricorn had engaged another and then another. The peace of his house was broken by constant dissension, and he assumed by the look of the house and the sounds of voices coming through strongly as he opened the door, an argument was even now taking place, though why Iris, the daily girl, should still be there

.he could not imagine.

As he approached the beautiful double-arched drawing-room, he found no pleasure in the sight of his cherished possessions, because another nasty surprise was waiting. The noise was not, as he had assumed it to be, that of a quarrel with Iris. It was nothing to do with Iris. It was merely the normal tones of his aunt, Dolly Merlino, the last person he had expected, or at this moment wanted, to see.

As usual, Dolly, built like a small tank, with her long hennaed curls flowing down over her magician's cape, which was decked with stars and moons, looked incongruous in that room of delicate colours and graceful furniture; most unusually, she was clutching Mrs Dermott's arm and shouting in what appeared to be a most friendly manner. Neither of the women noticed him, though Mrs Dermott usually had an attentive ear for his entrances. But now that respectable Scot – despite the hour fully dressed in her serviceable black, with shoes, not slippers though, as he knew, one foot was still bandaged – was absorbed with Dolly, gazing on her with sympathy, instead of trying to ease her out.

'It's not right,' Dolly was booming. 'Never 'eard of such a thing. So 'ere I am and I don't know what our Merle is going to say about it.'

At this moment Dolly in a crisis seemed far too much. Capricorn hesitated in the hall, tempted to run off quietly and stay the night in a hotel. But Dolly caught sight of him, and it was too late.

'Merle,' she thundered. 'What are you 'anging about for? Come here!'

Thus invited into his own parlour, he had no option but to go.

'Gawd, you're late,' she grumbled. 'I'll tell you what, I'm tired out.'

Capricorn, in spite of his own weariness and distraction, felt a jolt of surprise. In all the years of her life, he had never known Dolly to admit to tiredness or indeed – for she was a woman who liked to lie abed until well after noon – to seem to be tired, in spite of her years.

'I'll go and get supper for you both,' Mrs Dermott said, with this new, strange consideration for his aunt. Dolly and Mrs Dermott had been enemies for as long as they had known each other, more years than either of them would care to admit. 'I've got something all ready for the Super.'

'I'm sorry I ever said all right to Nelly and Tilly going with Mark the Magus to New York,' Dolly grumbled, referring to her sisters who were usually part of her act. 'Dollars or no dollars. Carrying the show at the Palladrome every night, with just those silly bits of girls and comics who couldn't get a laugh if they got down and tickled the audience, and all that after I finished taping the Merlino show this afternoon, it's getting on my nerves. Oh, what an audience tonight. Might'-ve thought they was in church.'

'We'll eat over here, Mrs Dermott,' Capricorn said, indicating the small table by the window overlooking the garden which he still used sometimes when alone, although he now had a dining-room. Tiredly, he wished for a moment he had left things as they were. At least Mrs Dermott hadn't mentioned the new daily girl. Perhaps she had become used to her. But what on earth was Dolly doing here instead of going to bed in her own house in Paddington? He didn't want to ask; certainly she would tell him anyway.

Mrs Dermott brought in cold meat and salad, but, to his further surprise, Dolly didn't seem to be hungry.

'Give us a drink, Merle, for Gawd's sake,' she said, pacing about instead of sitting at once at the table. Dolly was always a hearty eater. Without waiting for him to serve her, she poured a much too large glass of gin with a dash of orange.

'Went without letting me know a thing about it,' she informed him obliquely. 'I didn't even know it was tonight, until that Davy Phipps what thinks he's a comic started chipping me as he came off. Supposed to warm up the audience, my God, he has 'em crying, or praying.

'"Where's your tiara tonight, Doll?" he says. "Are you going to wear it on the platform?"

'And everybody giggling, knowing I didn't know, and I was the only one who didn't. Hadn't even brought my good fur coat, the tiara or nothing. And I came out after the show and looked to see if there was a car waiting for me, and all there was was a note left with the porter at the stage door.'

Her face darkened with the memory of insult.

'"Gone to award dinner, see you later."

'So I called him up, there and then. I guessed it was at the Goat's Club. Still guzzling and swilling they were, but I made them drag him to the phone.

'"Didn't think you'd want to come," he says, all innocent. "Thought you'd be too tired." Me,' she added, purple now. 'Me, who's never tired, and lucky for him I'm not or where would he have been all these years? Afraid to have me there, he was. Afraid the photographers would take my picture and not his. And so they would, because I'm the star and who is he?'

She was bellowing at the top of her voice.

'Nothing, that's what he is, nothing. No talent, me and the girls fed him and clothed him and done all we could, and he goes and gets the award without me. Not even a seat for me on the platform. You bloody fool, I told him, going up there in front of all the bigwigs, Sir Hugh Brody who's known us for years, without your own wife? And do you know what he said to me?'

She spluttered on her gin and her green marble-like eyes bulged ominously. 'He says, "But you're not my wife, Doll."'

She banged her glass down on the well-polished Pembroke table and for once Mrs Dermott, observing, didn't even sniff in disapproval. Capricorn now understood. A certain female consciousness had formed this strange bond, although, apart from their biological similarity, any likeness between the chaste and hardworking Scots war widow and the uproarious, bohemian Dolly, with her plethora of lovers and husbands, would be hard to find.

As for Dolly's complaint – he remembered now that Tod Parks, her lover and companion for so many years, had been due to get an award, something from the record industry for selling a million copies of a record. What was it called? 'They murdered the working lad.' He put his knife and fork down and considered, but he could think of nothing to say. In truth, Dolly was not Tod's wife, and she had reminded him of that fact on every day of their long association.

Tod, who played the ukelele, through the years had got a little work here and there, with a great deal of prodding from the Merlinos, and had made some appearances on television through his friends at Broadcasting House. Always he had lived in the shadow of the successful Dolly and her sisters, like Cinderella in the hearth, often treated with extreme brutality as Dolly, when in a temper, was liable to throw him down the stairs.

With the odd whirls and eddies of public taste, while Dolly had some time since reached the zenith of her career, suddenly Tod's star had come into the ascendant. His pale face and form, which had never looked young, now did not look old either. His odd, hesitant playing, his nervous aspect, his working-class songs, had taken the fancy of a very young public. Tod Parks had become the rage. His act, surrounded by a group of young rock players and an Indian boy playing an electrified *banshri*, could draw many thousands of young-sters to outdoor concerts and bring in tremendous receipts. In fact, he was now a bigger star than Dolly, even with her sisters, and Tod, he saw, was feeling his oats. It was hardly surprising.

He drank some of Mrs Dermott's good coffee, knowing it would keep him awake, but he didn't suppose he would sleep much anyway. Might as well enjoy the small creature com-fort. His mind slid away to wonder what Bridey was being fed, if anything. It was an effort to respond to Dolly.

'What do you think I could do?' he asked.

If he could get away from Dolly, he would ring up Burke at the Yard. Then he told himself he was being foolish. He had only left there half an hour ago, nothing more was likely to happen on the Lawdon case, certainly until the morn-ing.

'Go and arrest him,' Dolly bawled. 'Abandoning his wife. You go and get him, in front of everybody, there'll still be plenty of 'em hanging on, boozing and yarning to the last. *He* doesn't have to get up tomorrow to do a tape, no, not after I've kept him all these years. What's the good of having a nephew in the Force –' she looked at him accusingly – 'if you don't look after your own? Do something. You're a cold fish, Merle.' It was his aunts' lifelong cry. 'You're always arresting people, half the time for nothing, bloody interfering lot the police.' She was working herself up into one of her famous tantrums, and Mrs Dermott was watching now with some care as to the glasses and the china plates.

'What are you still sitting there for?' she screamed. 'You think it's all right what he's doing, standing up there and getting the award as if he didn't owe me nothing? You think it's all right –' she glared – 'because of you hanging round her ladyship all these years and never marrying her either.'

She made to fling her glass, empty, at the full-length portrait of his friend Rose, which smiled down benignly into the room, but Mrs Dermott caught her arm gently but firmly.

Capricorn sighed at this bit of typical Merlino logic. It would be a waste of time to point out that he could hardly propose to the devoted wife of the Dean of Cicester. Dolly was merely upset, too upset to go home to a house that would be, for the first time since the Parks-Merlino invasion, empty. He could not think of anything to comfort her. Tod was paying Dolly back for her very cavalier treatment of him over the years and there was nothing anyone could do about it. If Nelly, the eldest of the aunts, were at home, she might be able to talk to him. Nelly was the most sensible one of the highly volatile group. But Nelly was abroad. Dolly was quite capable, he knew, of making for Tod with the breadknife when he did come home. Perhaps Mrs Dermott had the same thought.

'Don't upset yoursel',' she counselled. 'Don't fret 'bout him, he's not worth it. Stay here tonight. I have the spare room ready made up. That'll teach him a lesson,' she said slyly. 'When he comes home with his award and no one to show it to. It's well known,' she added caustically, 'that men don't understand much. That women can't be put upon all the time. Iris has left,' she threw out to Capricorn casually. 'After she did the bedrooms this morning I had to do them over. Your bed not even slept in and she managed to crumple the counterpane. Double work for me; I had to clean up after her, lipstick on the towels, hair all over the basin; drank out of the milk bottle and put it back in the fridge.'

She folded her arms over her chest, her head nodding slightly, an attitude that Capricorn knew well boded no good.

'What a relief now she's gone,' he said carefully. 'She certainly didn't fit in.'

As Mrs Dermott looked a little less formidable, he took the opportunity to turn his attention to Dolly and ease her to the stairway.

'We'll think of something in the morning,' he said sooth-ingly, and slightly mendaciously, as he knew he would be well away before Dolly rose. 'But by then, I'm sure, Tod will be ashamed of himself and ready to apologize. As Mrs Dermott says, he'll certainly want to show you his award – a gold record, is it? And he'll probably be worried that you're not at home.'

Rumbling like a distant gun, Dolly allowed herself to be led away, her hard, determined tread muffled by the carpet. As he stood over her by the stair rail, Capricorn noticed that her red hair – her own tonight, she must have left her wig at the theatre – was getting thin. For the second time that day he felt an unexpected pang of pity. Dreadful Dolly, the virago of stage, cinema and television, was suddenly human and vulnerable. The gorgon was a woman in disguise.

Dolly turned back at the landing.

'Where was you all night, anyway?'

'A new case,' Capricorn said. 'The murdered Fawn. You must have read about it.'

'Saw it on the telly,' she replied. 'A big tart. What about the bobby's wife, then? Forget about her, is it? Tarts more important than wives,' she added, her new situation putting her for the first time in her life on the side of respectabil-ity.

'Manning's heading up a team,' Capricorn explained, very

tired. 'If I can get this case finished up quickly ... of course,
she might be released quite soon. We have no ransom note
yet, but –'

'Poor cow,' Dolly interjected, yawning. 'Likely she's
done in already. Gawd, and she was the only one of your
police wives I could stand for twopence. Not like the others,
all starch and carbolic. Likes her drop of wallop, Bridey, and
smokes like a chimney. And there's one that likes a joke.
Times I've had her in fits,' Dolly said, gloomy. 'Not like that
bloody audience tonight. Laugh – they're afraid their faces
would crack. Should have gone to "the modern dramah".'
She mouthed the words with mock earnestness. 'You know,
all misery, and you can't make out what's supposed to be
happening, and they get the sets on the cheap.'

'I didn't know you knew Bridey Lawdon,' Capricorn said,
surprised.

'Course not,' Dolly said, with a return of her usual spirit.
'You're a detective, what would you know?'

Her insults seemed to cheer her for a moment, but her
brow darkened again.

'A good sort,' she went on, 'and she would have given it
to Tod hot and strong. So where is she? And where's her old
man? Probably chasing some tart. Just because she's plain
and ordinary, she isn't good enough for him, I suppose, that
bobby. 'Specially since his brother is a Lord.'

She grumbled off beside Mrs Dermott, muttering about the
duplicity of men. Capricorn didn't bother to correct her
remarks about Lawdon, who was stunned with fear and
grief. Dolly was just working off her ill humour. Instead he
lit a cigarette – he had begun smoking again the last few days
– and as he drew, gratefully a clouded breath, he reflected
on Dolly's idea of Bridey.

It was perhaps not so surprising that they knew each other;
Bridey, with her interest in people, had a wide acquaintance
and a great knowledge of London life, especially its seamier
side. People said she knew enough to shop half the villains
from Dulwich to Islington, but she never helped her husband
in that way. Dolly usually disliked women, other than her
sisters, and her relationship with them was stormy enough,

as it had been with her female lodgers in the war and post-war years. But if she thought Bridey plain, Dolly would not feel threatened. Women rarely thought Bridey attractive.

Capricorn remembered his friend Rose trying to persuade her to use a little make-up, to do something with her straight brown hair, still hardly touched by grey, other than to tie it back with a bit of ribbon when she thought of it, or a bootlace if pressed for time; Rose looking sadly at Bridey's clothes, tidy but plain, obviously bought with small expenditure of time and money. But men noticed Bridey's well-made, full-bosomed form, hardly plumper than when she was a girl, her clear skin, bright eyes and good-humoured countenance. Dolly was right that Bridey liked to laugh, her face would light up, she would cock her head and glance obliquely and burst into a clap of laughter. Yet Dolly was shrewd enough, Bridey was not erotically alluring – except perhaps when she wished to be. She was every man's favourite sister. Every man's sister – in hostile, careless hands.

Too restless to sleep, he called the Yard again, but there was of course no further news. He switched his call to Copper who, fresh from his holiday, was still working, and they went over the results of their investigation so far in the case of Muffy Mirro. Capricorn had been holding Hoggett only while his clothes were checked for blood, but Hoggett during the course of the day had developed a fear that the unknown murderer might return to try to kill him and was eager to be detained. It could have been an assumed fear, but Capricorn told his junior it looked genuine enough.

During the afternoon and evening Capricorn had person-ally interviewed many of the neighbours in and around the street where Muffy had lived. The nearer neighbours knew of her living there with the group, and many unflattering remarks were made, but no one had noticed a visitor that night. They were not likely to have noticed if there were any visitors; they had eaten their dinners, drawn their curtains and settled in for an evening's look at television, and were yawning over calamities in far corners of the globe while Muffy was being sliced to death next door.

One of the local housewives had remarked that only that

very morning she had seen a strange red-headed man drive
up in a fancy sports car with a blonde whom he treated in a
very familiar manner. Capricorn relayed that to Copper
without comment, but Copper merely roared with laughter.

'Trust the old girl not to notice an axe-murderer on the
loose,' he said unfairly, 'but watch her put the finger on
anyone who gives a pretty girl a kiss.'

Capricorn couldn't complain, as Copper's work that day
had been prodigious. The winnowing process was well under
way. Lists were drawn up of the Fawns who were to be
interviewed, the photographers, and all the people in the
Fawn and model world who had the slightest acquaintance
with Muffy. Copper had seen the Fawns in the London club
and had also visited Barton's, the toy factory in Haversham,
the new satellite town north-east of London. Verbal inquiry
and a search of the records proved Muffy's mother to have
been a Mrs Dortman. Her husband, a German national, was
long dead and Muffy, whose name, it transpired, was Hilda,
her only living child. Mrs Dortman's co-workers didn't know
much about her; apparently she had not been a talkative or
friendly woman and she had lived in her caravan on an open
stretch of heath outside Haversham. Many of the women
who had known her by name or by sight were not even aware
of Mrs Dortman's death. When her absence from the factory
floor had been noticed, they had merely assumed she had
gone elsewhere.

'Like a gyppo she lived, in that caravan. That girl of hers,
a saucy piece, had gone off on her own a while back.' Hilda
was remembered as a pert young thing, 'very developed,' a
woman had said, with a sniff. Others reported she had
curried favour with the foreman by as much display of her
charms as was possible in working overalls.

'The way it's shaping up, guv,' Copper told his chief
plainly, 'it's quite a job. As far as the names on these lists
are concerned, I've seen one or two already, and I can tell
you this: young Hoggett wasn't the only pebble on her beach
by a long shot. Quite a girl, was Muffy. I don't know about
that talk down at Barton's, those women might be just a lot

of old cats – snaggle-toothed and stringy-haired, or fair, fat and forty most of them, just the sort to get their daggers into a good-looking young bird – but from what I got around town she and the *Fawn* photographer were pretty thick. And according to the girls, she was a terrible tease with the customers and they don't know if it stopped there. Anyway, why don't you get some sleep,' he said with the familiarity of many years of friendship. 'I'll see you first thing in the morning. I'm staying in town.'

Capricorn hung up unhappily. What Copper was saying was in line with what he had discovered himself. He had been in touch with the Fawn management. At the moment they were not co-operating with his request for the names and addresses of the members who had known Muffy Mirro, although they knew they would have to in the end. Giving themselves a chance to warn the customers in question, no doubt. He could, and would, get a court order to examine their books, but there would have to be extensive interviewing of the staff to try to narrow down which of the hundreds of Fawn club members Muffy had known outside.

He would not get back on the Lawdon case, that was obvious. He might as well go to bed and try to sleep. Try not to think about Bridey, on some remote farm perhaps, or kept drugged in some city flat not so far away ... No, he told himself firmly, he simply must not go on like that. Lawdon himself was keeping an iron control; Lawdon, who would be working without let or cease. And so was Manning. Manning, the best man in Special Branch, the best detective in the whole of the Force, for that matter. Manning was tenacious and tireless. With Manning on the case, if Bridey was still alive her chances were good. And it might turn out to be a simple matter, he told himself. A straight swap: Bridey for a few terrorists being held in gaol. Of course, the Powers-That-Be declared they would not bargain with terrorists, but there was precedent for it.

Feeling a little better, he started up to his new sleeping quarters, a room with a balcony over the garden. But before he reached the first floor he heard a car drive up and stop outside. There was a light knock, he opened the door, and there stood Manning himself.

'Thought you'd want to know what's happening,' Manning said. 'So I stopped in on my way home.'

Capricorn took him into the drawing-room, poured them each a brandy and sat down to listen, his heart pounding. Even in his anxiety he could not help noticing Manning's chameleon looks. In the pool of lamplight by the empty hearth the grey man in his dark clothes looked like any male caller who might have stopped in after a night of city pleasures.

'No ransom note yet,' Manning said. 'No demands. But I'm taking the MAYDAY thing seriously. Notified Interpol, but we're not waiting for them, of course. Called everyone I know from China to Peru, but no one has ever heard of them. A split-off group, most likely. Took this name for the occasion. I tried our friends the Americans – they're in a shocking state of disarray at the moment. Drew a blank. I spoke to your old friend Delaney,' he told Capricorn, 'mentioned your name, and that Bridey was a personal friend and so forth. He'll let us know if he gets anything. The Continent – nothing. Even approached the other side,' he said bluntly. 'A few people owe me favours.' He did not elaborate, and Capricorn did not inquire. He had worked in Intelligence himself, and he knew that that world had its own rules. 'But nothing as yet,' Manning continued. 'It doesn't mean anything, of course, except that they'll be hard to find.'

Capricorn nodded. New groups sprang up constantly. Young hotheads who couldn't wait for their own leaders to act. There seemed to be no difficulty in getting money and weapons and plenty of support for almost any kind of subversive or revolutionary activity.

'The Irish are high on your list, I imagine,' Capricorn said. 'Lawdon picked up quite a few of their men last year. Bridey being Irish would make no difference to them, they would consider her a traitor, no doubt.'

Manning, who knew as much about the IRA as any man in England, hesitated, swirling his brandy round in his glass – Manning drank very little.

'Logically you're right,' he said. 'And yet – it doesn't

follow their pattern, you know. If it had been a bomb in the Lawdon house, Lawdon himself shot – I would say yes. But this kind of kidnapping, the silence, the long wait before the demand – it smacks more of a young, unknown group who want publicity more than anything else. It's a sure way of getting spread all over the telly. Think – four days ago no one had heard of MAYDAY – now it's a household word over a great part of the globe, courtesy of satellite.'

He grimaced. Manning had a Luddite attitude to television.

'And there's another thing, the name itself. You have to think of Communists – Saviours of the Workers of the World. MAYDAY – their special day. Some kind of Marxists. Not much like the Provos.'

His eyelids drooped, giving him a sleepy look, but Manning wasn't sleepy.

'Mayday has another meaning,' he said abruptly. 'Pilots use it for air emergencies. To anyone familiar with air traffic, those words are dreadfully ominous. That name could have sprung from the brain of a pilot.'

The idea might seem far-fetched, but Manning's hunches were sound far more often than informed guesswork would explain.

'No, it doesn't have the earmarks of an Irish job to me, though of course we're not ruling them out.'

Deep in thought, he sat back in his chair, whistling some unknown, unrecognizable tune, as he often did as he concentrated. The whistle was not loud, but it was penetrating, and soon Capricorn heard a heavy tread. There at the door was a reconstituted Dolly, arrayed in one of Mrs Dermott's nightgowns. Too long and too narrow, it gave Dolly the look of a red-topped sausage bursting its skin, but she was not self-conscious and she advanced on Manning with the air of a Queen of Love and Beauty come to accept homage. As Capricorn well knew, male company and any hint of merriment was enough to draw Dolly from her bed – he imagined her death-bed would be no different; she would try to carouse with the angel Gabriel.

Manning, who had met her before, greeted her with

courtesy, quite prepared for chat. It was Manning's way to talk to everyone who came into his path, Capricorn remembered with some exasperation, driven himself by a sense of dreadful urgency; Manning claimed that some of his greatest successes had come from talking to people who seemed to have little connection with his work. But Dolly could be no earthly help in their hunt. Nevertheless, under Capricorn's eye, next to his ebullient aunt, Manning turned into an audience, a familiar of the music halls, and Dolly's devoted fan.

Dolly poured herself a glass of brandy and beamed on Manning, whom she easily accepted as an admirer.

'Knocking off as usual,' she said brightly. 'Gawd, glad I'm not in trouble with you two, the pride of the p'lice.'

It was half past three.

'Quite right, Miss Merlino,' Manning said. 'And I even missed your show tonight at the Palladrome, worthless creature that I am. I did have some business near here, though, and that's why I stepped in. So I hope you'll go on paying your taxes for the Metropolitan Police.'

'Don't talk to me about taxes,' Dolly said and groaned. 'I ought to scarper off, like everybody else. But I can't leave poor old England while she's down. What business was you on?' Tact and discretion were not in Dolly's line. 'D'you mean to say they've got Bridey Lawdon hid round here?'

'I wish I had the faintest idea where she was,' Manning said. 'No, I was actually working on some other business that I had to do personally. An investigation I was on before this started.'

Capricorn looked up, shocked. He had assumed that when Manning was put on the Lawdon case he would have temporarily dropped everything else. Although Special Branch, like Central, always had a heap of cases they were working on, a matter like this would surely have been one for his exclusive attention.

'Saving the Empire, eh?' Dolly chortled, her good humour quite restored.

'No, we're not working to keep a great country safe any more,' Manning said, the brandy perhaps acting on his tired state. This was not the way he would usually speak before an outsider. 'Just shoring up the bits.'

Dolly took this as a joke and laughed heartily, and chatted away, unaware of any tension, entertaining Manning with stories of Bridey Lawdon: Bridey singing in the pub, Bridey dancing Irish jigs, Bridey on what Dolly called a Save-a-Tart Committee, faced with a group of girls who wanted union recognition and higher pay. Then the clock struck four, and Dolly went upstairs to call her sisters in New York, who should just be getting back to the hotel after the show.

'Our number of actually working agents is so small,' Manning said to Capricorn, in some sort of explanation after she went. Manning, who missed very little, had noticed Capricorn's start. 'I've been walking round the edges of something big. Or I think it is. I've run into enough odd shapes and edges that I think can add up to an elephant. So what can I do?'

He stared into the smoke that hung between them, his eyes unfocused, an attitude that meant, Capricorn knew, he was brooding over one of his enduring fears and vexations. Manning believed that England and Western civilization were heading for destruction and that certain official practices were hastening the day of doom.

'Did you ever work out how much we spend on people in offices, collecting information by nice, polite, legal means? Reading reports, evaluating published material? And if you think we're bad, the Americans are fifty times worse. A huge proportion of their intelligence budget is spent on clerks who can read foreign languages and stuff data into a computer. And in the meantime the opposition, when they want to know something about us, or to get something we've got, send in well-trained men and suborn the possessors of information or steal what they want and walk away with it in their hot little flesh-and-blood hands. I sometimes think,' Manning said bitterly, 'that if our people saw them stealing North Sea oil in buckets, they would name a team to study their import data and evaluate it in terms of decades to see if we should believe the evidence of our own eyes. I can't just drop this,' he said slowly, 'but I promise you, I'll do everything for Bridey. I've got a lot of good men working for me.'

Capricorn faced his friend with a frightened cold feeling in the pit of his stomach that no amount of brandy could warm. He understood what Manning was saying all too well. Only now did he realize how much he had relied on Manning, personally, to find Bridey. Manning, who had no family, no friends outside the profession, no hobbies or interests other than his work, no distractions of any kind and who, once he started a job, would pursue his goal with seemingly no need even for food or sleep – Manning with his brilliant abilities was the one man in whom he had absolute confidence. If anyone could find Bridey, he had been sure it was Manning.

Now Capricorn could see that Bridey was merely one worry in Manning's day. He would do what he could, but his real concern was for the larger matter. He was worried about great events, and Bridey's kidnapping was no great event, except to those who loved her. A statistic, an unfortunate wiped out in a revolutionary struggle. He had an absurd desire to cry out: 'But it's Bridey!' As, he supposed, those who loved the victim always did. But he realized clearly what perhaps he had always known: individuals meant little to Manning. He was a kind and chivalrous man, but his great love was his country, and her safety was his concern.

Capricorn felt something close to despair. With all the good men working on the case there was no one who he personally felt was adequate if it proved – difficult. If the kidnappers' demands could not be met. If they were not acting in what might be called good faith. Lawdon himself was normally good enough, but in this matter he was hardly clear-minded. He would want to throttle every revolutionary he met, rather than coax or wheedle information as Manning could. He stared at Manning, who for once was looking like a tired and discouraged detective, and cursed that he himself was tied by the tail to the case of the murdered Fawn.

Above their heads the lamps burned with what seemed now a useless light. Moving to the window he looked over the garden but outside it was still dark; the moon's face hidden by drifting cloud.

FOUR

4 MAY

That morning they hadn't bothered with the blindfold. Bridey tried not to wonder why. Instead she tried to concentrate her thoughts on Charlie and probably Merle and the others who must be looking for her. Very likely someone had noticed that pretty silver car – but perhaps her captors had changed cars. She rather thought they had.

They had been quarrelling all through the night. The dark boy and girl talked to each other in French and she hadn't understood much. '*Putain*', they said, over and over – she knew what that was. When she and Charlie had been on their honeymoon in Normandy they had heard a man screaming at a woman in a café. She had asked Charlie what *putain* meant and he had told her, blushing to the ears. Poor Charlie, who had liked to think of himself, then, as a man of the world. Did they mean her? A bad name, to degrade her? She had listened hard but they had said nothing else she could make out. 'Too soon' or something like that came up often, but what it meant she couldn't think.

When the Irish boy – they called him Michael – came, they had to quarrel in English, but mostly they kept their voices hushed. Once Michael's voice had risen, it seemed in protest.

'Ah, he's crazy. When he made the trouble he was quiet enough; now he's screaming in fright. That all is nothing, I tell you. They say prayers and give the girls money –'

'She didn't need money.' That was the chill voice of the girl. 'And she wouldn't say her prayers. So they must have talked about something else.'

They moved out of earshot. They left a guard now outside the cellar. She could tell by the sun coming in through the bars that the weather was still lovely – Bridey imagined Michael on a kitchen chair sitting by the door. An open door – he would want a bit of warmth and light. But that would mean he wasn't afraid to be seen.

But they weren't afraid to be seen. Their off-duty time was spent upstairs. If they had neighbours it would be no good to keep the blinds down – nothing would make people curious quicker than that. She had heard splashing sounds in the night, like a boat on the river. Would the police think to search along the rivers ... there were so many. The Thames had river police, but these young people would be more knowing than to hide on the Thames bank.

Not knowing where she was made her feel so helpless. And lonely – they had tied her hands in the front now so that she could feed herself. Through the long hours she had pulled and twisted at the cords from a frantic urge to do *something*, and then she would get dull and hopeless. It seemed she was as far from ordinary life as a dead cat in a ditch. She wasn't used to a lot of quiet sitting, even to say her prayers. Always on the gad, the housekeeper at Lawdon Court used to say. When she was at home the wireless was going all the time. The call-ins half the night when Charlie wasn't there. He laughed at her for that – Charlie.

She turned her mind away, but tears pricked her eyes. How she missed him. Here in this godforsaken place he seemed like something so good she wondered that she had ever had him at all. She'd never deserved him, she knew that. And yet – she had to admit – she'd sometimes had critical notions. When she saw Gervase so respected and Charlie just a policeman. Thinking if he'd had more go in him he could have been a Commissioner, which was silly. What sort of Commissioner's wife she'd have been she didn't know. Never given a proper dinner-party in her life; people always ended up with her in the kitchen. Yet how saucy she'd been! Many a time she'd told his friends that the best wife for a policeman was a servant, the old-fashioned sort. Cooking, scrubbing, not so fussy about a man's hours. And Charlie, she'd thought, had never wanted a lot of clever talk and book learning.

A chair scraped on the floor outside at the end of the passage. Michael was fidgety. Careless – she clung to that idea. It was just carelessness when they hadn't re-tied the blindfold that morning. It meant nothing. They hadn't decided – of course not. If they had decided to kill her they would kill her, no need to wait about and risk being found themselves. Or wear the masks.

She could see they were growing careless. Obviously they pulled the masks on – stocking caps with great holes in them – just before they came in. Michael's hair was wiry, and the cap was caught up in the back this morning; the sun had shone on fair curls, and she'd noticed grey strands in the gold. Prematurely grey. She'd recognize him anywhere. If she got out.

It was no use to get morbid. In fact, she probably felt like this because of the drugs. They had pumped something into her yesterday, not sleep stuff, but something new. It had made her light-headed. Like when she went to the dentist; the pain killer would make her giggly all day. She hadn't been giggly yesterday. They had kept asking her questions, especially the girl. They soon found she knew nothing of Charlie's work – only that he wouldn't try for the job of Commander. She was surprised now that she had told them that. Most of the time they asked about her work at St Anne's. That must be what they were talking of before. Girls, prayers, money. Why had they cared about her work? It was since then they had been quarrelling.

It made no sense. St Anne's. The last thing that would interest these young people. A little plan she had had, helping the nuns because some of the girls found it easier to talk to a married woman. Sometimes the girls decided to have the baby after all. And there were the ones who came troubled in mind after they had done the deed and could hardly bear to face the sisters. She had thought of herself as a sort of rope, a handy household article, which could pull the floundering creatures back to safety. She knew what happened to a girl who lost all respect for herself. And there were a lot more like that than anyone would believe. Some of the worst-seeming girls on the streets were those who felt the guilt the most, going on, trying to harden their hearts and pretend they cared for nothing.

But why would these young people know or care? That girl with the hard eyes, what was it to her who had babies and who didn't? Never would she have known girls like Connie, Hilda, Alma and Beryl – Beryl, that poor girl who'd changed her mind in her eighth month, got herself a back-street abortion and died with her sin fresh on her.

Her mind rattled round the words she'd overheard. Who was the 'he' who had caused trouble and was now frightened? 'Wouldn't say her prayers' – that sounded like Beryl. 'She didn't need money.' Beryl had needed money. Surely they weren't friends of Beryl who blamed her – or the father who was frightened – no, that was absurd. Bridey had never asked, but Beryl had told her that she had no notion who the father was. Hilda hadn't needed money, but she'd had the wretched operation before Bridey met her. It made no sense at all. They must be talking about something else.

Perhaps they'd misunderstood something she had said while she was drugged. She remembered Merle and Charlie talking about that one night, and how easily it could happen. That Mr Manning had been with them. Charlie said he was the best detective in Special Branch – they called him the grey ghost. He hadn't looked like a ghost, he'd looked like any policeman, or any other man who had dropped in unexpectedly. They had talked but she hadn't been listening much, throwing a quick supper together, wondering if there were enough chops, and peeling extra potatoes. Then she made the drinks strong so they wouldn't notice the chops had overdone themselves a bit on the grill.

They had been talking about drugs and torture – Merle and Charlie talking, Mr Manning rather quiet. He had asked her to call him George but she still thought of him as Mr Manning, just as she would always think of a priest as Father. Charlie asked why; she had always called Merle by his name, and he was impressive enough. But Merle was different, she had known him so long, and his dark good looks would warm any woman's heart. He hardly seemed to age like other people, and when he gave her his special smile she would feel as flighty as the village girl she had been thirty years ago.

Drugs and torture – there had been something in the news. Charlie and Merle were strong against such wickedness. Not

even useful, Merle had said. If you injure people, they'll talk,
but they'll say what they think you want to hear, not
necessarily the truth. Drugs made them babble, and who
could say what was real and what was a confusion in their
minds?

Charlie had agreed. Both of them said there was nothing
like skilful questioning. If they answer, Mr Manning said
sombrely. For some reason it had made her shiver. A strange
man: Charlie said the grey ghost *was* his work. He had no
family, no other interests at all. No one knew him well,
except perhaps Merle, his only close friend. Even his nick-
name was not a familiar one. A real Special Branch man, not
like Charlie, on loan. Rory had called Special Branch the
secret police. That might be why she was here ...

Had they decided to kill her? The question rattled round
in her head. If they had asked for ransom, certainly it had not
been paid. Would there have been negotiations? She couldn't
know. Although it seemed now she had been here half her
life, she didn't think it was more than a week, perhaps less.
Miss Impatience wouldn't want to wait long. She spoke as
though she were in charge. Bridey hoped fervently that she
wasn't. Would it be likely, such a young woman – young
enough to be her own daughter? She didn't know that either.
Usually the men wouldn't talk in front of her about things
that were upsetting. And she had never been one to dwell on
what she couldn't help. It seemed sensible. Now she wondered. How did the police find people? Could they ever find
her?

She stared at the opposite wall, where the plaster was
flaking from damp and neglect. No repair work done in this
house for many a year. An old place, condemned as insani-
tary and abandoned, probably. Perhaps even now men were
combing all the old abandoned houses – but how many might
there be? All the long roads of condemned streets waiting to
be pulled down, thousands of houses in London alone. That
thought wasn't cheering.

Her head still hurt. She felt alternately hot and cold, and
her cough was worse. Now she felt another familiar, drawing
pain. Always careless about dates, but she knew what that

was. What could she do about it? Silly to care, but she did care. If she told the girl it would be like talking to the wall. When the three of them had asked the questions, the girl's grip on her arm was the only one to bruise. In her drugged state she had thought the girl like the kind of child who enjoys tormenting animals. Yet there hadn't been much enjoyment in those glittering eyes: hatred, loathing even.

Bridey stirred uneasily. No one had ever looked at her like that. Not even Rory when ...

They were passing her door again and she could hear snatches of their talk. The girl's high voice was the easiest to catch.

'... in any case. The police should be made to suffer for their crime. Apart from the question of Comrade Ali ... We will tell the world their perjury and deceit is the reason for the execution.'

Bridey's stomach gave a lurch, and sweat beaded her forehead. She had been right ...

'... Scotland Yard ...'

It was the dark boy.

'So-called British justice. They never could have proved anything against the Colonel.'

'They've planted evidence before.' Michael's voice, deeper, but it carried.

'But a fingerprint ...' The dark boy – were he and the girl Arabs? Bridey thought that they were – was mumbling, and she could not make out all he said.

The girl, as always, was crisp. 'They paid the experts to lie. The virtuous British. We'll make them pay in blood.'

'... a policeman, then. Not a woman ...' Michael again. He was trying to help her, but he was moving off, towards the garden, it was agonizingly hard to hear. 'And not the Prime Minister's daughter, or even the lady ...'

So it had been Cynthia they were after.

'This woman will hurt them more. There's only one Prime Minister, and not so many lords or ladies. Now every policeman will be terrified for his own. It's better than Lady Lawdon. Her husband is mostly a fool. Very likely he doesn't understand what he does. And better than a Prime Minister's daughter; I'm glad she went abroad. A Special Branch wife ...'

The girl, of course. Cynthia, then, had only been a second choice. The Prime Minister's daughter had gone to America and saved herself. If the Mini hadn't broken down the day before and gone to the garage, Bridey Lawdon would still be in her own kitchen. It would be Cynthia, or her maid, or some entirely different person here in this cellar.

'... exchange for your Colonel ...'

Your Colonel. Michael was with them, but he never sounded like one of them.

'... other arrangements ...'

'... too soon is let off ...' That was Michael; but she must have misunderstood. It made no sense.

'... Comrade Ali, you fool. Remember he is reinstated.' The girl, sharp, clear. 'And call me Natasha: war regulations.'

The boy again – Natasha's brother? She treated both boys like an elder sister. '... matter now ...?'

Michael said something low. Probably he swore. He wouldn't care much for rules.

Bridey stared at the stone flag she was sitting on, seeing nothing. Execution. Certainly they were planning to kill her. Nothing else made much sense, but that she understood. But Michael, or whatever his real name was, he didn't want her dead. But would he help? If he came in she would have to try to talk to him.

Natasha's voice, angry. '... report you to the Colonel.'

'Ah, and him still in prison and might stay there twenty years.'

'He'll be released in a week.' Natasha was passionate now.

'In-sha-Allah.' The dark boy was quieter.

'We don't wait for Allah any more.' The girl was scornful. 'I'll show both of you.'

She ran down the passage and flung the door open. Not much light came from the doorway, but Bridey saw with great distinctness. The girl wasn't wearing a mask at all, and she was carrying a gun slung round her shoulder. Bridey's heart banged against her chest so hard it hurt – Not now! Not now –

A hand shot forward and grabbed the gun; two hands were on the girl's shoulder, pulling her back.

'Don't be a fool,' the dark boy said. The boys didn't have their masks on, either. 'Wait for orders. Remember how angry the Colonel was when you blew up the plane. We lost the hostages and the money.'

Natasha's thin, handsome face was sullen. Bridey couldn't see the boys, further back, too clearly. Her heart quieting, she heard the tap of the girl's feet, the clang of the heavy key in the lock at the top of the stairs. The boys moved away. Michael had not even looked at her. This frightened Bridey again. Her stomach was clenching itself like a fist, and she felt sick.

Michael said something she couldn't make out.

'... high,' the Arab boy said. 'Don't know where she got it, against the rules ...'

'... when she blew up the plane?'

'... not. She said afterwards she just wanted to show a woman could do it. A hundred people ... didn't like it. But she gets her way. Always ...'

Another light tap on the stairs. The dark boy moved almost as quietly as the girl. At the top of the stairs he unlocked then relocked the door. Even Miss Impatience was always careful with that. Not like the garden door – they were in and out of that all the time, and Bridey hadn't heard the click of its lock very often. But then there was always at least one of them in the downstairs passage. No hope there. Except that it was Michael ... Michael. She felt sure he didn't want to kill her. Perhaps she could talk to him ...

They'd said at St Anne's she had a rare tongue with the young girls. Boys she didn't know as well nowadays, though years back she could twist her brothers round her finger. She had to try. Salt tears ran into her mouth, though she hadn't realized she was sobbing. Dear God, she didn't want to die.

Michael came at last. Her heart banged. She had to try

now. He brought her food – as always, bread and cheese. The others brought water, but he brought a mug of stewed tea. Terrible stuff, he must leave it on the hob all day, but usually she thought better than nothing. Now she couldn't get it down.

Ask him to do something for you, she told herself. Helping people made them real to you, she knew that. Charlie said she made every tart in London one of the family. Charlie ... she pushed the thought aside.

'I need something for that time of the month,' she said bluntly.

It was ridiculous, but he blushed. He had put his mask back on, but she saw the flush come up under his eyes. Like a young peasant boy who had never left the farm. Children, they were, children-murderers. Out in the world on their children's crusade.

'Tell – Natasha, then,' he said.

'As she just wanted to kill me, I don't suppose she'll trouble herself,' Bridey said. She was surprised that her voice was so sharp. I sound as sour as Eileen, she thought. No way to attack the boy. And how I must look, dirty as a pig, my hair – it felt lank against her face. It had needed washing that day – She had tied it up in a scarf. What had happened to the scarf?

She watched Michael's eyes, trying to guess his reaction. They went blank the way a child's do when it doesn't want to answer. He knew she spoke the truth.

'Mm,' was all she got from him.

No more than a grunt. He went out and that was the last she saw of any of them for most of that day, except when the Arab boy brought her supper. But when it grew dark she heard the sound again of a boat going into the water, and the slap of oars.

Going to get word to their Colonel perhaps, to settle the date of her execution. A dark thought on a dark night. She tried to turn her mind away, but it would not stay away from them. Them. A funny way to have to think of people, but she supposed she'd never know who they really were, or why they were together. Was their Colonel young, too?

She had thought of them on a children's crusade – but she had never liked to think of the real Children's Crusade. It had always left her puzzled and miserable, and it made her more miserable now. A strange feeling it gave her to think of that, like the Lord and his Creation out of kilter. It was one of the many things she knew she could never understand, and the priest couldn't explain. He had given her a catechism and told her to study but it had been no use. There must have been good people then but they let it happen. So were they good? She didn't know. Most of the time she didn't think of it.

She had told herself that everyone knows what a good woman is, and she had done her best. Well, not quite. After she'd taken more whisky than a good woman ever needed she'd giggle a bit and decide the devil wasn't dead in her. But she hadn't had that strange wrenching feeling of a dreadful wrongness for a long time, yet here it was, back again, just as the feelings of stupid Bridey, long forgotten, had come back. It was these children and their crusade – all mixed up with Michael's hands, big, fair, his palms calloused like a labourer's, his dirty nails – his hands, Jack's hands – what strange god were they following, all beyond her knowing?

FIVE

5 MAY

Despite his late night, Capricorn woke very early with a start, because in his sleep he had remembered something, something that might be useful. Not in his own case, but in the search for Bridey Lawdon. The sun was already filtering round the edges of the drawn blinds as he woke, giving his room a dim light with all his familiar objects, the solid chairs, a massive chest, here a bronze figure and there a well-loved sketch, looming mysteriously as something seen but only partly recognized under water.

Without waiting even to rub his eyes he telephoned Manning at his flat, that dun-coloured space in a rabbit warren which he called home. Manning would be up with the sun and once gone would be hard to find. No one worked harder and longer than Manning. He was, in fact, ready to leave when he got the call. He listened to Capricorn's story without interruption.

'... it might not be anything,' Capricorn apologized. 'It was so long ago I had completely forgotten. I was at the Lawdons' wedding. Bridey was happy of course but she had a tearful moment in the garden after the champagne and she told me then that her cousin had come the night before and scolded her half to death for her treachery to the cause. A die-hard IRA man, it seemed. Of course, that was more than twenty years ago –'

'A lot more,' Manning said. 'Rory Collins. One of the main leaders of the Provisionals. No relation to his illustrious namesake. A wild man – the Dublin government would like to get him as much, or more, than we would. I had it from Lawdon the night after Bridey was taken. I might have liked to know before,' he said grimly. 'But Lawdon had not wanted to embarrass his wife. He said there had been no meeting or correspondence between them since the wedding so he thought it unimportant.'

'Oh,' Capricorn answered somewhat blankly. Just wakening, the information had seemed vital, he couldn't say why. But of course Manning would know. He couldn't be expected to relay every scrap of information he collected to someone who wasn't working on the case.

Early as it was, Capricorn had heard Mrs Dermott up and about. No matter what time he left she liked to have his breakfast ready for him. Capricorn had always enjoyed the attention but after the strictures he had received, and with Iris gone, he felt guilty. Now Mrs Dermott, fully dressed and wearing her apron, appeared silently and put a cup of tea in his hand. She drew the curtains back and opened the long windows to the balcony. Fresh sweet air came in with the pale sunlight, blossom-scented. The leaves were thick and full already on the chestnut tree, blown about by a very light breeze. That had helped to give the room the strange, quivering, underwater light.

'As you know, I haven't believed it's IRA,' Manning said. 'But I put through some inquiries to be sure. You know the problem. Every time we use an informant it places him at risk. I didn't want to do it, but it had to be done. I got word back, and the answer is no.

'Rory Collins is believed to be in Belfast, but no one knows of any plan to kidnap his cousin. It isn't thought to be even a remote possibility. He is mad only in the sense of being a total fanatic. He would know Bridey Lawdon simply isn't important enough to make the job worthwhile. Besides, in spite of what Lawdon said, the men who are close to Collins believe he is still fond of her. Unlike the more illustrious Collins, he's not a man who bothers himself much with women, but was thought when they were young to have a yearning for Bridey. Thanks for telling me,' Manning said in a voice making it clear he was anxious to go. 'But I don't think there is any lead there.'

Sipping his tea, Capricorn walked out on the balcony to clear his mind. His garden was at its best, tender green and all the spring flowers out in glory. A blackbird was perched in the hedge, singing rapturously, but although Capricorn saw and heard, the sights and sounds hardly registered.

He knew Manning too well. The fear that had troubled him the night before returned and deepened. Manning was doing his job as he always would but Capricorn was aware of his – reluctance was too strong a word, but it came to mind. Manning had not wanted to risk a valuable agent to get information on Rory Collins. Manning's mind was on the defence of the realm, and not on the rescue of one woman.

He, Capricorn, had his own job. He showered and dressed quickly, and went downstairs to find Mrs Dermott already serving breakfast to Copper, who made an unexpected, cheerful sight, his foxy red head gleaming as he sat by the window to the garden.

'Morning, guv,' he said amiably. 'Had a good bit of shut-eye? Lucky you've got a young man on the job.'

Mrs Dermott took his porridge plate away and brought him a large dish of bacon, sausage and eggs with mushrooms and hot rolls – Copper was a favourite.

'Young in stomach,' Capricorn observed, and commanded a more modest meal for himself.

'It's all the work I've done,' Copper said, sunny. 'I don't like that Fawn outfit – I think the next move is to get a court order to look over their records. They don't want to give us a thing, I can tell you. I was up and round to that Simpson who manages the Dean Street club where our Muffy disported herself. Lives in a little flat just off Piccadilly. Thought I'd catch him with the dew on him and he might be less cagey. He was frightened, but he wasn't talking. I'd like to know who really owns that little lot.' Copper frowned. 'I did dig out of him that Harry Harper, who started the rotten mess, sold out about two years ago and now it's owned by a limited company. FCC.'

Capricorn noted the 'rotten mess'. 'I didn't think you younger men objected to the Fawn phenomenon,' he commented.

'Don't like birds in cages,' Copper replied. 'Anyway, Simpson only mumbles about his running the place himself and that the money goes to a firm of solicitors. If ever I saw someone trying to keep quiet about some skulduggery, it's Mr Simpson.'

'It may be that the real owners don't want to be publicly connected with Fawn,' Capricorn said thoughtfully. 'Or there could be a tax question – his attitude might have nothing to do with the case.'

'He sweated a lot,' Copper replied briefly. 'I'd say Mr Public School Simpson was worried about more than taxes.'

Capricorn took his reference to public school to mean not necessarily contempt for Simpson's education or social status but an indication that his upset, being so visible, must also be profound. He had lost his characteristic calm. On the other hand, Capricorn thought, for many people the question of taxes and tax avoidance was quite enough to destroy any amount of calm. Still, Copper's judgement, especially about people he had met, was usually sound.

'Start the court order business straight away,' he said. 'It's too early to rule out anyone, but the Fawn connection seems the most obvious area to look. I can't believe it was Hoggett, and if it wasn't he, or someone who knew her as a Fawn, that leaves only a wandering maniac.'

'Or some nutter who had seen her picture and found out where she lived,' Copper said thoughtfully. He had arrived at the stage of drinking Mrs Dermott's excellent coffee and smoking a cigarette, and looked pensive. 'It's too easy, you know. She was in half a dozen catalogues as a model, picture, measurements, name, and of course the agencies have her address. All of them swear officially that the lists are confidential, but they will tell you on the quiet that there's no way to stop them being sold. It's not the owners of the agencies, the good ones anyway, but anybody in those offices can make photocopies and sell them and how could the boss find out? And a lot of the grotty operators sell them themselves – they make more money out of that than from the agency bookings.'

The two men who had worked together on so many cases looked at each other. The Mirro murder was already taking on the aspect of one that might never be solved. Contrary to what the public might believe, this often happened early in an investigation. Most murder cases were not difficult, the passions inspiring them were obvious, the killers not clever at covering their tracks. Sometimes they didn't even want to; the sense of guilt and penitence was not lost in England. But Muffy Mirro, with all her public advertisement, her invitation to any sadist with the price of a magazine, her accessibility –

'Worse than that,' Copper went on. 'Who's to say it wasn't someone local, not anyone that knew her but some dirty old bastard who saw her and followed her home? P'raps when she got off the bus coming home?'

'And then came round and hung about until he found her alone? It's possible,' Capricorn said doubtfully. 'Though she hadn't taken a bus home for quite some time. Of course, it didn't have to be a night prowler. She was seen in a lot of pubs – and she might have inflamed the local tradesmen, for that matter. Let's stick with the most likely before we worry about the rag, tag and bobtail,' he said. 'I'll leave you to take care of the legalities. When you get the membership lists, and any record they might have of members' guests, take a couple of men and start winnowing through. Only a few thousand, I expect.'

'Might not be so bad. They get a lot of foreigners, and some would be out of the country on the murder night. And I've got a few ideas of what to look for. I talked to some of the Fawns when I was over at Dean Street last night. Funny tart, our Muffy. Mixed up as they come. Had a fancy for young stuff, all flailing loins, but then she would have ideas of being a Pompadour. Bragged to the other girls about being given lush jewels and rambled on about being the darling of some millionaire sheik.'

Capricorn remembered the magazine article, with Muffy's description of her imaginary flat where she lived surrounded by angora cats and heaps of jewels, gifts from important admirers.

'Actually,' Copper went on, 'she had about fifty quid in a Giro – I checked on that yesterday afternoon.'

Fifty pounds in a post office account; not much for a

would-be Pompadour, Capricorn reflected; not a very high scale for the wages of sin.

'None of the girls know of any boy-friend except Hoggett and the *Fawn* photographer – though they're sure she had plenty. The photographer is out of it, by the way. He was at a class that evening and stayed with the group for coffee and drinks – or something – until after midnight. At Kenyon's studio,' he explained.

Kenyon, the greatest of all fashion photographers, had his studio in Belgravia. Yes, that let the photographer out. Too bad. Capricorn pushed his coffee cup away.

'I have to pick Bly up, we're going on with the canvassing.'

'He'll love that,' Copper observed. Capricorn's habit of doing certain tasks usually relegated to subordinates was not always appreciated by his equals in rank.

'Bly's all right,' Capricorn said. 'You might follow up on the other members of the Rotten Apples. Make sure they were all performing that night. Nobody slipping into town to see Muffy while Hoggett was with his parents. She might have had a fancy for drums, accordion or penny-whistle, or whatever they play now.'

'Bongos, keyboard and fender bass,' Copper said. 'Gawd, you're out of the Ark, guv. Bad as Meg. Wanted me to take her to a symphony concert. Me!'

'You don't appreciate WPC Hardcastle,' Capricorn said drily. Copper's latest affair with the Commissioner's daughter was causing some embarrassment. 'She seems a very pleasant young woman.'

'Nice girl,' Copper said absently, 'that's the trouble.'

'Speaking of girls,' Capricorn dropped the matter of Copper's private life that wasn't nearly private enough. 'Who does the actual engaging of the Fawns?'

'That's easy.' Copper consulted his notebook. 'You want Miss June. Each of the clubs has what they call a Wendy Doe.' He pulled a face. 'One of the girls who's getting on – that can be nineteen with the Fawns – but has some brains. She's in charge of the girls on the premises. I talked to the Wendy Doe at Dean Street, but you'd think she was deaf, dumb and blind. She's been told to keep quiet and she's doing what she's told. But they tell me that Miss June in the main office, that's one June Halliday, has control of the engaging and dismissing of Fawns for any of the places. She has something to do with the magazine as well, but I don't know what.'

He gave Capricorn an address, and the two men rose to go. Capricorn went to his study to call the Yard before he left, but the telephone rang before he got there and the receiver was picked up by Mrs Dermott.

'Yes, she is,' she said in her grimmest voice. 'No, I'll not be waking her. The poor woman needs her sleep, working as hard as she does. I'll tell her that you rang up.'

She put the instrument down firmly.

'It's him,' she said. 'Wondered where she was.'

Capricorn had quite forgotten his aunt, sleeping upstairs. Well, if Tod had rung up to find Dolly, he was not quite indifferent. Things there were not so bad ... He hastily dialled the special number. 'Nothing more,' Burke's voice told him, and the line clicked and was dead. They had no time to waste in that office. It was already a quarter to eight.

Outside, Copper was looking about the square. 'Lovely bloody day.'

The sun warmed the grass in the little park. A woman was walking a big white Borzoi that barked excitedly.

'Bridey still missing?'

Capricorn had a lump in his throat and couldn't speak.

After they separated, Capricorn took the Tube east. In the tunnels his mind was full of a suggestion he wanted to make to Manning. Manning wouldn't like it, he had to think of some tactful way ... While he was still considering, the train came up from underground and rattled the rest of the way in daylight, and Capricorn hadn't had the fidgets or even a light sweat. Bly was ready for him when he arrived at the police station, but that was the last good thing that morning.

Canvassing house to house was always a long-drawn-out process, but now it was particularly annoying. There were very few people at home. All the women in the district worked now, Bly told him. As soon as the kids were old enough, and often sooner. 'It's a new world,' he said, shrugging his shoulders, as if he thought but poorly of it. 'Not so bad for the men. They get the cars, stereo and so forth. But the women are always rushed off their feet. In the old days, if you went house to house, the women were pleased to stop and chat for a few minutes. Now they rush home just in time to line up at the butcher's, rush to put something on the stove, rush to wash up in time to get a bit of a sit-down and watch the telly, and a nosey-parker policeman is nothing but a confounded nuisance, ruining the programme and the sooner they get rid of you the better they like it. Your only chance is if they watch ITV,' he went on gloomily. 'They might give you a word during the adverts.'

They found an old-age pensioner at home, partly bedridden, a man who lived alone with the assistance of a home help and Meals on Wheels. But he hardly bothered to look out of the window any more, he told them, and could be of no help.

'All rubbish,' he grumbled. He was still in his flannel pyjamas, but wore slippers and shuffled a little round the room, staring at them through rheumy eyes. He knew of the Mirro-Hoggett household by the noise which had stopped lately, he said, pleased. It was a pity it was the girl killed and not the bongo player who kept him up all night. 'Think we was a lot of savages rahnd 'ere. And the police don't do nothing.'

He accepted a cigarette from Capricorn and then dismissed them with a scorn that was perhaps deserved, Capricorn felt. Was it not the function of the Metropolitan Police to preserve public order?

As they continued the search it was obvious that Bly had not exaggerated. They found only mothers of very young children who were too busy to bother watching the neighbours by day and too tired at night; the blind and the deaf, the very old and infirm. One young mother made a plea for the eviction of the Rotten Apples, claiming the drums kept her children awake at night.

Only one old woman said she had seen someone approach

the Hoggett house on the night of the murder: she lived directly across the street, between the boarded-up houses. Her own house was neat and well-kept. They first saw her sitting at her window, her head peering round the curtain, cocked-up like an inquisitive bird's, bright-eyed, with her short white hair brushed up into a cockscomb on the top. The door was ajar; they entered to find her in a rocking-chair, a story-book little old lady in a tidy red and blue dress.

She had seemed delighted to see them.

'I'm Joan Bullen,' she said, 'I've lived here fifty year. I know everybody and I know everything that goes on. Can't get about so much, – she pointed to a bandaged ankle. 'But here I am and here I stay.'

Mrs Bullen was a great chatterer. Capricorn guided her to the night in question, and she said that yes, she had been watching from the window. She watched all day and when she went up to bed she watched from there for a while, too.

'That street lamp out there lights up the house across the way and I see all their goings-on. Better than the stuff on the telly,' she informed the policemen. 'Nothing on there that you can't see better out in the street and it's real, not a lot of made-up stuff.'

Her eyes sparkled even brighter. 'I saw those boys go in as squatters and I told my daughter Marj, I said, no good will come from that lot, wait and see. Killed her and carved up the body, I know all about it.'

She chattered on, mentioning details that had not been in the published reports and Capricorn wondered which of Bly's men had been telling tales. So did he, judging by the stern look on his face.

'And you saw someone walk up to the house when, Mrs Bullen?' he asked.

'It was between ten and eleven,' she said positively. 'I know because my daughter helped me upstairs just before ten, 'cause she wanted to watch something that was coming on ten o'clock. And I heard when it went off at eleven, and then I went to bed. Always go to bed at eleven. Bed at eleven, up at seven. Early to bed, early to rise. The early bird catches the worm.'

She gave a little cackle.

'You saw someone go up to the house between ten and eleven,' Capricorn prompted.

'Oh, yes, I saw him all right. Young feller. He rings the bell; the door opens and he goes in, and I thinks to myself, that's not one of the lot that lives there. That blond tart is up to no good.'

'Did you see who opened the door?, Capricorn asked.

She hesitated. 'Couldn't say for sure,'she said reluctantly. 'I thought it was the blond tart, but the hall light wasn't on.'

'And did you see the visitor leave?'

'Oh, no.' She shook her head. 'He didn't leave while I was watching. And I kept my eye on that door.'

'Did you see them through the windows?'

Mrs Bullen sniffed. 'Not over there, not with her. The boys, they never had no curtains at all, but she was a sly one. Curtains up as soon as she went in, and always drawn at night. Thick ones, with not even a shadder showing. That was *her* type. I would've watched to see when he left but once it was eleven I went to bed. Always go to bed at eleven. Early to bed –'

'A very good idea,' Capricorn said. 'And did you notice anything about the man who went in the door?'

'Carrying a plant in a pot, he was, the silly date. Fancy giving a plant to the likes of her.' Her high voice quavered with amused contempt. 'Her with a front garden and a back garden all in rack and ruin – they throws their old boots and rubbish right on the beds of crocuses and iris and glads that Mrs Harkhorn slaved over all them years.'

'A plant?' Capricorn said, with the first hope he had felt on this case bubbling up. The old woman was talking fact. She really had seen someone.

'Yerse.' She described the plant accurately.

Bly glanced at him with a hope equal to his own.

'And what did the man look like?'

'Oh, he was foreign. You know, one of them.'

'Them?'

'Yerse. One of them. Not just a foreigner – 'e was a Paki or what you call 'em now. Well, what would you expect? All sorts round here these days. Don't know where you are. Might as well be abroad, because abroad has come right here. But here I am and here I'll stay.'

'Yes,' Capricorn said. 'I'm sure you will. But what made you think the young man was a foreigner? Was he wearing Indian clothes?'

She looked at him with impatience.

'No, 'course not. Wore a suit and tie. Artful, like they are. But I could tell,' she said in triumph. 'Foreign. Dark hair and dark face. You think I don't know a foreigner? You should chuck 'em all out,' her voice rose to a shriek and her face flushed. 'Chuck 'em out. Out, out – that's what I say –' Her face was scarlet now, her chin trembled like a swollen crop. She tried to hop up; Bly caught her arm and she shrieked something the men could not make out, her face distorted by rage: the bright little bird become a screaming macaw.

She gulped and found speech again.

'Chuck 'em out –'

The door opened.

'Now, Mum, do be quiet.'

A harried-looking middle-aged woman, matronly in a pair of trousers and a print blouse partly covered by an apron, came rushing in and put soothing, capable hands about the old woman.

'You've got her worked up,' she said reproachfully. 'What are you doing in here? I only went up to the baker's for a minute. They don't deliver any more.'

The two men explained their presence.

She gave them a pitying glance.

'You know the doctors only let her out of St Luke's if she takes the pills,' she explained. 'And she mustn't get worked up. Ever so healthy she is,' she said with pride. 'Never would think she's almost ninety, would you? And the doctors say she's all right if no one gets her excited.'

'Unfortunately,' Capricorn said, frowning, 'she had been giving us some valuable information when –'

While they spoke the competent daughter had laid the old woman on the sofa, removed her shoes and covered her with a quilt. Mrs Bullen closed her eyes and went off into a light doze, her head cocked peacefully upon the cushions.

'Oh, I don't know about val'able,' her daughter said uncomfortably. 'She'd say anything ... foreigners, was it? Usually it's foreigners. Never liked the girls going out with Yanks years back in the war. Then she was in the Home a good few years and when they let her out and she came back there was a lot of foreigners moved in and she took against it dreadful. But you can't take notice of what she says. Gets things all mixed up with what's on the telly. Sometimes she thinks it's Germans moving in.'

The old woman woke up with a start.

'Hitler!' she screamed. 'Hitler brought a plant. I seen his moustache! Chuck him out!'

The two policemen escaped with apologies. Outside they looked at each other.

'Phew!' Bly said, shaking his head.

'But she was right about the plant,' Capricorn said, uneasy.

'One of the uniform men has been talking,' Bly said, 'that's obvious. They've been posted outside, supposed to be watching the house. They get bored and start talking to the neighbours. Not many to talk to, now. Nobody wanting to give a bobby a cup of tea. I'll inquire, but they're not going to admit they were slacking on the job gossiping with old loonies, no matter how forthcoming the loonies are.'

As if in support of his words they saw the old woman back in her place at the window, her bright eyes watching them with eager interest.

Capricorn made his way back to the Yard, Bly having promised to return that evening to talk to the rest of the neighbours when they got home from work.

'I'll get what I can out of them between the defrosting and the time they find the milkman didn't deliver and they have to run round to the Off Licence,' he said, sighing.

Manning's men, looking grim and tired, had nothing to tell Capricorn on the Lawdon case. Manning himself was out.

The exhaustive investigation that had taken place in the area where the abandoned car was found had produced no results at all.

Burke blinked up at Capricorn, pushing aside a cup of cold tea, and banged his pockets in search of cigarettes.

'Early in the morning in a residential neighbourhood,' he said bitterly, 'and no one, *no one*, noticed anything. You'd think they were all deaf, dumb and blind, or that anyone with the use of their senses must have been somewhere else. Can you believe it?'

Capricorn gave him a cigarette. He could believe it. The area where Bridey had been kidnapped was a wealthier one than the East London street where Muffy Mirro had lived, but possibly a lot of the women there, too, had jobs. Or they could have been taking their children to school, or conducting play groups, involved with the many activities that kept women away from home.

When Copper came up to his office his news was not good either. He leaned against Capricorn's desk with his usual negligent air, but he had been far from negligent.

'Got the order,' he said, 'but they're still hanging on to the records. Obstinate sods. Simpson came up with some cock-and-bull tale that there are no central lists, that each house keeps its own. Members can use facilities of other clubs by means of a special kind of key card. I have a few men checking round, but I'll bet my last quid they keep a record of everyone that's in and out.'

'They could use just numbers, a computer system,' Capricorn said.

'Yes, but those slave markets like to have a personal touch. "Hello, Mr Fatpockets, how nice to see you again." Oh, and there's a big fuss from the Fawn lawyers. Close-mouthed as oysters, client-solicitor relationship and all that. The Commander had a word with them and finally they came up with the hot tip that FCC Ltd is a wholly-owned subsidiary of Inter-Konto AG, registered in Berne. And if that's not enough, the Rotten Apples, as part of the Warlock Five, were playing in Oldham that night until eleven. You have any luck?'

'Yes,' Capricorn said bitterly, feeling remiss. He should have been contending with the lawyers instead of running about like an Aid. To no purpose. 'I've placed the murderer at the scene. A villainous-looking foreigner, complete with potted plant. Unfortunately he turned out to be a figment of someone's imagination.'

'Funny figment,' Copper said, 'plant and all.'

'Unfortunately the witness is certifiable, in fact, already certified,' Capricorn concluded. 'Anyway, keep at those lists. I'm going to look round.'

Copper, who knew quite well that his superior should be in his office directing, and not 'looking round', did not indulge himself with a quizzical glance. Without discussion, he knew the nervous drive that would not permit his chief to sit, calm and still.

'I hear Manning's got all the best men on the Lawdon case,' he said with seeming casualness. 'They're using the dog teams in some areas ...'

'He thinks she's in this country, then?'

'It's the most likely guess. Nothing to lose by looking. What the old grey ghost thinks ...' Copper shrugged.

The Chelsea studio of the *Fawn* photographer was locked. It bore a printed sign: 'On Location.' Nothing indicated where or how long the absence would be. Capricorn looked at the notice blankly. Although it was lunch-time he had been unable to eat. The photographer, although cleared of suspicion, might have had something to say. Like a mechanical man, Capricorn had made for the next place on his list. Two pigeons, darting purposefully at crusts by a dustbin, squawked as if deriding his aimlessness.

The trained Scotland Yard detective went on with his routine. As he went back to his car a woman crossed his path, hurrying, a blunt profile tilted eagerly into the sunshine. His heart stopped for a moment, his hand reached out, he blurted 'Bridey!'

The woman turned, surprised, and he was staring into the face of a stranger. With a muttered apology he was in his car, but suddenly London was full of women who looked, for an instant, like Bridey Lawdon. He drove through Belgravia on his way to Cambridge Circus and FCC Ltd. For the first time in his life, London and its size seemed infinitely depressing. The maze of streets, the thousands upon thousands of buildings between Chelsea and Cambridge Circus alone. And Bridey could be in any one. Cellars, attics, sheds, warehouses – The fine buildings on this street could not be ruled out. One terrorist group had made a so-called 'People's Prison' in a tent in a drawing-room. And that was just London.

He knew what Manning's men were doing. It was all they could do. Check on the whereabouts of all known terrorist groups. Meet their usual informers. Blanket the area where Bridey had been kidnapped, looking for the slightest of leads. Inquire all over the world about MAYDAY, trying to pick up some hints. Undercover agents of different governments who had infiltrated various student movements would be approached as the most likely informants – some through official channels, others through the 'private network' that agents themselves developed. It was a wide net – with, unfortunately, a wide mesh. MAYDAY could be the smallest of minnows, and probably was.

For himself, he had only one suggestion, and that Manning would most likely refuse. Suddenly, he thought of Lawdon. It would be against police etiquette to go to Lawdon over Manning's head. Manning, his old friend, would find such behaviour unforgivable. But a cold, lost feeling inside hardened into a determination to do it. He would finish up his Fawn work for the day, and he would see Lawdon. Probably it would be a vain gesture, but every chance must be taken, no matter how much etiquette was transgressed or old friendships broken.

After making the decision Capricorn felt slightly better. Soon he was parking his car in a lot near Cambridge Circus and walking to the building that held the offices of FCC Ltd. Fawn Club Communications. It sounded very businesslike, quite removed from warm flesh and erotic yearnings, ready, perhaps, to be listed on the Stock Exchange. He remembered Inter-Konto AG of Berne, even more remote, a world away from Muffy Mirro, stark in a pool of her own blood, her flesh cut into ribbons, the F carved into her breast.

FCC was on the fourth floor, one of a row of doors in a green-painted corridor. No magnificent views here, no splendour. The Fawn organization that spread itself so richly in the clubs, so lavishly in the magazine, didn't otherwise bother with appearances. Their main office kept company with Grrr! Exterminating, Briskett's Plastic Twine, and Jeevey's Teas, Importers. Jeevey's had come down in the world.

Inside was a small, windowless reception room, with a plain, spotty-faced girl presiding over a metal desk, a small switchboard and a typewriter. He asked for Miss June Halliday and sent in his card. He was fortunate, Miss June was back from lunch and the girl pointed out an appropriate door, the only one other than the entrance. Miss June's room was larger and lighter – it had a window on the street – but otherwise was a companion to the reception office. File cabinets, a plain desk, metal chairs; no more money had been spent here, obviously, than was absolutely necessary, and Miss June had added no touch of her own.

She sat behind her desk looking up at him, and he had a feeling he had seen her before, but he could not think where. As he introduced himself and stated the reason for his call he studied her, but his memory did not serve him. She was a small, slight woman between thirty and forty; obviously she had been pretty, but the prettiness had gone. The slimness of youth had become angular, her complexion was now wan and tired-looking, her long, smooth, light brown hair seemed too young for her face in both colour and style. A permanent vertical frown-line marred her brow. She wore, as so many women did now, a trouser suit. Hers was of grey flannel, well cut, and her shirt was of heavy white silk. Her cuff-links he recognized as coming from a famous jeweller. Despite the mildness of the day she looked pinched and cold, and as they spoke she took a fur jacket from an adjacent chair – sable, but well worn – and huddled into it.

She was obviously not pleased to see Capricorn, but instructed her receptionist not to put through any calls or

announce any other visitors until Capricorn left. She
answered his preliminary questions without fuss. He
refrained from discussing the membership lists – Copper was
dealing with that. Possibly she was relieved; certainly she
was fairly frank.

'Yes, I engaged Muffy – Hilda she was then, of course –
myself. I engage all the Fawns. There was no reason not to.
Her appearance and personality were exactly what we need.
Her lack of experience made no difference – we have a
two-week training course which teaches the girls all they
need to know – in fact, we prefer girls who have not worked
as cocktail waitresses elsewhere. Our methods and rules are
quite different from the average lounge, and it's easier to
start fresh. Hilda had a good reference from the factory
where she had worked and that was all that was necessary.
We do need references,' she went on to explain. 'Our girls
serve wealthy patrons and their guests, men who often carry
large sums of money and have valuables on them – watches,
rings, cigarette cases. The atmosphere of the Fawn Clubs is
very relaxing; our members must not have to be on guard.
So every girl is carefully checked for honesty and stability.
We don't want anyone with a tendency to drug-taking, heavy
drinking – certainly none with a record of prostitution. That's
really all I can tell you. I don't see the girls after they are
engaged, unless they have to be dismissed. The girls in each
club house are under the supervision of their Wendy
Doe.'

As she spoke she had taken a folder from the file cabinet
and spread its contents before him. He saw a picture of
Hilda Dortman when she had been engaged, a little younger
than she appeared in the *Fawn* photograph, the face fresh
and laughing, not quite as stunning without the careful
make-up Fawn had taught her; instead of the erotic symbol
she was a healthy young German-looking girl with a frank
sexual appetite.

He turned the pages over: application for employment,
filled out in a large, childish handwriting, conditions of
employment, contracts with *Fawn* magazine; weekly reports
showing figures and giving comments as to her demeanour,

check marks against a printed list. In most cases Mirro had been checked as 'Satisfactory'. Once or twice she had earned demerits from drinking on the job, and some late entries were marked against an X. He inquired about X.

Miss June shuffled her papers and huddled a little deeper into her jacket, obviously preferring not to say, but resigned.

'X is arranging, or attempting to arrange, a meeting with the customer outside the club. Strictly against the rules. Of course, they will do it,' she said, and shrugged. 'We know that. It is something impossible to stop. But the rule is made so that they will at least be discreet and cautious and not solicit openly in the clubs.'

'What happens when they are caught?'

'Naturally, it's annoying. The Wendy Does try to stop it before it happens – that's one of their jobs. We don't want to have to dismiss a girl after the expense of her training and outfitting – all the costumes are made to measure for each girl, and they are provided with several outfits, so that they are always fresh. But now and again we have to make an example. To be frank – we don't usually get rid of a very successful, money-making girl, but when they start to get a little older and they are not as useful – That, in fact, is when they usually begin to look for some other – arrangement, shall we say.'

Capricorn looked at the practical, businesslike woman before him with distaste. He wondered how many young girls had been edged into prostitution from this office.

'You say "money-making",' he pointed out. 'Do the girls work on a commission basis?'

'Oh no. It is simply that, as you probably know, Superintendent, the proximity of pretty girls causes a man to spend money. A simple matter, and quite legal, I believe.'

She certainly knew what was legal, he reflected. She had been very well prepared for her post. He wondered how much she was paid. Not as much as she should be, he guessed. Like Jeevey's teas, she had come down in the world. The material signs were there, and others. She had the poise of a businesswoman, but not the confidence that goes with a good income and a pleasant bank balance. He wondered if she would not have done better in a more honourable business. But that was not his affair.

Irritated, he wondered where on earth he had seen her before. She showed no sign of recognizing him, but then, Miss June was giving nothing away. Already she was replacing the file in the drawer and he knew, if asked, she would say she knew nothing other than what was on the official papers. As far as she was concerned the interview was over.

'Did you have her mother's consent for her to work at the Fawn Club?' he inquired.

'She told me both parents were dead,' Miss June answered.

Capricorn remembered Hoggett's story of Muffy going to her mother's funeral while they were living together, which was after Muffy became a Fawn. But the girl could have lied. He wondered for a moment why the authorities in question had never got after the Fawns for employing young persons at night as, by all accounts, most of the girls were below the legal age for such work. Miss June must cover herself legally with false dates of birth. And she was careful, he imagined, to engage girls about whom no complaints would be made; girls who were unprotected, or who were poor enough so that their families were glad of the wages, and not inclined to kill their golden goose.

Miss June had not asked him to sit down, and now she bent to her intercom, obviously ready to tell her receptionist to put her calls through. But Capricorn was by no means finished. He did not mind being left on his feet; he knew how to use his height to advantage. Now he looked down upon her with a steady gaze and demanded, 'Who are your employers, Miss Halliday?'

She looked up, startled, even less pleased than when he first came, but she was held firmly by his gaze and let the switch on her machine drop.

'FCC Ltd, of course.'

'And who is FCC Ltd?' He had no reason to mention that he knew of Inter-Konto AG – hardly a useful bit of information in any case.

'I imagine the information is filed with the proper authority,' she said coldly. 'I have no personal knowledge of the make-up of the company. I deal with the accountants and the solicitors –' she named two firms, 'and of course I have charge of the Fawns and the Wendy Does. I work with, but am not, except in the matters of staff, senior to the various club managers. The magazine, though part of FCC, is a separate organizational structure, and I deal with them by contract.'

It was a set speech, prepared by a legal pen, he concluded.

'Did you run the Fawns for Harry Harper?' he asked, ignoring her statement. She fidgeted between the arms of her metal chair. She made Capricorn think, suddenly, of a small animal caught in a trap and, as he often did when he thought he shouldn't, he felt sorry for a witness he was harrying.

'I had more or less the same position when Mr Harper was the owner, yes.'

'And exactly who engaged you when Mr Harper sold?'

'Mr Harper told me he was making arrangements for me to continue. He put me in touch with the accountants and the solicitors. The individual club managers remained the same and there have been few changes since.'

'I am sure the new owners were very happy to have someone of your experience,' Capricorn said smoothly. 'And I expect you were given a rise in salary to reflect that.'

She stared, nonplussed for a moment.

'I certainly don't have to tell you that,' she said. 'It could have nothing to do with your inquiry. But I see no reason why I should not; it would save you the trouble of poking elsewhere.' Her voice was crisp. 'My salary was not increased. In fact, it is somewhat less than it was under Mr Harper's arrangements. Mr Harper was extremely generous.'

She stood. 'I must ask you to excuse me now, Superintendent. I have a lot of calls waiting.'

'Just another question or two,' Capricorn said pleasantly.

'Did you know of anyone that Miss Mirro was seeing outside club hours? Any relationships she had with customers – for instance, the ones for which she received those X notations – or any members of your staff?'

'I think I have already explained,' Miss June said coldly. 'I did not see Mirro after I engaged her. When there were contracts to be signed they went to the Wendy Doe, who got her signature and returned the documents to me, and I have them in the file, as you have seen. I have not spoken to her since her original interview, and the only thing I have heard is the comment of the Wendy Doe at the Dean Street club. When I get an adverse report for two weeks running on the weekly form it is my practice to telephone to discuss the matter. The Wendy Doe stated that Mirro was suffering a little from swelled head after her exposure in the magazine.'

Miss June made the comment with a straight face. Capricorn reflected that she must have no sense of humour.

'It was not a question of her actually making appointments with customers,' she said, as he had been sure she would. 'Merely the kind of flirting that interferes with work. It happens frequently enough,' she went on. 'Most of our girls come from poor homes and a little flattery and attention from men of means who seem important to them turns their heads. They begin coming in late, doing the less exciting part of their work, like cleaning and tidying up tables and so forth, in a sloppy way or neglecting it altogether. You get loud talking to attract attention from parties other than the ones they are serving, laughing too much, refusing to take reasonable orders – we call it the star syndrome. Muffy had it rather badly. On the other hand, she had done very well in her work for the magazine and it was arranged that she take two weeks off without pay. It was not exactly a penalty,' Miss June explained. 'She was quite willing to do so. Of course, she intended to try for a modelling career and the films, but we knew what she would find. It is best to let them get it over. Apart from *Fawn*, she would only be offered work by lesser publications, or the pornographic studios. She was much too big a girl for fashion work. And I doubt that she had a chance with the films. She was not talented, and she didn't have the necessary dedication and drive. We expected her to return.'

'She might have found a rich patron,' Capricorn suggested.

'I'm sure she would have, eventually,' Miss June said drily. 'It seemed her obvious fate. But for the moment, I understood from Marian, the Wendy Doe, she was entangled with a young musician – but you probably know about that.'

'Yes,' he said. She didn't mention the *Fawn* photographer, though he was certain she had heard about that, too. The interview was over. He left her shivering in her worn furs, bending over her intercom.

The spotty girl at the reception desk looked after him with an amorous gaze. Was it in tribute to the personal charm of a middle-aged detective, or was she practising to be a Fawn? He decided on the latter. She was probably working for substandard wages on vague promises of Fawnhood which would never be kept.

But why would the efficient if chill Miss June be working for less than her previous wage? Of course, with Harry Harper there might have been a personal relationship, though Harry's taste was usually for the florid, buxom sort. As Capricorn arrived at the ground floor he was still puzzling over where he had seen her before. He made a mental picture of her with a fresh complexion and rosy cheeks, without the frown-line in the middle of her forehead. The sense of recognition was strong, but the circumstances still eluded him.

There was a public telephone booth in the vestibule. He tried to pass it, but his feet walked into the booth and his hand was dialling.

'It came.' Capricorn had never thought that Burke's voice, flat, weary, could evoke such emotions of suspense and dread. 'Typed message on the most common sort of writing paper – the kind you pull off a pad. No prints on the letter. A big emblem – WW with an S written through with the head of a snake. MAYDAY in a horseshoe round it. Postmark W1.

They want a million pounds in gold and a bundle of assorted terrorists, only one of them in our control.'

'Oh,' Capricorn said blankly. He felt sick, though he couldn't think what else he had expected. Even a communication like this was better than nothing. He asked a few brief questions about the progress of the search, wrote down the names of the wanted prisoners, and then let Burke go.

He scanned the list. Apart from the one in England, there were three in prisons in various countries in Western Europe, two in South America, and one in Israel. He wished savagely that each country shot captured terrorists upon conviction. That would end these exchange kidnappings. He could see no connection between them; they seemed like a job lot. Japanese, an Arab, a West German, a Cuban, a French student, an Irishman – and him held in Dublin. All, except the Irishman, of the left, but of widely different backgrounds, beliefs, goals and aims – the kidnappers could have stuck a pin down the list of convicted terrorists.

What hope for Bridey? These demands could never be met. They seemed to have been chosen not to be met. Perhaps they were just put there as units for bargaining. That should spread out the negotiations and give MAYDAY a long stretch of publicity. But they must know it would increase their chance of capture. If they *were* holding Bridey. If she was still alive.

He stood in the telephone booth without noticing the flurry of people rushing past, office workers going back to their jobs after lunch, a little late, jockeying for places in the lift. For no reason at all except that he had ceased to think of the question, his mind served him up the answer which had eluded him earlier; he knew where he had met June Halliday before. He saw her plain: younger, less tense, in evening dress, dark and glittering, with a little fur jacket, perhaps even the same one she wore today, or something similar, but new. She had been in the club known then as the Top Hat, once owned by Charlie Bonomi, jovial proprietor of many clubs and a few other enterprises besides. Pete Moletta, a very different man, cold and crafty, had been his chief lieutenant as well as a prominent villain in his own right.

Moletta had managed the club briefly for a time after Bonomi's death until it was sold and reopened under a new name. Or at least the ownership had been transferred – Moletta was not in good odour with the licensing authorities. Nevertheless, he had taken Bonomi's place as king of the nightclub world. June Halliday had been with Moletta. It came back to him now. Improbable as it seemed – Miss June had the air of a certain background, different from most of the waifs and strays who made up so much of the nightclub world and fell victim to the charms of such as Moletta – she had been Moletta's girl.

Moletta – had he been the banker for the original Fawn owner? Harry Harper, just a few years from being a Cockney barrow boy, could easily have been a front. Very likely he was. And was Moletta, with whom Capricorn had crossed swords before, still the owner of FCC Ltd, having disposed of Harper? It seemed all too likely, yet it didn't jell. Why would Moletta be keeping Miss June on reduced wages? He might have no feeling for a former mistress, but he certainly knew the value of that cold efficiency.

Capricorn shook his head to clear his mind as he stepped out into the street. Trying to think about two cases at once was dulling his intelligence. He remembered Hoggett – Hoggett should be released. An Aid had been sent to check out every detail of his story, but Capricorn had no doubt that it would all prove to be true. He wanted to talk himself to the Fawns who had worked closely with Mirro; the photographer, as well as the Fawn clients who, he hoped, were already being winnowed by Copper and two detective-sergeants.

With the matter of Bridey shuttling through his head – was she dead or alive? All the murdered women he had ever seen floated in a ghastly procession before his mental gaze – he felt an intense aversion to his own planned routine. For the first time he understood the listlessness of depression and melancholy. It all seemed a great deal of toil. He resented the fresh-faced girls walking about town, some still going back to their work after a late lunch, others up for a day in town, to get theatre tickets perhaps and then go shopping.

At the parking lot in Soho where he had left his car he had to wait while an attendant cleared a way through a mass of cars, grumbling that no one had told *him* this car would be wanted again so quickly. In his enforced idleness, Capricorn watched the people milling about the narrow streets, not only the visitors but local women with shopping baskets coming back from the market; pale-faced, furtive-looking men, some expensively if not well dressed, slipping about on doubtful occupations; several respectable-seeming business-men darting into a massage parlour on the corner – one of Pete Moletta's enterprises. Then he caught sight of Miss June, still huddled in her shabby sables, scurrying along like a frightened mouse, disappearing down the same steps, obviously on a sudden search for Pete Moletta.

SIX

5 MAY

Half an hour later Capricorn was not in any of the places where he had intended to be, but instead was standing reluctantly, with a grim look, in the middle of his Aunt Dolly's living-room, under the eyes of two Paddington policemen, separating the furious, implacable Dolly from the terrified Tod. The blue-clad constables were the only sober note in the room. The aunts had their principal rooms done up in high-camp Victorian style. The red plush and satin, the imitation gas-lamps, the what-nots and bric-à-brac, gave an air of fancy dress which suited the aunts, who were usually in fancy dress themselves. But now Nelly and Tilly were far away, only represented by a thousand dark photographs in the front hall, with their dead sister Milly, Capricorn's mother, and his father, The Great Capricornus. Most of the ornaments were in shards and bits over the flowered rugs, Dolly was a red-faced fury in her flannel nightdress with, for some reason, her diamond tiara on her head. Tod, scratched and bleeding, had a picture-frame round his neck, and was clinging to a constable.

The constables withdrew on Capricorn's appearance. He was somewhat relieved to observe that no notebooks had been taken out: Dolly was to get away with one more breach of the peace and assault. Relief turned quickly to anger; she was infuriating, claiming his time and energy as if he were a small boy still, trotting round the provinces with the Magic Merlinos, and not an overworked Chief Superintendent trying to have done with a puzzling and sordid case.

Pete Moletta's presence in his sauna-bath emporium had been denied, but as Miss June was also still missing Capricorn had received this information with scepticism. Before he left Soho he had telephoned Copper about the release of Hoggett, and had the unwelcome though expected news that

Hoggett's alibi had been verified by patrons of the Three Crowns, and the more unwelcome and unexpected news that the Paddington police were looking for Capricorn as his aunt was being restrained from physical assault with apparently murderous intent. They had been called in by neighbours who were accustomed to Merlino rows, so this must be a more serious attempt than usual.

Torn from the comforting arms of the constable, Tod, grimy and sweaty, now clung to Capricorn, who looked at his almost uncle-in-law with distaste. Tod had always been inoffensive-looking: pale, small and thin, with a shock of tow-coloured hair – he resembled a rabbit. His success, Capricorn thought, did not sit well upon him. Tod's hair was long; despite the time of day he was dressed in something like cloth of gold, one earring and a huge mandala on a chain round his neck. It seemed unsuitable for the man who rose to fame singing of the trials of the working lad. Perhaps in concession to this the wide gold trousers were stuffed into hobnailed boots.

'What's it this time?' Capricorn said briskly. If he couldn't settle this in five minutes, he would call one of the men back and let him arrest Dolly.

Dolly's green marble-like eyes rolled frantically.

''E's going!, she said, and choked in fury. 'Wants to go off and live in America! Threatens to sell the house out from under us! Us what took him in when he had nothink! Kep' him all the years!'

Tod, braver now in the presence of the Yard, drew himself up and dusted off his gold cloth, forgetting the frame for the moment.

'I have tried to explain to your aunt,' he said to Capricorn, in his high squeaky voice which had a new note of determination,'but she is being completely unreasonable. She won't listen.'

Dolly had never been reasonable and had never listened.

'You are planning to sell the house and leave the country?'

'It's in my name,' Tod said, 'and it's very valuable now.

It's much too big for your aunts by themselves. And I have
decided to leave the country, yes. I simply can't afford the
taxes any more.'

He caught sight of himself in the looking-glass surrounded
by bronze cupids which was one of the few breakable objects
in the room still left in one piece, and removed the
frame from round his neck with as much dignity as he could
find.

Dolly looked as though she would burst. For once Capricorn thought she had some justification for her anger.

'Wasn't it the girls and me what paid for it and everything
in it and for you from the year dot?' she stormed. 'Don't we
all pay taxes, and the first time you get off the dole you want
to run off abroad like – like Hitler,' she screamed, not
much to the point, but it was the worst insult she could
imagine.

Tod calmed down just a little and looked a trifle more like
himself.

'Doll,' he said, 'you wouldn't believe how much we're
making. That last concert we did up on the Isle of Man, we
took in half a million quid. I can't stay here. We can't keep
anythink.'

'A mill – You're lying,' Dolly said scornfully.

She glanced at Capricorn for support. He couldn't give
any. He didn't know the figures, but he had heard that fifty
thousand youngsters at least had squeezed into the concert;
it had been televised; a film had been made; a vast amount
of goods had been sold, records cut – it was possible. It
seemed unreal to Dolly, knowing Tod to be rather untalented
in his chosen field, and the rest of his group had hardly
mastered their instruments either – except perhaps the Indian
boy who had invented his own, an adaptation of the ancient
bamboo flute, now in plastic and wired to amplifiers and
loudspeakers, so that no one could tell if he played it well or
not – but in spite of, or perhaps because of, this lack, they
had gone to the top of the popularity heap.

'If you've made so much,' Capricorn said, trying to find
some point of agreement, 'why are you selling the house out
from under the girls?'

'That's neither here nor there,' Tod said, turning sulky.
'We made the money – it doesn't mean we've got it. Between
expenses and the taxes you get bugger-all left. And we've got
a few lawsuits, we might come out worse off than when we
started. I can use the house money. And that's why I'm
getting out.'

Dolly grabbed at the looking-glass. It was heavy, which
was probably why it had remained until last, and she struggled, trying to pull it down to smash on Tod's head. Capricorn was beginning to feel rather on her side, but he
restrained her with considerable difficulty in spite of his six
feet four inches and good physical condition.

'There will certainly be another lawsuit if you try to sell
this house,' he said sternly, though somewhat out of breath.
'But, Dolly, you must see your solicitors.' He remembered
that his aunts' lawyers dealt mainly with their professional
matters. He would put his own man on to it. 'I'm sure that
under the circumstances your interests, and Tilly's and
Nelly's, will be protected by the courts. If Tod wishes to
leave the country, that's his business. We can't stop him –
nor do we want to, surely.'

In appealing to Dolly's pride he found a response.

'Want him!' she said with contempt. ''Course we don't
want him. He can go to – to Australia if he likes.'

Australia had become the home, as far as was known, of
Dolly's legal husband. This alliance had prevented marriage
between Dolly and Tod during their long association, which
had bothered Tod but not Dolly, ever, until this point.

'We've never wanted him,' she said tersely. 'No looks, no
guts, no talent.' She added another negative, concerning
Tod's physiognomy and sexual prowess. 'We were sorry for
'im and we looked after him – spent thousands on 'im we
have. We was grateful, 'cause when we was down and out
'e let us move in 'ere, but it wasn't his house. He
was a squatter in the war – he didn't go and fight, not
him.'

All of which was true but they weren't getting anywhere.
But perhaps Dolly was getting herself into a better frame of
mind. He wished Nelly, the most sensible of the aunts, was

at home. Normally he would have called on Bridey for help. Bridey.

'I don't care about his going for myself, but you can't help thinking what a sod,' she said with scorn. 'Calls himself a revolutionary and a good Party member and all he can think about is the lolly – "They murdered the working lad",' she mimicked, in a high whine and with a woebegone expression very like Tod's in performance, extremely comic – all the Merlinos were accomplished mimics, and Capricorn in all his grief and vexation was almost shocked into laughter. 'D'you know, with all his money he owes his dresser back wages for three months? Him and his People's State.'

Tod smiled, a superior little smile which Capricorn had never seen before.

'Now, Doll,' he said, sitting himself down on a velvet chair festooned with bobbles, after pushing off a broken Dresden shepherdess and a bon-bon dish. 'You don't understand economics. That's exactly why I'm leaving. I have to go to stop my money being used to support this rotten crypto-Fascist state. Pull out the wealth of the producers –'

Dolly screamed at the word. 'Producers! You lazy good-for-nothing –'

He ignored her and went on sunnily. His speech was obviously prepared, rehearsed and much used. ' – Pull out the wealth of the producers and the state will sink into oblivion and the new workers' party take over.'

Dolly sneered. 'And isn't America a crypto-Fascist state, then? And won't you be supporting that?'

He didn't blink an eye.

'Ah,' he said, 'in the United States the dissolution process will take longer. It will last my time,' he went on in great hope. 'Besides, my manager has thought up a few dodges.' He sounded more like himself. 'Off-shore islands, you can have a corporation and –'

'Bleedin' hyprocrite,' Dolly said. 'I always knew the Party was a fool to trust you. Let them help you out and get you jobs all these years and –'

'Let it be, Dolly,' Capricorn said, thinking of the time passing and all he needed to do. 'Let him go. Surely,' he said cunningly, 'you've got more than one string to your bow–'

'More fish in the sea than ever came out of it.' Dolly nodded in agreement so vigorously that the tiara almost fell off. She put it in Capricorn's hands. ''Ang on to that. I had to wear it,' she informed him, 'because that sod said he might claim it. He says he's entitled to half of everything I've got as an unmarried husband. Men's rights, he says.'

Dolly was about to explode again. Fortunately, Tod seemed to be arraying himself for departure; settling a Sherlock Holmes cape about his shoulders, and completing his effect with a French beret. Capricorn, to distract Dolly while Tod escaped, asked for a cup of tea.

'Tea?' Dolly said in surprise. ''Aven't had any in the house in years. I'll get you some Guinness, if the char hasn't had it all. She's probably drunk in the basement now, that's about all she does,' she added, unfairly, and went to the basement stairs and hollered.

'Well, I'm off,' Tod said at last, after a long, searching examination of his appearance in the looking-glass. 'Sorry Doll's upset. She can't understand,' he went on smugly. 'I've just gone beyond her, that's all.'

Unfortunately at that moment Dolly returned carrying three bottles of Guinness, and Capricorn braced himself for another explosion and probably the hurling of bottles. But no explosion came. Dolly's mood had gone through one of her mercurial changes. Perhaps she had sampled the Guinness.

She looked at Tod with a half-smile.

'Gawd, if you knew how silly you look,' she said without heat. 'You think you're so clever, but you ought to wait till our Nell comes back before you sign anything. If you didn't get nothing out of that concert it's because Nell wasn't managing you. You're too dopey to manage yourself – a dancing bear's got more sense than what you have.

'And I'll tell you what,' she said folding her arms and looking pensive, gazing at Tod through half-closed lids, 'I've seen your act. You think you're the star and so you was, but you ain't going to be long.'

'What are you talking about?' Tod said crossly. It was nervous crossness, because, as both Capricorn and Tod knew, Dolly had a sure instinct about the profession. It was Dolly who had seen the possibilities of television before anyone else, and Dolly whose indefatigable work had made the Merlinos the stars they were. 'It's my group. I hire who I want and I give 'em the sack.'

'That Yuman Sadness,' Dolly said softly, 'you watch out for 'im. They like him here and they'll go mad over 'im in America. They got a million like you,' she added.

'Suman Sabnis?' Tod said incredulously. 'Gawd, 'e's a joke. That thing he's got makes an 'orrible row. Even we can't stand it and you know we use ear plugs. Only brought 'im in to make a change. Visual impact, my agent calls it,' he said grandly.

'Visual impact all right. I seen it. He came out in a turban and with bandages on his feet and started all that holy, holy stuff – the kids was eating it up. Yuman Sadness they call 'im. He's going to push you out of your own turn, mark my words.'

Dolly was cheering up as she predicted disaster, and Tod was looking more and more cast down.

'Just jealous,' he said as he left, but he was considerably chastened, although he attempted a jaunty chorus of 'There's no business like show business' in a quavering tenor.

Dolly looked about her in the now quiet living-room. Apparently her housewifely feelings were not entirely dormant because she kicked at some broken china with her slippered foot.

'I'm not going after him, Merle, you don't have to worry. If you're in a hurry to be off, I'll take this wallop to Boohoo.'

Relieved at her calm, while wondering for a moment who Boohoo might be – the much maligned char, he supposed, or perhaps the cat – Capricorn picked his way through the debris to the hall.

Dolly followed him.

'Still looking for 'oo done in that Fawn? Terrible, eh?'

Her eyes gleamed: she loved gory horrors. Capricorn felt unable to talk about a mutilated corpse. He looked instead at the photographs of Merlinos, past and present, good professionals, most of whom had eked out modest livelihoods. 'Who would have thought that Tod could be a star?' Tod's lack of talent had been a family joke for more than a quarter of a century.

'I don't think he'll last,' Dolly was reflective. 'But it's the kids who like him, and what do they know? They've never heard anything decent. Cor, Merle, d'you remember our Milly singing "The boy I love is up in the gallery"?'

He did remember, with an odd ache in the heart for his aunt who had died in America, as he left the thoughtful Dolly on her doorstep – he hoped it would turn out to be her doorstep – and drove back to Soho to try to find Pete Moletta.

But before he was to find Moletta the case had taken another turn. The results of the post mortem were due in and he telephoned the lab from a public box along the way. The Divisional Surgeon had been correct. Death had been caused by the first slash to the throat and had come quickly; most of the other injuries had been inflicted after. One interesting discovery was that Muffy had had an abortion not too long before. In spite of this, she had had sexual intercourse shortly before her death.

'Rape?' Capricorn asked the pathologist, who was Hardy, a short, tubby, cheerful man who spoke English and not professional jargon, and who was imperturbable on the witness stand, as defence counsel knew to their cost. 'Doesn't appear to be,' he answered. 'Apart from the first gash there was no sign of any struggle. I would say, definitely not. Nothing else remarkable. She had been a young woman in perfect health, strong and vigorous. Fine set of organs,' he added regretfully. 'She'd had a meal about two hours before, cheese and bread.'

Typical of a woman alone, Capricorn thought. His own Mrs Dermott, left to herself, fine cook that she was, would do the same thing. He remembered the one plate in the sink. Muffy had not had company for dinner. And now he could be almost certain that the attacker had been well-known to her. She had let him in – had there been an appointment? They had made love – and then the attack, out of the blue. Why? Who?

As Capricorn drove through Dean Street he noticed men with women going into the Fawn Club. It was only five o'clock, two hours before its usual opening time. He inquired of the doorman and found out that a private party was going on, a wedding party in fact, the doorman told Capricorn, with a shrug of his shoulders for the oddities of taste.

On impulse, Capricorn went inside. Simpson, the manager, was absent but he found Miss Marian, the Wendy Doe, a pretty young woman who wore the Fawn costume but with the addition of a transparent skirt to mark her change of status, and, when she was out of sight of the customers, a pair of spectacles. Miss Marian had weak eyesight; Capricorn could see, faintly, under the heavy Fawn make-up, the adumbration of the lines that would score her forehead a few years hence. He remembered Miss June. As Copper had observed, the Wendy Doe was nervous, but she had been well-instructed, and repeated Miss June's words carefully.

Despite having worked with Muffy Mirro very closely for a year, she insisted that she knew nothing more of her than she had reported to the main office. The Wendy Doe was obviously more concerned with preserving her job than finding the killer. Capricorn remembered one of Dolly's songs: 'Nobody loves a fairy when she's forty.' This girl couldn't be much more than twenty: did she consider she was fading already?

Even Copper's charm had failed to loosen her tongue. Yet Capricorn, observing her carefully, judged that despite her provocative garments there was a respectable air about Miss Marian. Unlike the more well-bred Miss June, Marian was uneasy on the wrong side of the law. He bore down with the full weight of a Chief Superintendent of Scotland Yard and ordered her to write out the names of the customers who had used the club in the last three months. They might have to go back through the rest of the year that Muffy had been at Dean Street, but that would be a good start. She hesitated, but quailed under his stern gaze, and finally did as she was told. It was not as laborious, nor as difficult, as the devious Simpson would have had the Yard believe. Most of the time it was the same group of men who returned again and again, with a few newcomers joining each month and the members occasionally bringing guests whose names were, as Copper had believed, taken down.

Capricorn watched the girl sitting at her desk, which was a bench made of plastic, but imitating a split log; a pot of white pansies gave off a fresh, pleasant scent – the whole motif of Fawn was rural. Her handwriting was neat and legible; her actions were thought out, her files in excellent condition. This was another young woman who could have succeeded in a worthwhile business, and for the second time that day he wondered at the attraction of nightclub life.

As she gave him the names she looked at him apprehensively. He relaxed and gave her his once-famous smile, so carefully trained by the Merlino aunts the better to please their public.

She smiled back, her soft, short-sighted eyes beaming.

'These are the names we have,' she said. 'Of course, you know, a lot of men give us false ones. Even the credit cards are sometimes made out in the false names, but nobody cares as long as the bills are paid.'

She leaned towards him, her long brown heavily-scented hair brushing his arm as her fingernail tapped against a Brown here, a Smith there, and oddly enough, two Farouks. The barriers once down, she went all the way.

'We know who they are really,' she added, giving away some prominent persons, 'but if they like it that way ...'

And that, after all the fuss, was that. Forgetting or ignoring her instructions, she also gave him the names of the other Fawns, fortunately present that day, who had been closest to Muffy in proximity and in friendship.

'Not that she was much for women, Muffy,' she went on. 'She was the sort of girl who only likes other girls to show off in front of. Always going on about mysterious admirers who gave her jewellery. But her trouble was,' she said

judiciously, 'she was hot stuff. She liked the young fellers
and even if they've got it, they don't give much away these
days. Too many girls ready to go to bed without even a
thank-you,' she said dismally, regretting the days when such
things were better arranged.

'You mentioned to Inspector Copper her musician friend
and the *Fawn* photographer,' he murmured. 'Do you know
of anyone else?'

The Wendy Doe shook her head vigorously, causing her
Fawn ears to tremble.

'No, but we wouldn't, none of us,' she said. Her voice had
the ring of truth, very different from the flat tone of her
prepared tale at the start of the interview. 'See, Muffy was
a terrible story-teller, always wanting us to think her lovers
were so posh and rich. Well, she could've had a rich man,'
she said, and shrugged. 'I'm supposed to stop the girls from
getting off with the customers, but you can't watch 'em
every minute. But they're nearly all old geezers. Muffy
couldn't have fancied them baked on a dish with parsley. So
when she came in with her stories about spending a night at
the Connaught or Claridge's with some millionaire, the girls
thought she's been with someone all right, but God knows
who. Could've been anyone from a young porter on the
Underground to a bobby,' she added, giggling, 'but I'd say
they was always young.'

So much for his case, Capricorn thought wryly. Miss June
was an accomplished liar; this girl was truthful enough, but
they had both said the same thing, the very worst thing from
a detective's point of view.

The Wendy Doe, perhaps belatedly remembering her
orders, claimed she couldn't pull the girls away from their
stations during this very busy time. The wedding party was
indeed large; champagne and hors d'oeuvres comprised the
whole of the wedding breakfast and the girls were constantly
on the move. Perhaps because of the champagne all the
guests looked happy, yet Capricorn wondered how the
women liked being served by these almost naked maidens,
whose youth and beauty of form, in the soft moving lights
representing moonbeams through drifting leaves, were

breathtaking.

Capricorn was almost overwhelmed himself, but there was something in Copper's remark about birds in cages. There was something of the slave market here, mitigated today by the presence of the women guests. Dressed as they were in expensive outfits, carefully coiffed and with make-up liberally applied, they came a poor second in attractiveness to the young girls, as was becoming very obvious by the surreptitious activity of their men.

When Capricorn caught the girls at the bar for a few words he found to his exasperation that they could add nothing to what he already knew. Muffy never went out with the others, did not visit their homes or invite anyone to her own, and told them nothing except her fantasies. They had not known that her name was really Hilda Dortman; they knew nothing of her mother or the caravan, and they only knew about Hoggett because he had appeared at the club. The *Fawn* photographer had babbled, not Muffy.

Capricorn spent the longest time with Muffy's 'best friend', Désirée, a very slender girl with dark eyes and hair, an oval face which looked angelic until she spoke. She had been, before Muffy's arrival, the most popular Fawn.

'Call *her* a Fawn,' she said, 'I mean, it was ridiculous. More like a cow, she was, and some of the men didn't half take it out of her. Her front jiggled something terrible when she walked. Tony Blatter – you know him, he's in a lot of shows on the telly – he's one of our regulars and he always sang when he saw Muffy "Drink a pinta milka day". 'She relished this sample of humour with a smile which showed an entirely adorable dimple.

'Her and her rich men and her jewels. Well,' she concluded with some satisfaction,' '*she* never got out of the East End.'

Désirée was caught up in a rush of business and he saw her sway off with a tray of thin champagne glasses elegantly poised, her breast a prow through the sea of tightly-packed guests, the sleek and rounded hips a magnet to the eye of the most hardened and unsusceptible, which, he thought ruefully, he was not. Or would not be, if his spirits were unweighted with grief and anxiety. It was as well no one here knew who he was, it was hardly seemly for a Chief Superintendent to appear to be enjoying such sights on duty.

'Over the side, Super?' Capricorn turned to see a familiar sneering face, looking more good-humoured than usual at catching a Chief Superintendent *in flagrante delicto* as it were. 'Have a drink, it'll quiet your nerves. The champagne's good.'

'Not like the stuff you serve in your clubs, eh?' Capricorn said absently. 'What is it, Très Gaie, or Belle Paris, vintage vinegar and lemonade?'

Now that he had the names he wanted it was no longer so important to track down the owners of Fawn, but, since the gods had brought him Moletta, he might as well inquire.

Moletta smiled, the half-smile that was the furthest limit of his gaiety, gratified at what he considered a tribute to his business acumen. 'Heard you were looking for me,' he said casually, 'but I had to show up here, friend of the groom. Very nervous – only his third wedding.'

He was actually sipping the champagne, but slowly. Moletta was not a drinker and never gave anything away. No use beating about the bush, if Moletta was to give information it would have to be a trade, an IOU that Moletta would collect at his convenience. But it should be done.

'I saw Miss Halliday,' Capricorn said bluntly, 'and she didn't seem anxious to enlighten me about the present ownership of Fawn.'

'What makes you think I would know?'

Moletta leaned against the bar, his dull cold gaze following the undulating bodies of the girls with a certain detached interest.

Moletta couldn't know – though he might suspect – that Capricorn had seen Miss June going into his place near Cambridge Circus.

Capricorn lifted an eyebrow.

'I thought you knew everything that went on in the West End. Your manor isn't it?'

Moletta smiled again at this witticism.

'Fawn is all over the country,' he said. 'You know that.

Too big for us local lads.'

'Wasn't too big for Harry Harper,' Capricorn said. 'Thought you might have set him up.'

Moletta neither confirmed nor denied this. He was watching the Wendy Doe. Her spectacles removed, she was still very pretty. As she took a parcel and a scarf from an incoming guest to hand to the cloakroom girl, a five-pound note passed from hand to hand and her smile beamed as she leaned over to tuck it into the only possible place upon her person, the top of the little Fawn boot.

The Fawn costume was so designed that when its wearer bent downwards the maximum possible of young curves was exhibited to the viewer's gaze, and the Wendy Doe's transparent skirt increased, if possible, the attractions of the view. But Moletta only remarked, 'If this was my place I'd get rid of that Simpson. He ought to be here – those girls are walking off with all the profit. I'll tell you something for nothing.' He rested with one arm outstretched along the bar, not bothered at all that he was hindering the girls in their work and causing a strain in their wide Fawn smiles. 'I hear that Fawn is in financial trouble.'

Capricorn was inclined to dismiss this gift as worthless. Money was pouring into the Fawn Clubs, and from what he had seen expenses were very tightly guarded. It probably just irked Moletta to see girls allowed to keep their own tips – he would never do such a thing, which was probably why the girls in his clubs were never as young and pretty as these.

'Who did Harry Harper sell to, Moletta?' he said abruptly. 'Who is behind FCC Ltd?'

Moletta smiled, this time actually showing teeth, large gleaming teeth. 'Inter-Konto AG of Berne,' he said agreeably.

Capricorn wondered if anyone had ever tried to knock those teeth down his throat. Moletta noticed this uncharacteristic onrush of rage.

'Edgy, aren't you?' he commented. 'All in a flutter at the Yard, I hear. Lost Lawdon's wife. Can't help you there.' He stroked his long pale chin. 'Not local work, you know that. A lot of little grafters have a soft spot for Irish Lawdon.

Always good for a touch with a hard luck story. Word would come round if anything was known.'

He looked at Capricorn's face. 'You haven't been so diabolical to me, guv,' he said meditatively. 'I'll really give you something. 'Course, if I need a favour I'll apply.' He glanced mockingly at the Superintendent, responding to the grief, which he saw as weakness, and despising it. 'Inter-Konto is an Arab outfit. They have an Egyptian rep in London who runs things. I'll even give you his name and address.'

He took out a card and a thin gold pen, and wrote something on the back. He handed it to Capricorn as though it were a tip.

'Now you really owe me,' he said, and turned his attention back to the girls.

Capricorn swallowed hard and looked at the words in Moletta's small tight hand.

Hakim el Hamed, he read. Mouna Import-Export. There was a number on Greek Street.

Various persons, slightly inebriated, were trying to thrust champagne upon him; someone murmured about a toast to the bride and groom as he made for the door. But while everyone's attention was on the libidinous remarks Capricorn was followed and caught in the entrance hall. His arms were clutched, a heaving round young bosom was pressed against him, the strong but pleasing scent of the Wendy Doe assailed his senses.

'He gave you Mr Hamed's address, I know he did,' she said, her rather lovely weak eyes blinking at him distractedly. 'There'll be trouble – and all for nothing. Mr Hamed couldn't have had anything to do with – with Muffy. He's a very nice man,' she added mournfully.

So he's mixed up with you too, Capricorn thought.

'I suggest you take great care of yourself,' he said, hoping she would pay attention.

'Oh, you don't understand,' she said breathlessly, her little hand clutching his arm.

'Wendy Doe,' one of the girls called, sticking her Fawn head into the doorway.

'I must go,' she muttered, 'but you're all wrong –'

She disappeared with a flutter of flying skirt. Capricorn found himself back in the street, in the workaday world, caught up in the usual press at that hour of people trying to get home from their jobs, while others were arriving for their pleasure. Perhaps Moletta was not entirely wrong and Capricorn had been more affected by the proximity of the young Fawns than he would care to admit; certainly his nerves were on edge, and his mind was taken up with the question of where he could find Charles Lawdon that night: would he go home or continue searching the streets? Without doubt, as he walked the short distance from the club to the Greek Street address given him by Moletta, his observation was not as sharp as usual.

All he noticed, when he arrived at his destination, was that the office of this apparently rich international company was in even shabbier quarters than FCC Ltd. The building was three storeys, old without distinction, and whatever its original purpose had been, was now converted into offices. It was dingy, and the door to the street, unlocked, badly needed a coat of paint.

Capricorn entered to find himself in a corridor illuminated only by the fanlight. He peered round, searching for some indication as to which door belonged to Mouna Import-Export. The tiled floor was cracked, sagging and whole tiles were missing. Capricorn, for once not looking where he trod, caught his toe in a hole and pitched forward.

For a second it seemed as though he had kicked a fuse. A blast roared in his ears; the floor cracked open; a chunk of the ceiling fell as Capricorn was hurled backwards. Something smacked against his head as he reached his arms out to break his fall. The door before him crashed open and through the dust and flying fragments he saw a youth stretched on the floor, his head covered in blood.

SEVEN

5 MAY

Bridey had been sleeping little. Her body by now was too bruised and stiff to find rest, even on the bit of blanket that Michael had thrown on the floor for her after the first day. Her pain was worse; she had a sick headache. And her cold was worse too, settled deep in her chest; she had spells of coughing that left her raw. She thought she had a touch of fever. Fear would not let her eyes stay closed; as sleep started to come she would see the door bursting open again and Natasha there, the gun aimed in her direction. Bridey would start awake, but the nightmare never disappeared. It was only beginning.

The Arab boy had stayed outside her door in the night. She had heard him restlessly padding up and down – not the staccato steps of the girl. But to her relief it was Michael who brought her breakfast again – and the few things she had asked for in a small brown bag. Then he turned to give her the privacy she needed – but, desperate, she called him back.

'If you don't want a murder on your conscience, you'll have to help me get out of here,' she said.

Plain speech, after all, was the only thing that came to her mind.

'That girl will kill me without a thought. Yet I'm no help to you dead.'

If only he didn't wear that stupid mask, she thought. As if a face were the only thing that identified a man. She would know him anywhere from the set of his shoulders, the sound of his tread. But the mask made it so hard to judge his response.

Michael didn't leave her in doubt for long.

'No help alive either,' he retorted, after a moment, just as blunt as she. 'I don't decide, but if I did – why should I save you? What have you done for us, all the years you could have helped?'

She couldn't pretend she didn't know what he meant – she might have been talking to Rory. His little kindnesses then – they had been merely the acts of a boy used to some politeness to women, not that he was, at bottom, different from the others. His cause; their cause. The Children's Crusade. She felt a terrible weariness. How could she explain to him that she had never understood politics and never would? Bad enough in Ireland, but in Palestine – only the Lord himself could solve that, and he was the one who started it. Or was that sacrilege? She was no theologian, she had always relied on the parish priest to tell her the rights and wrongs.

'Helped in what?' she said, though she knew she wasn't helping herself now. 'To set bombs in the Tower and blow up little children?'

'We're helpless within the power structure,' he said doggedly. Words someone had taught him from a book. This boy wouldn't think like that. 'Curse the dhirthy English' would roll more easily off his tongue. 'If what we do is violent, it's because that's all people like you have left us.'

The words came by rote, but there was feeling in his voice, for all that. He believed he was doing good, like all the other crusaders. People always thought they were doing good, in her experience. Even the girls who wanted to get rid of their babies – better for them not to be born unwanted, they would say. And mean it. Although it wasn't cold, she shivered. Someone walking over her grave.

'What have you to do with those others?' she said, without much hope. 'D'you think they care at all for Ireland?'

'The oppressed people have learned to work together. It's our only strength.' His book talk again. His voice didn't have the ring of emotion now. Likely he was beginning to doubt what he was saying. She thought of the brother and sister – never had she seen anyone less oppressed than Natasha. Her face, seen clear, had had a matchless arrogance. English royalty would look modest, humble beside her.

Perhaps Michael followed her thought because he went on

doggedly, 'We're lucky that there are those who could sit back, rich and safe, but throw in with us anyway. With pity in them.'

She snorted. That girl had as much pity as a cat. Why she was doing what she did Bridey couldn't know, but it wasn't from compassion, surely, tenderness or love for others. She had heard them quarrelling about the mess in the house. 'Dirty pig,' Michael had called her. 'Kiss my cunt,' Natasha had answered with a contempt that went deeper than his. Bridey had flinched – familiar as she was with the language of street-women, she had never got used to such talk from young girls.

'Well, I'm not rich and it looks as though I wasn't safe. You've enough sense to know a housewife when you see one. I might not have joined you, but that's no reason to break the Lord's commandments and do murder. And I've done you no harm. I keep my house, do what I can do, and don't meddle in what I can't understand.'

Once again, he flushed up to the eye-sockets, but this time with anger. A temper like Jack's, too.

'Do you think that lets you off?' he said, in his own voice at last. 'You think you can sit back and enjoy the comfort of your kitchen, with half the world starving and armed men like your husband to keep them down, and then cry you don't understand? Well, now you know. *It doesn't let you off.*'

He slammed from the cellar door. Her talk had only made things worse. If they could be worse. But Michael was a strange lad. After he had put the sentence of death on her, he came back with another large brown bag. She was frightened for a moment – but it was no knife, gun or rope. It was a big, rolled-up rubber mat. He threw it at her, like a bone to a dog, but he had meant it to ease her bruised body, after all.

She was weak and deeply chagrined. Not until now did she realize how much she had clung to the hope of the Irish boy taking pity on her. But she had just been deceiving herself; he was as set in his notions as the others, and she was nothing to him. Terrifyingly, she could see herself as he saw her, smug and careless. But what *could* she have done? Her running about for the nuns – it seemed the best she could do. He was right about the hungry world, she knew that; Cynthia raised money for Oxfam and Bridey had given what she could, but of course it wasn't enough. She knew that too, yet if she had starved herself it wouldn't have helped one poor child.

There had been the children close to hand – her play-group for crippled children. A memory came sharp from many years before, when she had taken a class to a musical version of *Peter Pan*. They had loved the song,

'I won't grow up, I won't grow up,
I will never go to school
I will never eat my spinach,
nor obey the golden rule –'

And now these young people in their masks, so close to play-acting and yet it was real. Michael – he had said Charlie carried a gun to keep the starving in their place, but that was rubbish. Charlie looked for murderers and – Well, it was true that Charlie would lock up Rory and his like if he caught them. How many murders had Rory done? She couldn't, wouldn't think of it. Charlie might shoot him first. But that wasn't to keep people hungry. Surely no one was hungry in Ireland now. Even the refugee Arabs were fed, not well, perhaps, but fed. Gervase and Cynthia were always raising money for them, partly in memory of old Lord Lawdon – he had been on a Commission to Palestine and he loved the Arabs. Yet these youngsters had wanted to kidnap Cynthia just the same.

She rubbed her tired head. For all that, the boy was right in a way; there were hungry people still. And the good Lord would think it wrong that some ate and did not concern themselves. A professor on the wireless had said there were too many people – at that point her mind stopped as it always did. It *was* too deep for her, and that was the truth. She wished she could stop her thoughts from jumping round, like nuts in a rolling barrel. But the boy was right about that too; it didn't let her off.

At least he had brought the mat. She rolled onto it, and it

gave her a little ease. She looked at the package and
wondered how she would manage with her hands still tied.
If only they would give her some water and soap to wash in
– but for one of their strange reasons they would not. She had
used some of the tea on her hands and face, and now she was
thirsty. But if she were to die – resolutely, she turned the
thought away. Despair was a sin. Somehow, that thought was
heartening. She managed to tidy herself a little, but, ham-
pered as she was, it seemed to have taken an hour. Then she
tried to eat some of the food but her mouth was so dry and
soon her mind was at it again.

No use to deceive herself. They intended to kill her, now
or later. Wait for orders, the boy had said. But he expected
them to come. He and Michael were good soldiers, the girl
a bad one, but it would be all the same for Bridey Lawdon
at the last. Michael would not help her. She had to think of
a way to escape without his help. She had heard him walk
down the passage to the chair by the door. The others had
not come back down. If he were alone sitting with the door
open and the sun on him, he might fall asleep, great sleeper
that he was.

Suddenly she remembered something that brought a
quickening of her pulse. Something that had *not* happened.
When Michael had left the second time there had been no
scraping of the key. She always listened for the turn of the
key, but then she had been too crushed by her failure, too
bewildered by his odd little kindness, to take notice. But
some part of her noticed.

Yet her excitement, she cautioned herself, might all be for
nothing. If the passage was as she imagined, if Michael did
fall asleep by an open door, still she never could creep past
him. With her feet tied, her one shoe dragging, she could only
slither on the floor, much too slow, or hop which would
waken even that country boy.

She brought her knees up close to her chest and tried to
push her hands between them to reach her ankles, but the
ankle ropes went too high, she couldn't open her knees
enough. The wrist ropes were too high as well to part her
elbows much. Whoever had taught those youngsters to tie up

a prisoner had known what he was about. She strained against the rope until her wrists turned dark red and started bleeding, but the rope would not give. Pushing down on her left side, she twisted her knees to the right and reached down. The mat helped the pain in her bruised bottom, but her tied wrists banged uselessly against her lower calf. No wriggling could get her fingers to the rope. She tried bending and reaching the other way but it was the same. She lay back against the wall, panting, the tears pricking her eyes. Her arms were too short and plump, and her breasts were sore and strained from her struggle.

She glared at the ropes. To think of a grown woman being beaten by a length of old kitchen line, the sort she'd shoved in a drawer with a few wooden pegs almost every other day of her life. The very homeliness of it made her as angry as she was frustrated. But it wasn't like her new kitchen line, she noticed. It was like the old one, brown with fuzz sticking out. The new one with the pink loops was much thinner, smoother and blond – nylon. It wouldn't stretch and it was almost indestructible, the man had told her when she bought it. This was real rope, and rope always had give in it. The one on her wrists was freshly tied – the girl had done that yesterday. But from all her wriggling she thought the ankle rope had given a bit.

Her shoe had no laces; it was not much more than a slipper. She scraped her foot against it until the shoe came off. That was the easy part. She shoved one foot down in a quick, skin-burning thrust – her tights had been in shreds long since. With one ankle bone just below the other she wriggled and pushed and slithered. Her back hurt and she braced it against the wall. Without the mat she didn't think she could have borne the pain.

She went on for what might have been an hour, two hours, three – she didn't know. At last, with most of the skin of her right instep ripped away, and with the heel of her left foot so cut into by the rope that she was sure she must be lame, she got her right foot out of the bond. Suddenly the pain was nothing, nothing at all. If only she could have done the same with her hands ...

Already she was on her feet, the left only dragging a bit. The door made a squeak as it opened – her belly tightened to a knot. But there was no sound from down the passage, except a steady breathing. She tried the door again and crept out. There were three feet of stone flags, the same as in 'her' cellar, another green-streaked wall. A staircase, leading to the locked upstairs door. A big calendar, with the days marked off, hung from the post, but she had no attention for that. At the end of the passage, very much as she had imagined, was the door open to the garden. And Michael. He was sitting on a kitchen chair, his head resting on the wall, without his mask, a gun in the hand that rested on his knee. He hadn't heard her step. The sun was warm and he had nodded off.

She was seized by a sudden elation. Those others, they would not bother to keep a look-out with Michael on guard down here. She crept by, holding her breath. Like a miracle, her feet were on grass. The sun was so bright on her face, she could hardly open her eyes. She hung back against the wall until she could see, blinking rapidly. Her heart sank. Beyond the small patch of grass was water, but not a river as she had thought. Looking round she saw she was on a tiny island, with the water lapping up to the hedges. Sweating from the sudden heat and fear, she edged round the house to be sure. The house was in the middle of a small lake.

Bridey was a good swimmer, but her hands were tied. There were no shears handy by the hedge – but there was a row-boat with its oars drawn up behind the privet bushes, out of sight from the shore. A quiver of hope ran through her. At the back of the house the channel was fairly narrow. She could paddle with one oar, but could she get off without them hearing the scrape of the boat? Michael would not wake, but if one of the others came to the window she was done for. All at once, in the bright sun she was cold, shivering. If she stayed still and hidden, no one would notice her absence until they brought her evening meal. It would be easier to get away after dark ... but it wouldn't be dark yet. Not outside. The days were long now. The boat sat, a mute temptation. She could see the further shore, bushes, trees. No sign of human life. No good to risk a scream or even try to signal.

Nor was it any use to try to wait till dark. Should they come looking for her there was nowhere to hide. She had to take the chance. And Natasha and the Arab boy *might* not hear. After quarrelling most of the night they could be asleep, like Michael. She summoned her courage and made a swift, silent dash for the bushes. It was only a few feet, but exposed as she was it seemed endless. As her hands touched the blessed planks of the boat she crouched as low as she could get, surely out of sight from all but the topmost window. Past the bushes the ground was mud to the water's edge – it shouldn't make much noise. Her back to the lake, Bridey gave a good heave into the water and turned – to see Natasha, stark naked, springing up from a rubber mat over a gravel bed, pushing the barrel of a machine-gun up into her face.

EIGHT

6 MAY

'Mindless violence,' the Commander's voice came grumbling over the telephone. 'I'm glad you're all right, old fellow, but one can't help thinking – not so long since the worst thing a policeman was likely to face was a punch-up with a villain with brass knuckles. Now – why, it's only a year or so since you had a bomb in your house –'

Capricorn listened politely but impatiently. For once he had no interest in reflection. He was ready to leave the hospital and wanted to be about his business. Already he had tried to reach Lawdon, but of course he was out. Perhaps he wasn't going home at night at all. Capricorn escaped at last in a state of keen irritation not entirely caused by his headache. He had a slight scalp wound from falling masonry, and his head had been partly shaved. A small bandage covered with pink sticky plaster at the peak of his crown looked like a dunce's cap.

It had happened many times in his career that he had been injured in the course of duty – more than the average policeman, certainly more than was usual in the higher ranks, due to his fondness for doing so much legwork himself. He had been reproved for this on more than one occasion. What annoyed him so much now was that he had not been injured in the course of duty at all. It had been merely a stupid accident. Certainly a bomb had been detonated. The Yard had quickly found it to be a simple affair in an attaché case, the sort that the IRA had been leaving about London for years. It was a small bomb, not intended to do much damage except in a crowd of people. The experts believed it was an 'aborted mission'. The bomber had become nervous. Delayed perhaps in reaching his assigned target, he had left it in the first open doorway he had passed.

Capricorn had started a hare that perhaps the bomb – very

quickly prepared! – had been set by the mysterious Hamed alerted by a telephone call from the Wendy Doe at Dean Street, though it seemed hardly likely. But he was soon cleared. Early that morning Capricorn had met the youth who had been injured in the bombed building. He was a young Arab, Tüssün Hamed, the mysterious Hamed's son. Capricorn had to accept that the bombing was accidental. Hamed would hardly have wanted to blow up his own son, even to put off an inquisitive superintendent.

The main damage had been to a plaster partition wall, but the youth had been caught by flying glass, as well as getting a bang on the head from a falling fixture. He had lost a lot of blood, and the doctors, after giving him a transfusion, wanted him to stay another day in the hospital, but the youth had signed himself out on his own responsibility. Clearer thought suggested to Capricorn that a bombing by Hamed would have been stupid – there was nothing to stop Moletta giving the information to someone else.

Back at the Yard he spoke to one of the men on the demolition team, who told him cheerfully that it was very likely his own stumbling about in the hallway that had set off the bomb's mechanism.

'You walked into that one like John Q. Public,' the man said. Capricorn, who within twenty-four hours had been accused of concupiscence and amateurishness, found that despite his profound worry and sense of dread he was not beyond feeling mortified.

There was no chance of seeing Hamed yet. No other bombs had been found; the engineers had found no structural damage, and emergency repairs had been made, but Hamed, nervous, had taken himself off, no one knew where. The young Tüssün, a sulky youth, had already told Capricorn he knew nothing of his father's business affairs. And so Capricorn put an inquiry through Interpol, and then gathered up Copper to go over the Dean Street list.

The results of the court order had produced little more than Capricorn had already received from the Wendy Doe. The members fell into two groups, London businessmen and visiting foreigners. Only a few country members availed themselves of the entrée to the London club, merely a dozen were noted in the last three months. After a quick rundown, it was found that only a half dozen of the foreign visitors had been in the country on the murder night. Of those, two were still in London, the other four had returned to their homes. Inquiries about the missing four were sent off, and Copper and two sergeants started the job of checking first the foreigners and then the London businessmen. An Aid reported to Capricorn that the *Fawn* photographer, David Baker, had returned to his studio and Capricorn, too restless to stay in his office, set out again for Chelsea.

The broad sweep of the Thames sparkled in the noon sun. All London was clothed in fresh green, and chestnut flowers were everywhere as Capricorn made for the studio just off Cheyne Walk, but today none of these spoke to him; there was no lifting of the heart or refreshment of spirit. Even the girls in their spring clothes did not please him – too many had merely left off their shawls and jackets, and their boots and jeans were not fresh in the bright light. There was too much traffic; the Embankment stank from petrol.

Baker's studio was not fancy but it was well-equipped. The walls were covered with blow-ups, mostly society women, elegantly dressed, and Fawns, hardly dressed at all. Muffy Mirro occupied a whole wall. Baker himself was a tall, rangy young man not yet thirty, good-looking in a virile and open-air way. He sounded completely silly, but Capricorn knew he must have talent or Kenyon would not be bothered with him.

He was very ready to speak of Muffy with no encouragement.

'I adored Muffy,' he explained, running his hands through his hair in an engaging manner. 'She came here the first time for a session of photographs for *Fawn*, but she stayed for hours, and I took hundreds of pictures for my own collection and to place elsewhere – though don't tell Fawn that. They think they *own* their girls. She was inspired. Muffy was – she was visual sex incarnate.'

Capricorn thought he remembered that phrase from the *Fawn* article.

'Look.' Baker gestured at the wall. Most of the photographs of Muffy were the usual sex goddess poses, but one caught Capricorn's attention. She was clothed, in jeans and a leather jacket; the jacket was open half-way to the waist and she wore nothing beneath; she sat astride a motor-cycle and laughed into the camera. There was little make-up on her rather large, glowing face, and the shot sang with energy.

Baker was rambling on. 'When I finished shooting we made love for hours – it was the only natural thing.'

He and Muffy had planned to marry, he told Capricorn. He seemed ignorant of her engagement to Hoggett and unconcerned that he had been married already. His wife had been in London at the time of Muffy's death, so although their love-affair was blazing, he had not seen her for ten days before. He repeated his story of being with Kenyon that night and had no more to add.

It was a curious affair by his own account. He knew nothing of Muffy's real background. Although she had told him she shared quarters with a musical group she had not elaborated. He had never been to the East London house; she always came to his studio. Capricorn learned that Baker had never taken her out anywhere; their affair was conducted from beginning to end in his studio. Their only venture out of doors to the street below had been to take the shot on the motor-cycle with which she had arrived one day for a sitting.

'It was her motor-cycle then?' Capricorn asked. It was an expensive machine for a girl with only fifty pounds in the world, and there had been no motor-cycle among her effects. But Baker knew nothing about it. He had not asked.

Nor had he known about her abortion. Capricorn believed his surprise at this news to be genuine.

'She said nothing about being pregnant,' Baker said, slightly puzzled. 'But then, she wouldn't. I don't think Muffy was into the family scene.'

Capricorn brought up the subject of other boy-friends, but it seemed that Baker had not known even about Hoggett until he had seen the newspaper stories.

'She never mentioned anyone else,' he said vaguely. 'I

didn't ask her. She didn't ask me, come to that. We only talked about each other.'

She had told him that she wanted to leave the Fawns; she didn't feel appreciated and was hoping for work in films. No definite plans had been formed; their time together had apparently been spent in photography, love-making and, Capricorn suspected, smoking cannabis.

Except for his talent, Baker seemed to live in Cloud-Cuckoo Land like Muffy herself. He had no idea who might have wanted to kill her; he knew of no one who had shown any interest in her and who might have felt rejected or scorned.

'Did you know anything of her background, that she was half German, for instance?'

'Of course I knew that,' Baker said, staring.

'She told you?'

'I could *see.*'

Of course, he could see. His brains were in his eyes. Sighing irritably, his head throbbing, Capricorn made to go. He believed this young man knew nothing. Baker was talented, Hoggett was not, but they were curiously alike in their lack of interest and knowledge concerning the vital, beautiful young woman they seemed to have shared. Capricorn tried to visualize Baker, jealous, following Muffy home, quarrelling, murdering and performing those strange, sadistic mutilations with a handy knife. But the picture would not form. Baker was without passion, without even a keen interest, except perhaps in his work.

Already Muffy was forgotten, he was regarding Capricorn's head, his eyes narrowed. His hand, surprisingly gentle and yet firm, turned Capricorn's chin and brushed the hair, which Capricorn had combed over the taped bandage, the better to display the wound.

'I like that,' he said thoughtfully. 'A good head, with a touch of the macabre. Could you stop for a few shots?'

Capricorn, with a fleeting thought of John the Baptist, declined.

Baker sighed. 'God, I get so bored with this stuff.' He gestured limply towards his work.

'Those whores from Fawn – except for Muffy, just adding machines under the skin. And old society bitches for the class mags. You know Kenyon's work,' he said broodingly. 'But when he started it was different. Those models he used were fantastic. Now *La Belle* wants *them*.'

He glanced at the cosmopolites, who did look, Capricorn had to agree, somewhat overwhelmed by their clothes.

'After two facelifts they look like mummies. I'd like to show them in a winding sheet,' he said vengefully. Giggling, he showed Capricorn a few shots where he had superimposed grave clothes and a coffin round a celebrated member of the 'jet set'. It was wicked, but Capricorn was shocked into a smile. Baker, like Kenyon himself, was quick to catch the look of death. Baker turned it to ridicule; Kenyon, the greater artist, had shown Old Mortality as companion even to the gayest of girls, flouncing in their summer dresses.

Capricorn looked at the one portrait that lived, worthy of the master. A girl, very slender, with intense dark eyes which subdued her fashionable gown into a background. Baker had caught, or created, a look of severe purity, an olive-skinned Joan of Arc.

'Very good,' Capricorn said thoughtfully, the art lover for a moment superseding both the detective and the man.

''T's all right,' Baker said indifferently, his attention veering off as he examined a negative. 'Tima – a stupid bitch like all the other stupid bitches, but she's young and she has bones. Pity she's so stinking rich, lousy Arab, she might have made a half-way decent model. Thinks she's too bloody important to give a proper sitting. Hyped up with coke half the time.'

He glanced for a second at the portrait.

'I'm putting that in for the *La Belle* Kenyon prize. It's all right,' he repeated, 'but it was just luck.'

The policeman in Capricorn told him this was a dead end. His search for Muffy's killer would be in the long check of the Fawn customers, the wearisome house-to-house canvassing. Bridey would have to wait to be rescued without his help. As he left, the dark eyes of the girl in the portrait seemed to follow him with derision.

NINE

6 MAY

At first the disappointment Bridey felt, after a brief taste of freedom, was almost too much to bear. For she had been so close. Afterwards, from the noisy quarrels among her captors, she knew she had been right. They had all been dozing – and the Arab boy fast asleep. Unlucky for her that Natasha had chosen to sunbathe, screening herself from the boys by the hedge. For Bridey to be poked back into the dark cellar after having the clean air, the blue of the water and the sky, the patch of green grass strewn with buttercups, was like being shovelled back into her grave.

The girl had pushed her with the snout of the gun, and Bridey had got a crack with the butt on her head before she was flung into her cell. Her feet were tied again so that the rope bit. There was blood in her hair, and later a big bump on her forehead, and all the time a bad headache, but apart from the one blow there had been no beatings. Natasha had made one reprisal, though. Kneeling down beside Bridey, she had taken off the rope binding her wrists and replaced it with a handcuff of heavy wire that kept the wrists crossed and dug into them so hard that after a time Bridey could hardly feel her right hand.

Michael looked, and Natasha said they should have used the cuffs from the beginning.

Natasha had screamed at Michael for his sleeping, and then when she saw the things he had bought for Bridey: 'You fool.' Her voice had been heavy with scorn. 'Don't you realize any chemist will remember a young man –'

Michael said something Bridey had not heard. Swore at the girl, most likely. '... Woolworth's,' he ended.

'And if you had been arrested for stealing ...'

'Ah, I'm a professional.'

Michael laughed.

The girl had responded, quieter. Then she had given orders in a tone that carried.

'Since you've been asleep today, you can take two turns on the look-out tonight.'

Of course, they must watch the shore so that they could not be surprised. There was some moonlight. How would they see in the dark of the moon ... she supposed they intended –

'Give your orders to your brother,' Michael answered angrily.

So the dark boy was Natasha's brother, as she had thought.

'He can listen to you if he likes. I follow the Colonel's orders while I'm here, and I don't want to hear a lot of talk from any woman – let alone a slut that walks round naked, worse than a prostitute off the docks –'

Natasha had screamed for her brother.

'Kerim,' she called in her anger. Bridey wondered if that was his real name. He had had a fight on his hands but they quieted down at last.

Bridey, if she had not been so cast down, might have been amused at the quarrel. Whatever these crusaders had in common, the West Country Michael and Natasha, whoever she was, were still in different worlds. When Bridey had a moment to think, she realized she had been right about the girl. The lean brown body that she had seen had the look of care and money. A cherished child brought up to luxurious young womanhood. Straight limbs, clear eyes, glowing skin and shining hair. And accustomed to her way. To her, Michael was a servant and he knew it.

But whatever Michael might think about his companions, it would make no difference to Bridey Lawdon. When it came to the point, he had made that clear as clear could be. It had been Michael who helped bundle her back into the cellar, and he was the one who had turned the key with a heavy, final sound in her prison lock.

TEN

6 MAY

As Capricorn left Baker's studio, the scarlet of a street telephone booth beckoned. He must call Burke; there could be news. But there was no news on the Lawdon case. One of his own men told him that Hamed had now returned to the bombed premises and would be there for some time, clearing up. For the first time that he could remember, Capricorn was not eager to talk to a potential witness. Hamed himself, involved as he seemed to be with Marian at Dean Street, was unlikely to be the inflamed and murderous lover of Muffy Mirro, but he should be checked. More important, he would know the mysterious owner or owners of Fawn, any one of whom might have had some connection with the dead girl. Capricorn felt tired and listless, like an experimental rat on a treadmill, going through a set of motions. But he was the scientist as well as the laboratory rat; his brain directed him while his feelings protested he should be tramping round every corner of London, of England, looking for Bridey ...

His brain also reminded him of domestic troubles. Before he left the booth he made a quick call to Paddington to be sure that all was well. Everything was quiet. Tod had not appeared again. But for some reason not explained to Capricorn, and which he really didn't want to know, Dolly was excited and coy. She did just remember to ask how he was progressing in the search for Bridey – she had seen a report on television – and foolishly he explained he was not assigned to that case, though he desperately wished he was.

'Desperate? You? Fancy you getting all excited,' Dolly said sardonically. She was not one to let a perceived weakness go by. 'Anyone would think you was her old man. Bit of slap and tickle, was it?'

He wondered why no one had ever murdered Dolly. But he obeyed his brain like a good detective, and drove round to Greek Street. The exterior of the building was undamaged, but in the corridor fresh wooden planking covered the hole in the floor. The partition wall to Mouna Import-Export was replaced by uprights and closed off with plywood. He had been very lucky, Capricorn thought without enthusiasm, as he observed the direction of the blast. If he had stumbled a few feet closer he would have fallen right into it. The solid door and door frame of Mouna were still intact, odd survivors of the explosion.

The lock was broken, the door opened at his touch, and Capricorn was surprised to see Tüssün Hamed already back behind his desk that took up most of the room. He was still scowling. The white bandage round his head emphasized his dark skin and shining little moustache that gave him a foreign look, despite his European clothes, and did not at all prepare Capricorn for Mr Hamed the elder.

The rear office was not much larger than the front one. The man in his shirt-sleeves who was sweeping the dust off a filing cabinet with a brush and pan did not look like an Egyptian and certainly was no Arab. Of middle height, well-fleshed, his skin a light olive, with a balding head that appeared tonsured, he could have been a Greek perhaps, or a Levantine of some sort. His warm brown eyes smiled up at Capricorn as the detective introduced himself, and with great affability Hamed begged him to sit down.

'You were injured,' he said, with an air of mourning, 'so terrible – in this place – what could such criminals want here? But the other policemen said they thought it was a mistake. A mistake!' He sighed deeply. 'Who would think such things could happen here, in England?'

A look of sadness, which might have been genuine, suffused his features at this thought. 'But you were coming to see me *before* the explosion,' he went on, with great interest. 'What can I do for you?' His manner was obsequious.

Capricorn gazed, wondering. This was the man for whom the Wendy Doe at Dean Street had shown such warm and genuine concern – only affection and something more could cause that much anxiety. Hamed was illuminated by a bare bulb that hung from the ceiling, the only lighting fixture in the room. The small aperture onto a court in the back wall let in almost no daylight. The coat of Hamed's suit was on a chair, his white shirt crumpled and past its first freshness. It was open at the neck and showed a large quantity of dark curling hair. The girl was young and pretty – but there was no accounting for sexual tastes.

'I have come to ask a few questions about the Fawn clubs,' he said, 'with reference to the death of Muffy Mirro.'

'Very sad.' Mr Hamed looked unhappy. 'Unfortunate young woman.'

'You don't say terrible in this case,' Capricorn observed.

The brown eyes gazed at him. 'Ah, such crimes as these will always be. Even in England. Who can prevent such things? Women of that sort, unprotected ...'

Capricorn was irritated by Mr Hamed. What he said was true, but it was clubs like Fawn which were busy turning girls into 'women of that sort'. And the kind of protection Hamed might like to provide would no doubt be contrary to English law.

'It is quite likely one of your clients who is responsible,' Capricorn said coldly, knowing he had no right to say that. 'And you have not helped us, making it so difficult to get their names.'

Hamed spread his hands in a helpless gesture.

'But it is not easy for us, dear Superintendent. Many names given to us are false. And you must understand, a certain discretion in such places is always observed. Besides,' he said, sighing, 'little Marian has given you everything you need. She was quite right to do so. There is nothing more I can tell you. I am merely the London agent for Inter-Konto, collecting, collating figures and dispatching them.'

His eyes blinked sleepily.

'Doubtless you wish to know if I knew this Muffy Mirro,

but I have never met her. I heard of her only through Marian – and then the newspapers – dreadful. And to spare you time, Superintendent, on the night of the unfortunate girl's death, I was here in this office until very late. My accountant was with me, going over the books of Mouna Import-Export. A little tax problem. That is my main business, and a good, profitable one. In existence a hundred years,' he said proudly. 'I inherit from my mother, a blessed woman. I will leave it to my son, in-sha-Allah.'

'The Fawn enterprise is very profitable, I take it,' Capricorn said, refusing to be diverted.

'Very profitable,' Hamed replied, but the look of happiness was gone.

'I would like the names of the officers of Inter-Konto,' Capricorn said firmly.

'Of course, Scotland Yard will want this. I am sure you gentlemen can obtain it. But not from me,' Hamed said, smiling apologetically. His teeth were large, strong and very yellow. 'I have no secrets.' He rose and went to his filing cabinet, a single unit of four drawers. He removed two slim files, and showed Capricorn the typed sheets.

Capricorn took the address. It was a firm of solicitors, who, if questioned, would know only Mr Hamed and a bank. This investigation was like the old shell game.

'How did Inter-Konto come to engage you, Mr Hamed? As you say, your business –' his voice had an edge – 'after all is import-export, not young – girls.'

'Ah.' Hamed smiled. His look of happiness returned. 'The great Scotland Yard does not know that? But it is simple. Mr Harry Harper who began Fawn had his offices in this building. On the top floor. He used to complain – after a big lunch, too many stairs. He was a big man with a full belly. I, too,' he patted his soft round paunch with something between disapproval and delight. 'But fortunately I have no stairs. We got to talking. Mr Harper asked me to take charge of his books. When he sold out to FCC – they had their own book-keepers, accountants. But they kept Miss Halliday and myself. I am merely a clerk. I have nothing to do –' he looked regretful – 'with the charming young ladies.'

'Except,' Capricorn pointed out, 'the Wendy Doe at Dean Street.'

'Ah!' For some reason Hamed fumbled in the top drawer of his desk, found a pair of gold-rimmed spectacles and put them on his nose. He gazed at Capricorn earnestly. 'That is not what you think, perhaps, Superintendent. Miss Marian is a fine young woman. Not flighty. I have known her since the days of Mr Harper when she was an ordinary Fawn. She would bring the records to this office. Steady, reliable, her mind on her work. She saves her money. I would like to marry her,' he said unexpectedly, 'but –'

He paused. He looked at the door behind Capricorn. It was a little ajar. Capricorn clearly remembered closing it behind him. Perhaps the catch was loose, after the bombing. Hamed tiptoed to the door, his big plump body ludicrous in an attitude suitable to a slender young dancer. He peered round, and sighed, perhaps in relief.

'He's gone,' he said. His tone was that of any parent of an adolescent child. He shook his head. 'You can't get them to settle down to work these days. And we lost so much time with the explosion, and the police and the engineers, and Tüssün going to the hospital. He does almost nothing as it is. What do you do with children in these days?'

Capricorn had no response to that, except the familiar sense of relief that he didn't have the problem, but he remembered very clearly that in the hospital Tüssün had declared he knew nothing of his father's business.

'He told the truth,' his father said dolefully. 'He should, but he doesn't. I only ask him to begin studying the books, but after half an hour at his desk he runs away. Always off to his friends. I did my best for him,' Hamed went on. 'More than I can afford. His mother, my late wife, was an Arab woman and she stayed with her family. She would not travel. When Tüssün was of the age, I sent him to the American University in Beirut. But he did not stay there. As they say, he "dropped out". He sighed again. 'What is to be done? He learned nothing, but he is a Pan-Arab, and a Moslem fanatic. He forbids me, his father, to take Marian for a wife. She is not an Arab, he says. And a lot more besides. She is an angel,

Miss Marian, to put up with him. All is nonsense – these are not the words of the Prophet. And my mother, his grand-mother, was a Greek.'

Capricorn, who was almost crushed with his own troubles, nevertheless felt an unwilling twinge of sympathy. He believed very little of what Hamed had told him, but about this son he was telling, Capricorn was sure, the simple truth. He had a moment of passing wonder how children, all over the world, seemed to have got the better of their parents, remembering the short shrift he himself had received at the hands of The Great Capricornus. The fact that he had had no desire to be buried alive at six years old had made no difference to a showman in need of a novelty in his act.

Hamed was still talking volubly when Capricorn rose to leave after copying down the name and address of the accountant for Mouna. The accountant, he was sure, would confirm what old Hamed had told him of their working together at the time of the murder, but it had to be checked. Capricorn noticed the very few papers in the wire baskets on the desk. Everything cleared away perhaps after the dust and debris of the explosion – or hidden from the prying eyes of the police. The telephone had not been dusted, and had remained silent during the interview, possibly still dam-aged.

Capricorn's first impression remained; this office seemed a very humble parent for the glossy Fawn business as well as Mouna Import-Export – if it existed. Not that such arrangements were unknown in London, he could think of more than one large organization with dark, cramped offices in the City. There was a very English touch here – pride of place on the desk was given to a pot of flowering violet-col-oured pansies.

The half-wrecked small front office, windowless, held only Tüssün's desk which was bare and had no telephone. A waste-paper basket held a discarded bouquet of white roses, only slightly wilted in the close airless space.

'Look,' Hamed said sadly. He rescued the flowers and put them in a tumbler. 'Marian brought them. Left from the wedding party. She loves flowers, that girl. She should have a house and a little garden.'

The sadness faded at the thought of these delights.

'She gave them to Tüssün, you see. She does everything to make friends. But he cares for nothing, that one. Perhaps he will go back to his mother's family.'

A faint look of hope lit up his features and he smiled again, warmly.

'Goodbye, Superintendent. If I can help you, do not hesitate to call.'

He bowed from the waist – Capricorn felt that at any moment Hamed might call him 'Effendi'. The old fraud. Yet, when Capricorn turned back in the corridor for a last look at the place where he had stumbled and detonated the bomb, he saw Hamed outside his office door looking after him with a puzzling glance. It was not unfriendly – Hamed had the look of a man who perhaps would like to say more. But when he caught Capricorn's eye he changed his mind and went back, softly, into his office, closed the door and locked it, a gesture proclaiming a desire for privacy rather than safety, as a child could have toppled the plywood partition.

Capricorn went back to the Yard, knowing he had wasted his time, especially when Copper reported to his office. Copper had, as usual, been getting through a prodigious amount of work. He looked at his chief and laughed.

'Getting to be a real Aunt Sally, guv,' he said. 'You ought to be more careful.'

The Dean Street lists so far had been unrewarding. Capricorn went over the results of the first checks with increasing gloom. The two foreigners, on the night of the murder, had both been staying with English families well outside London. Nearly all the Englishmen had either stayed late at the club, or remained home all night with their wives. Of the exceptions, one had been with his mistress, three had been at the same all-night party, two had stayed with their mothers, one had been in hospital, and one was being entertained by a member of the royal family. Except for the four foreigners who had gone home and remained to be heard from, the situation was distinctly unpromising.

Although Capricorn and Copper remained at the task until

midnight, re-checking and collating the results, pausing only to eat a sandwich at Capricorn's desk, nothing useful was found. Not one of the Fawn patrons admitted to ever having been with Muffy outside the club. A few confessed they would have liked to, but in spite of her very on-coming manner Muffy had never, when it came to the point, accepted an invitation.

'A terrible tease, but nothing doing,' one man said tersely, and that summed up the comments of all the rest.

'Looks like our girl really didn't go out with the customers,' Copper said. 'In spite of all the carry-on. The girls said she liked young stuff – that leaves us with a nice choice of a million or so possible pick-ups.'

The evidence so far wasn't conclusive, but Capricorn agreed. It looked like Muffy's killer would not be found among the Fawn customers after all.

'So far the only one we've found with a motive is Hoggett,' Copper observed. 'Unless – there might have been somebody who knew her before she was a Fawn. I think tomorrow I'll leave Sarge to get on with this, and I'll go down to Barton's and that place where she lived in the caravan and see what young Hilda was up to.'

Capricorn could think of nothing better and they said goodnight. Copper headed for his country house, where perhaps Meg Hardcastle was waiting, but Capricorn got into his car and drove about the streets. He made for the districts with rows of condemned buildings, and searched doggedly through empty house after empty house, knowing that the terrorists were almost certainly outside London, yet feeling that no chance should be left unexplored. It was a comfort to know that Manning had felt the same way. In street after street he met teams of men, from Uniform Branch as well as CID, making the same search. Not only in London, he knew; all over the country.

'The moon's a help tonight,' one of the men remarked.

It was a help, but they found nothing except a few squatters and a great many rats. The light was cold on the dreary streets, and Capricorn, weary and depressed, his head hurting abominably, was glad to come across Lawdon, still

out searching, and to persuade the exhausted man to go home
and get some rest. Lawdon refused, but Capricorn bundled
him into his car and took him home over his protests.

'You'll work better after a few hours of sleep,' he said.

They both knew that Lawdon could not sleep.

'You'd better have a drink,' Capricorn said, 'it might
help.'

Lawdon insisted that he join him, and Capricorn, with his
mind on his idea, went.

They didn't go to Lawdon's study, but down to the
kitchen: Bridey's place. They sat there as they had sat so
often, watching her. Capricorn knew that Lawdon would
want to talk of his wife, and the kindest thing would be to let
him, but while Lawdon was drinking a stiff whisky and soda
Capricorn looked round. Lawdon had not been eating, he
was sure of that. He said nothing, but found butter and eggs
and made an omelette, claiming a hunger himself that he
didn't feel.

Capricorn waited until the food and drink had brought
some colour back into Lawdon's face, and then he told him
his idea of trying to get in touch with Rory Collins through
Bridey's relations.

Lawdon looked at him sharply.

'I told Manning everything I knew,' he said.

'Manning will do what he can,' Capricorn said, 'but
inevitably any inquiry he makes will be known to come from
Special Branch. Even if there is – anyone – who might want
to help, certainly they won't want to deal with him.'

'I've thought of that,' Lawdon said, frowning, 'but –'

To try to reach Collins personally would be of course to
go over Manning's head – it would not be well seen. But
Capricorn knew that Lawdon would do it – for his beloved
wife.

'There's almost no one left over there,' Lawdon went
on.

He lit a cigarette.

'Bridey's father died, you know. Her brother Jack is
somewhere in the United States – I don't know where. One
sister is in a convent – there is only Eileen, the schoolmis-

tress. I don't know if she – she'll have seen about Bridey in the newspapers.'

He looked up at Capricorn, blinking. 'There's no reason to assume the IRA is involved. If they were, most likely they would have said so. They're not backward –' He peered at Capricorn. 'What happened to your head?'

Of course, Lawdon had been too busy to have heard.

'A bomb,' Capricorn said, 'also not claimed by our Irish friends. But, Lawdon, Collins might have sources of information that even Manning doesn't have. A telephone call to your sister-in-law: it couldn't do her any harm. You might say you think the IRA is involved. That might provoke Collins to something –'

'You're right, of course,' Lawdon said. He rubbed his forehead. 'I haven't been thinking straight. Excuse me.'

He jumped up, as if any action was a relief and went upstairs to his study. The normally courteous, thoughtful Charles Lawdon was telephoning his sister-in-law at four o'clock in the morning. Capricorn rose to go, his purpose achieved, and met Lawdon in the hall.

The estimable Eileen had not reproached him or made a fuss.

'She's a fine woman,' Lawdon said, 'I don't know why we've seen so little of her. I told her I wanted to call, though there wasn't any news. Just to tell her that we were searching – though we had nothing to go on. She has a lot of sense. I did mention that it might be the IRA. She didn't say a lot, but I got the idea she would do what she could – if she could do anything. Manning thinks Collins is in Ulster, you know.'

He went with Capricorn to the door.

'It's odd, the things that come to mind,' he said. 'It must be years since I told Bridey what she means to me. How I need her ...'

The moon was hidden now, but Capricorn could make out Lawdon's face in the light coming from the hall. Lawdon watched him go, as if clutching at the last bit of human companionship. Chief Superintendent Lawdon, bulwark of the Murder Squad, one of the most respected men at the Yard, lost, lonely. There was nothing left to say. Capricorn made for home and his own bed, but not to sleep.

He lay listening to his clock chime the quarter hours. What he could do he had done, he thought, even though it meant that he had bypassed Manning. And not for the first time in this case, he remembered. The night after the kidnapping, in the shock and confusion, he had telephoned his old friend Delaney, now with the CIA. But Manning would not mind that.

It had been a long, unhappy talk. Delaney would do anything possible, he had said, but he couldn't promise much. It was unlikely MAYDAY was American-based; Americans turned revolutionary preferred to strike their own. Delaney's fears matched Capricorn's. Manning looked at the large picture: great political powers inspiring subversion and chaos. But the American talked of groups of young people, nudged into armed rebellion by professionals, no doubt, but going off by themselves, autonomous, self-destructive, deadly.

'Terrifying as bands of armed children,' Delaney, the father of eight, had said. 'You know, after the big shoot-out with the SLA where most of them were killed, the ones that got away made for Disneyland. Oh, sure, a tourist haunt is easy to get lost in, but ... It's what makes it so damned hard ... My God, they're ours –'

That had not been all. Delaney had talked of the Weathermen and other groups. 'Join the revolution and become an instant celebrity,' he grumbled, 'the easiest way to do it.' The Manson thrill killings. Tonight Capricorn's mind could not stop churning. Every published detail of the Manson murders came vividly to mind, the laughter of the killers, and the young woman victim wore Bridey's face. He was only released from the torment by the peal of the bedside telephone.

It was Burke.

'Hope I didn't wake you, but I thought you'd like to know. We've had a bit of luck. Very small and it might not help at all, but at least it's something. We're not telling Lawdon until the morning, though – he'd be straight down here, and he's got to get some rest.'

Capricorn told him he wasn't in the least sleepy and he'd been praying for a call.

'It's the scarf Bridey was wearing that day. We're pretty sure it was that day because Lawdon saw it the day before. It had been a present for her birthday and she'd been wearing it nearly every time she went out. A woman picked it up in the road on one of those very quiet, almost country-like streets in North Chingford. That doesn't mean Mrs Lawdon is there, of course. There are only a few houses on the street but they're all occupied by families known in the area. The woman apparently noticed it was an expensive scarf and took the trouble of dropping it off at the police station. It's one of those handwoven jobs and it had B.L. worked into the design. Very fancy, you might not notice the initials; but one up to Chingford Station, somebody spotted it and sent it along to us.'

'Probably that's where they changed cars,' Capricorn said. 'Wherever they were going they wouldn't want to arrive in a car which might have been seen that morning.'

'Manning agrees,' Burke said. 'We've shifted most of the hunt to points east. It *could* be a red herring, of course, but we have to follow it up.'

Burke wasn't sleeping much either. Capricorn thanked him and let him get on with the work. For a few hours Capricorn tried to doze, but for the first time it wasn't his own case that ran ceaselessly through his mind. Over and over, as if he were trying to use a psychic power in which he did not believe, his tired mind was trying to probe the world to seek out the hidden prison of Bridey Lawdon.

ELEVEN

7 MAY

Capricorn was up at dawn. It was to be another warm, beautiful day, but for once he did not stop for a moment on the balcony outside his room and look down at his garden. He would go straight to the Yard, he decided. His body felt somewhat refreshed, and his mind, though still troubled, was capable of work.

Mrs Dermott was up before him. 'Thought I'd get an early start,' she said casually, brandishing a huge duster. 'Now we're rid of that Iris I've been giving the house a good turn out. Your breakfast is ready.'

His appetite was small, but he was grateful as always for Mrs Dermott's coffee, and after two cups felt somewhat lighter. That scarf – it could be a help. North Chingford was London, but it was also the fringe of Epping Forest. Epping was no great, dense forest these days, but it could still give shelter to a small band of terrorists. Because most of them were urban, and usually kept to the cities, it didn't mean that the woodlands and countryside could be ruled out. If he were Manning, he would make an intensive search of the forest immediately.

His telephone was ringing. Mrs Dermott answered and came to him at the table. With the early sunshine on her face he noticed that she already looked tired – the women were right, he had to do something about that. Another Iris ...

'It's your poor aunt,' Mrs Dermott said. 'He's come back, making trouble. You'll have to go.'

Never had Capricorn thought to hear Dolly described as his poor aunt, especially by Mrs Dermott. But, angry, reluctant, he knew he would have to go – if Tod was making trouble, Dolly was capable of murder. In two minutes he was in his car and on his way to Paddington, driving furiously. If Dolly was awake that meant she hadn't been to bed. This row might have gone on all night. He found himself wishing the local men would arrest her – at least she couldn't get into trouble in gaol. Though, being Dolly, she probably could.

Tod was in the crimson parlour, in his working man's outfit today, faded blue denim and a peaked cap, decked with odd bits of washleather – a comic window-cleaner. He was accompanied by a small, frightened-looking man wearing spectacles, more conventionally dressed, who was trying to hide behind Tod from the furious Dolly. Seated in the big velvet armchair, crying and sniffing, was a very young, fragile-looking girl. She had a tender white complexion set off by the red hair that hung, bell-shaped, round her small pink ears. Her only visible garment was a dressing-gown that belonged, he thought, to his Aunt Nelly; her throat and feet were bare.

'This is Mr Cream, a private investigator,' Tod introduced one of the strangers, with a smug look. 'We came here first thing to get evidence – and we've got it! Your aunt,' he went on, 'has set her lawyers on me about the house. Well, if she intends to go to court, we'll get there first. Mr Cream can give evidence that your aunt is conducting a disorderly house. Boohoo is a prostitute: Mr Cream caught her in bed with a man in your Aunt Nelly's room just now.'

So this was Boohoo. Her sobs increased, racking that frail-looking body, but curiosity about the newcomer caused her to look up. Capricorn caught his breath for a moment. Her eyes were large, with the clear rich green of very costly emeralds. Swimming in tears they had a startling beauty – Boohoo was all English loveliness. Her tears obscured her vision; she wiped her eyes with Nelly's silk, embroidered sleeve and for good measure she wiped her nose with it as well.

'You bloody great fool,' Dolly said between fury and scorn. 'Call that thing a detective! Merle's better than that. No law against having a man in your bed – there wouldn't be a woman left out of prison if there was. What about all those kids at your concerts then, having it off in the fields, rolling round like a lot of swine in their own dung? You can't prove there was money passed – nor was there,' she added, recalling herself.

'There was fifty pounds in notes on the dressing-table,' Tod said triumphantly.

Boohoo sobbed again, and the dressing-gown slipped to reveal her milk-white knees and thighs. Cream was staring at her, fascinated and abashed.

'And 'oo's to say it's not 'ers?' Dolly said scornfully, not a whit disturbed. 'Fifty quid might be something to 'im –' she looked at the loose-lipped Cream in contempt – 'but it's nothing to a girl like Boohoo. She makes more than that in tips in half an hour. She's no tart, you fool.' She grinned at Tod with the malevolence of victory 'She's a Fawn. Goin' to be in the book this summer, the pictures are took already.'

Tod was shaken.

'If she's a Fawn, why wasn't she working, then?'

'Don't you think they gets a night off?'

Dolly's smile widened. She had Tod on her spear's point now, and she was going to drive it in.

'Not that I care what you do,' she told her almost-husband of so many years, 'it was just your busting in here like that what upset me. Now that you don't live 'ere no more – I've 'ad all your things packed up and sent to storage – here's the bill.'

She threw a piece of paper at him, grinning evilly, probably forgetting that she had not as yet put her teeth in.

'And don't come round no more. My 'usband wouldn't like it.'

'Yer 'usband?'

Tod's expression was comic, incredulity mixed with a sudden dismay.

'Yerse.' Dolly's hand fiddled with her curls like any coquette and Boohoo, forgotten, whimpered.

'The Incredible Ivan,' Dolly said. 'He's back in London and of course he's been looking for me. Made his pile in Australia, retired, and now he wants to get together. So I'll thank you not to 'ang round no more, making trouble between man and wife.'

Tod and Cream were already beating a strategic retreat.

Dolly slammed the door after them, and returned in triumph.

He needn't have come after all, Capricorn thought ruefully, Dolly was in good form. But perhaps it was as well – if Boohoo was indeed a Fawn.

'Oh, did I come it over 'im,' Dolly was giggling. 'Silly bloody fool never had any more sense in his head than in his arse. Caught old Boohoo right on the job, silly cow.'

'I've always told you –' she looked sternly at the girl – 'you should always put the money away before they takes it back. And fifty quid's nothing now, a good-looking girl like you – a lot like me at her age, she is, Merle.'

The girl wept afresh.

'You're embarrassing Miss –' Capricorn pointed out. He couldn't help looking at the girl. Surely she *was* a Fawn – belatedly he remembered seeing her photograph in Baker's studio among the rest. He had not thought of it at once – the photograph had been in black and white, and it was the girl's colouring that caught the eye.

'Oh, don't take notice of 'er,' Dolly said comfortably, as if Boohoo wasn't there. 'That's all cobblers. Always yowling. She looks smashing when she does it, see, and it drives all the old geezers mad. Made a lot of money when she was a Fawn, but she got the sack.'

'Didn't get the sack,' Boohoo spoke, her voice muffled by her sobs, and Capricorn started – it was rather as though a pet had found the power of speech. 'They told me I had to go to the country and I wouldn't. Know too much about it, see. Go there, and make up beds, and get pulled about terrible by a lot of dirty old sods and you don't get nothing out of it, and if you says anything there's trouble.'

Capricorn had many more pressing things on his mind, but he decided to have a word with the AC. The country places were not under the jurisdiction of the Metropolitan Police, but the AC. could be in touch with the County Constables. If some of the girls could be persuaded to give evidence, it might be possible to close up these pestholes.

'Same thing as the sack,' Dolly said, shrewdly. 'So I took her in when she give up her room. But I don't know what I'll do when Ivan comes home. Very respectable, my 'usband,' she said, with a new unctuous gentility that sat ill upon her.

Capricorn believed the return of The Incredible Ivan to be purely imaginary – he had disappeared before World War Two – and did not trouble to inquire.

'You worked at Dean Street, then?' he asked.

'And I was their best Fawn, except Muffy,' she sniffed. 'I would have been on the cover ofthe book except they said I wasn't big enough.'

She looked down at the half-open dressing-gown disconsolately. 'But the photo-feller said I had the prettiest pink ones he'd ever seen and 'e was going to do a big colour spread but then they took against me.'

'When did they take against you, Boohoo?' Capricorn asked quietly and with a sympathetic air.

'All of a sudden,' she said. 'They started up last week. When Muffy was killed I thought straight away that I might be top Fawn, but they come over all nasty instead, I don't know why. Unless it was that Désirée, she's a miserable bitch, telling tales to the Mummy Doe and she told Miss June. Always at it, Désirée. She's nineteen,' Boohoo added, 'dead jealous of the young girls. Pretended to be Muffy's friend, but she was always telling tales on her.'

Capricorn, very interested, elicited Boohoo's real name. She gave it reluctantly – and with reason. It made Dolly hoot. Her name was Ethel Krapp and Capricorn was sure of one thing – it had not been on the list that Marian had supplied to him. He thought he knew more about the reason Boohoo had been eased from her London job than she did.

'Said I didn't have the class for Dean Street,' she was grumbling, her tears rolling again. 'As if I was the only one led the old boys on a bit. We all did, they want you to, but they have to say they don't to stay all right with the coppers. If the customers didn't get a feel of tit and bum now and again those places would close up in a week.'

The words came from a young red mouth that once would have been described as rosebud. Capricorn couldn't help thinking that if this girl objected to the country Fawn Clubs, there must indeed be a case against them.

'It was right after Muffy's death, then, that this persecution began?'

Boohoo nodded, sobbed and made more use of Nelly's sleeve. Capricorn gave her his handkerchief and asked her some questions, but she could add nothing to what he had already learned. Hoggett and Baker were the only lovers of Muffy she knew for certain. Muffy, she said, as the other girls had done, was such a liar that no one knew what to believe.

This girl, at least, was not a liar, Capricorn thought; her frankness was awful. To his surprise, however, Boohoo did know about Muffy's abortion – Muffy had asked her where to go. She had wanted it without question, but afterwards had been upset.

'Very queer tart, Muffy,' Boohoo said pensively. Dolly had brought refreshment and the two of them were drinking Guinness, Dolly's favourite morning drink. 'Told me she was Catholic, but she wasn't Irish. Went a bit funny if you ask me.'

'Takes a woman that way sometimes,' Dolly said portentously. 'Well do I remember when it was our Tilly – that's what started her off.'

Capricorn was glad to be spared the rest of these recollections as Dolly sighed gustily and refilled her glass.

'The doctor gave Muffy pills and everything but it didn't do her no good,' Boohoo confided.

Dolly's eyes gleamed in Gampish relish. 'Twisted her tubes, I expect.'

Capricorn rose. He was wasting precious time. Miss Halliday had lost a good Fawn for nothing, it seemed. This girl could do her no harm. He would leave Boohoo and Dolly to their very female discussions. As he went to say goodbye he noticed that Dolly was dressed – very strange for her at that hour, considering she had been to bed the night before. His mind must be slow with worry for him not to have noticed this before. Instead of her usual loose garment, she was arrayed in purple velvet, very pulled in about the waist, with a wide panniered skirt in Elizabethan style, but instead of a ruff she wore ropes of crystal beads and zircons round her neck. The costume seemed warm for the day.

'I told you,' she replied to his inquiry. 'My 'usband's coming. Naturally it's something to get dressed for after all these years.'

So it was true, then. He would have marvelled if he had the time. Certainly for the moment it would be convenient for Dolly to have one man to play against another. The women had forgotten him before he was out of the door.

Dolly was telling a story about someone he didn't know. '... went bad inside ...'

His attention was caught for a moment by an old photograph on the wall, newly hung to replace one of Tod. It was The Great Capricornus in one of his most difficult escapes, emerging triumphant from a huge milk churn that had been welded shut after he was in it. His smile was wide, and only Capricorn knew how hateful that trick was – he had done it himself. After his father had been searched and placed inside, it was the child's job to fling his arms about his father and bid him a choked farewell – while he passed him a vial of the beastly stuff his father called 'Capricorn custard'. It was a mixture of hydrochloric acid with chemical reagents that could bite through the new welding in about half an hour, just good time for the crowd at the fair to be distracted to some other sight, returning to see The Great Capricornus triumphantly emerged. Only Capricornus and his son knew the misery of that half-hour in the acid fumes, and about the burns that they occasionally received despite the protective clothing. It was a wonder that his father's lungs had been preserved –

'I don't think Muffy went off inside,' Boohoo answered, 'it was her 'ead, more. Went to some religious place to get cheered up, proper daft.'

Capricorn stopped to listen, his father forgotten. Boohoo would speak more frankly, thinking he was gone.

'Our Till was took just the same,' Dolly rejoined, ''ymns and all.'

'Not 'ymns,' Boohoo said, 'just going and yammering with the old girls.'

'With them nuns? Gawd,' Dolly said, shocked, 'that's terrible bad luck. No wonder she got done in.'

Tod had left the front door open and Capricorn could plainly see, to his annoyance, a man walking up the garden path. The Incredible Ivan had been burly and black-haired. This man's hair and skin were grey; he seemed to have shrunk, and looked decidedly seedy, but Ivan it certainly was. Capricorn, with no wish to be delayed by a raucous family reunion, decided to slip out of the back door – he could question Boohoo again later. He was safely beyond the drawing-room when her voice floated again through the red plush portières.

'Is that all the Guinness? Don't think it was nuns,' she said. 'But some old girl who was in with 'em. Irishwoman.'

'Same thing' Dolly was clanking bottles. 'Irish is always bad luck. Never liked 'em on the same bill.'

'Nice name she 'ad, though. I was thinking of changing my name legal. Deed poll. Bridey something. What you think, Doll – Bridey Fair, I thought.'

But Dolly had seen her husband and was tanking out for her great scene. Capricorn, in a state of shock, made for the Yard. St Anne's – of course, he had known about Bridey's work with St Anne's. Not that she spoke much of her charities, but Lawdon had said something about it – it had been something to do with her work for the nuns, he remembered, that she had gone out on the day she was kidnapped. A girl called Alma, living in Bayswater, had been expecting her, but she had never arrived. But for Muffy Mirro to have known Bridey – the significance was huge in his mind.

To his great disappointment, Manning, whom Capricorn found in his office, was not impressed. Bridey, after all, had known so many people. Manning did not say so, but Capricorn was aware that Manning saw his enthusiasm merely as a product of his worried and overstrained mind – and perhaps as intrusive.

When Capricorn entered, the Special Branch man had been studying long sheets filled with columns of figures and computer print-outs, and was somewhat distracted.

Although the office had all the familiar look and sound of the centre of a great search: the ringing telephones, the crowded men taking down information to be collated and compared, the messages rushed in from other rooms, Manning himself, sitting quietly at his desk, might have been an accountant. For once his unpolicemanly appearance did not amuse Capricorn. He suspected immediately that his figures had nothing to do with Bridey Lawdon.

Manning saw his glance.

'You remember the job I was working on,' he said. He owed Capricorn no explanation, but their friendship, for two such reserved men, was close. 'No one will talk, but the figures speak for themselves. There's a big blackmail game going on in the UK, and possibly elsewhere, of Arab-owned enterprises. I believe this money is siphoned off by a terrorist group – very likely a new one. The others are well-funded already,' he said dryly. 'As they don't, as a rule, care to remain anonymous for long, it's a fair chance that they are, or have a connection with, our new friends, MAYDAY.'

Capricorn felt both apologetic and still impatient. Manning, a brilliant and indefatigable worker, would come up with a lead – yet tracing MAYDAY through financial records seemed such a long way round to reach poor Bridey.

Manning might have read his thought.

'You know Issa Rashid was on their list. He was PFLP, of course, but my information is that he split off from them two years ago.'

He fiddled with a pencil on his desk. For once this familiar gesture was as irritating to Capricorn as Dolly's playing with her curls.

'A usually reliable source thinks he might have been trained in Shantung.'

In the bright sunlight, amid all the clatter and noise of a working day, it took a moment for Capricorn to catch the reference. He and Manning, both bachelors devoted to their work, had a habit over the years of meeting when they could at the end of the day for a drink, usually in a quiet pub, always to talk shop. They had worked together in Intelligence many years before, so that although most of Manning's work was secret, he was always willing to talk to Capricorn at least in general terms.

In the mellowness of late evening, amid clouds of tobacco smoke, he had for years now expounded his theory that the true danger to the West was not so much the constant spying that went on, but the subversion campaigns mounted by the two great Communist powers. Undercover warfare, Manning described it, quoting Stalin, and he also spoke much of Marighela and his 'climate of collapse'.

It was an effort to remember now what Manning had said of the various schools for spies and subverters. But he did recall Manning saying that of course the Soviets tended to use their own citizens, well-trained at such places as the great Gaczyna school near Kuibyshev, whereas the Chinese, because of the physical problem, had to import foreigners to be trained in special institutions under the control of the Peking Secret Service. Shantung Province was believed to be the home of the school for Arabs.

Usually Capricorn was interested in any political origins of crime, as well as the safety of society, but now political implications were hardly foremost in his mind.

'We don't get them often,' Manning went on. 'Usually they stay well out of sight. The ones we get are followers and dupes – unless they defect. But Rashid is no defector. I've questioned him until I was blue in the face, but not a word.'

Manning was the most patient and skilled of questioners.

'I almost got a feeling he doesn't mind being where he is. Seems to like our cosy little cells.'

Capricorn had to be interested in Rashid. As the one member of the MAYDAY list in Great Britain, he was the only known link. Much as he trusted Manning he wished he could question Rashid himself. He believed it possible that Rashid was not averse for a time to staying in a British prison. It had happened before when a terrorist had fallen out with his masters or with his peers.

The whole Rashid affair from the beginning, he remembered now, had struck him as odd. From the arrest to the trial and conviction it had been amazingly simple. The bombing itself had been a particularly nasty one – set off in a waxwork museum favoured by tourists, it had killed one adult and two children and mutilated three others. The men first on the scene had found a fragment of the steel tube which had contained the detonator – fulminate of mercury. This useful fragment had borne Rashid's thumb- and fingermarks – an astounding bit of luck, which alone had meant Rashid's incarceration. The public had been overjoyed. The radical press, of course, had claimed that witnesses lied about this evidence – bribed by Scotland Yard. Capricorn himself had wondered about Rashid's own people – the Yard didn't like to talk about it, but the transfer of fingermarks could be done.

But he couldn't talk to Rashid – that wasn't his case. Instead he spoke to Manning about another subject much on his mind – the value to the searchers of finding Bridey's scarf. To his disappointment, Manning was much cooler about it than Burke – tied to his telephone now – had been. Manning pointed out that the dropping of the scarf might well have been a ruse. Even if it had happened, as Capricorn had surmised, when the kidnappers changed cars, that did not necessarily mean that the second car had continued in a north-easterly direction. Manning had put some extra men in the area, but they could not afford to denude forces else-where. There was the watch on the ports and airports – so far there had been only false alarms, but certainly it would be easier for MAYDAY if they could get Bridey out. Nor was Manning impressed with Capricorn's idea that the terrorists might have taken to the forest.

'They are almost always town people – I can't see them running to the woods. A comfortable farmhouse, perhaps, in an isolated place – and Epping is hardly isolated. Only a mile wide, most of it, and pretty well traversed.'

'Some of the Provos might be country-born, although they do, as you say, tend to drift to the cities,' Capricorn offered, knowing that Manning must be thinking his colleague from CID was trying to teach his grandmother how to suck eggs.

But their long friendship held against professional pride. Manning glanced up at him and under the shelter of the general pandemonium became confidential. His grey eyes were very tired.

'To tell you the truth, I've tried to make contact with the Provos – with Collins himself. Through a whole series of cut-outs, of course. Although, apart from that, we're doing all we can, from everything I know, we're getting nowhere. Nowhere.'

Capricorn's heart sank. It was what he himself had suspected, and been afraid to believe.

'And Collins might be willing.' Manning spoke slowly. 'It seems he was very much in love with his cousin Bridey at one time. We have to hope, anyway. Because this came in an hour ago.'

He took a sheet of paper from a meticulously tidy drawer.

It was a photostated copy of a typed letter, similar to the last, with the emblem SWW-MAYDAY.

'The original went to the documents people and the lab. But they won't come up with much. These people are trained.'

Capricorn hardly heard him. He was staring at the words. Unless our demands are met in full, on 13 May the execution of the Fascist Bridget Lawdon, agent of the British Secret Police, will take place. All power to the workers.

It was already 7 May. Capricorn, sick at heart, went back to his office to work on his own case with as much interest as might have been expected from the man in the moon.

During the day reports came in from Interpol about the foreign Fawn patrons who had been in London on the murder night. Two of these had given addresses of English friends where they had been staying; one had been in a hotel, he claimed, with a lady; another had been alone in his hotel but his presence there at the hour of the murder could be vouched for: after perhaps too much to drink he had left his

bath running when he went to sleep and the people underneath had called the porter, who had wakened him. The
damage had appeared on his bill. And, like all the rest, these
men had claimed no personal knowledge of Muffy Mirro.

The checking and re-checking of these and other statements took the whole day, and brought nothing but the clear
picture that whatever kind of men the Fawn patrons might
be it looked as though none of them had been responsible for
the killing of Muffy Mirro.

Evening brought some relief in the person of Copper, back
from his investigation of Muffy's pre-Fawn existence. Capricorn suggested he join him again for sandwiches and coffee
at his desk while they went over the report.

Copper agreed, not without protest.

'You at least used to be good for some decent grub. After
the work I put in today I thought you might spring for the
Florabel.'

'I imagine you'd enjoy the Florabel more with WPC
Hardcastle than another policeman,' Capricorn replied.

He received a very Copper-ish glance.

'Meg wants me to go down and meet her people. Well, guv
_'

They settled down to the report.

'Eleven hundred people working down at Barton's,' Copper said, 'so of course you can't be sure. But if anyone was
after young Hilda it was kept quiet. She and her mum worked
in the same section, and her mum was a Tartar by all
accounts. I went to the caravan park and talked to some of
the women there. Got them all excited.' He grinned. 'Big
policeman in the caravan while the old man was out. Would
you believe it, most of those women had given Ma the cold
shoulder because her old man had been a German PW? They
got married after the war. Long memories, some of those old
girls. Anyway, she talked to this Mrs Wilson. Ma did her nut
when Hilda went as a Fawn. Said she'd throw her out. That's
when our Muffy went off with Hoggett.'

'Did people know where?' Capricorn asked.

Copper shrugged. 'Not as far as I could find out. Ma
Dortman hadn't known where the house was. Told Hilda she

was going to the Juvenile authorities but Hilda said if she did she'd never come and see her any more.

'I suppose someone might have found out if they really wanted to. Just to be on the safe side,' he said casually, 'I made a check on the men in the other caravans. There was one Arthur Crabbe who'd done six months. Hiding behind bushes and exposing himself. Bothering women at the pictures. But he got married five years ago and no record of trouble since.'

Both men considered. The mild type of sex offender that Copper had described rarely went on to sadistic murder. Offhand, Capricorn couldn't remember a single case.

'I went back and saw him,' Copper said. 'He and his wife both work at Barton's. They both swear he was in the caravan that night. Didn't stir out after dinner. For what that's worth.'

'Anybody else see him?'

'The Crabbes weren't very noticeable, it seems. Kept themselves to themselves. When the neighbours lost Hilda they had nothing to talk about. Still carrying on about her and Hoggett. Plenty to say about *him*. Mostly carrying on about the row, between his guitar and his motor-cycle. Roaring up after he finished a job, sometimes at three or four in the morning. Old Ma Dortman threw buckets of water down on him,' Copper added, looking happy.

'Motor-cycle?' Capricorn suddenly thought of the Harley-Davidson in Muffy's portrait. 'Did you ask what make?'

Copper looked surprised, but as usual his inquiries had been thorough.

'Yes, guv. I asked. Not that anyone knew. It was nothing much. An old piece of junk, they said – a cheap make.'

Well, that was more than a year ago, before Muffy Mirro had become his housemate. He would have gone on to better things. But, if so, why had they found no motor-cycle among his possessions? Capricorn looked at the timetable that had cleared Hoggett. The time of death established by PM was no closer than Sherwood's ten to twelve. Gorbel's evidence had Hoggett at the Three Crowns on Clapham Common to 'near closing time' – eleven o'clock. But to a busy man that could be anywhere from half ten on. Hoggett himself had telephoned the police at midnight. Capricorn had estimated that the fastest Hoggett could have made the run in the decrepit camper was an hour, which seemed, for all practical purposes, to leave him out of consideration. But now he realized – somewhat belatedly – that he and Bly had only Hoggett's word that he had gone in the camper. His own work had been sloppy, he thought in discomfort.

If the boy did have a motor-cycle it was far more likely he had used that. And if it was new, and expensive, certainly he would have wanted to show it off to his old friends. A powerful machine would have taken him home in a lot less than an hour at that time of night. Easy enough to move it well away from the house before he called the police. Capricorn telephoned the Three Crowns and was mildly surprised to find it was already closing time, but Gorbel came to the phone. Capricorn asked him if he would make inquiries as to how Hoggett had arrived that night.

Gorbel snorted.

'I don't have to inquire superintendent. He came on that ruddy bike of his. Showing off, as usual. Right over the grass in front and knocked a branch off my Agatha Incarnata. A prize plant, that is. Rides as well as he plays, Hoggett. And too lazy to go round by the car park.'

That laziness or showing off might cost him something, Capricorn thought grimly. He telephoned Bly and told him about the new development and asked him to bring Hoggett into the station for further questioning. Bly was very interested, but Capricorn forgot about it almost immediately, for as soon as he hung up he received another call.

It was Burke. Capricorn had to listen closely; Burke's voice was very subdued. 'We've been holding the story back, but you might as well know – it'll be in the papers tomorrow. Trouble at Wandsworth prison.'

'Wandsworth prison?'

The name chimed ominously in Capricorn's mind.

'A flock of demonstrators turned up – not like them to arrive in the evening, but it was well timed. "Free Issa

Rashid!" Just chanting and waving placards, the usual stuff. Hanging on, hoping for the television cameras, the authorities believed, not taking much notice. But it was an exercise period and when a warder went to shoo Rashid inside – it seems he had a gun. The warder was killed at once. Rashid tried to get over the wall, a policeman outside was shot, we think by Rashid, and one of our men shot him. He died a few moments later.'

Capricorn, all thought of his own work fled, explained to Copper and made for Manning's office. He passed Meg Hardcastle, waiting in the corridor, and then bumped into Manning himself, on his way to the prison, doubtless. As he met Manning's glance, he had a quick impression that Manning would have avoided him if he could. He looked like a doctor who had to confront a patient he has found to be terminally ill.

Manning at least was frank.

'I don't like this at all. They often ask for a list when they really want one person, just to put us off their scent. If Rashid is the one they wanted, this looks as though they've decided against the exchange. If they ever really intended it.'

He looked steadily at Capricorn.

'We have to think that perhaps she is dead already.'

Capricorn couldn't answer.

Manning sighed. 'Not a word from Collins. They rounded up some of the demonstrators. They seem to be students. A few disappeared when the shooting started. Odds on the ones we've got won't know anything.'

Capricorn could agree with that.

'I'll call you at home if anything should come up,' Manning said. 'Or Burke will let you know. I'll be back later – Lawdon will certainly be in. I hate to face him,' he said candidly, 'but it has to be done.'

They parted in silence. Capricorn felt aghast and lost. His detective's mind had to wonder about the business at the prison – Issa Rashid was a wily bird: shot trying to escape seemed all too simple. Capricorn knew, despite all the radical press was going to say, that it wasn't the Yard who had engineered his death. But whoever was responsible, Manning was right: it meant no good for Bridey.

In one thing, though, he did not agree with Manning. For some reason, probably just wishful thinking, he could not believe that she was dead. As though he would know if she had died – though that was absurd, he had to tell himself. They had not been so close. There was no special bond – not man and wife, not lovers, no tie of blood.

Outside, the night was provokingly enchanting. The air was soft and warm; the moonlight bathed St James's Park, silver water, silver leaves against the shadows. Capricorn had left his car behind, only walking could calm him. A girl's dress glimmered by a tree-trunk – two hidden lovers, entwined in an embrace. The world went on.

He stared up at the blind windows as he plunged through the streets, wondering if Bridey was there, behind any one of them, hoping, praying to be found as he passed them by. A dog barked as he paused by an overgrown front hedge, and he went on reluctantly. As he turned a corner he was startled by the howling of a tomcat. Later, a constable watched him curiously as he paused outside a shuttered diplomatic mission, glaring up hopelessly at the locked, empty rooms.

His own house was dark, and he let himself in silently, so as not to wake Mrs Dermott. His body was tired enough now to rest, but his mind was still churning. He went straight to his room in the back of the house – oddly enough, it was dark also. Mrs Dermott usually turned on his bedside lamp before she herself retired. He went to open the curtains to the balcony to let the moonlight in, and then stood very still. Not for the first time in his career, he had a nocturnal visitor – a man who was lean, not tall, in close, dark dress. Capricorn had never seen him before, but as he took in the strong profile against the moon he knew it was Special Branch's most wanted man: Rory Collins himself.

TWELVE

8 MAY

After Bridey's attempt at escape, Natasha and Kerim brought her no food or water; only Michael came in once that day. Bridey ate and drank without appetite. The pain in her head grew worse. She knew she had to try to keep up her strength, but the portion of food was small and sometimes she couldn't keep it down. Her chest was so congested now it was hard to speak and she coughed constantly – she had the 'flu all right. She told Michael but his eyes were guarded and he said nothing. It didn't matter, she supposed.

Yet it frightened her that she felt herself grow weaker. She hardly slept now but lay awake, waiting for the chatter of birds at dawn – they were a link with the outside world still going on without her. Once she thought she heard a swallow's scream.

The great thing was to see the first faint light at the bit of window. She'd never been much for the books, but something she'd read or heard a long time ago came to her mind when she saw the light, even though she should have been thinking of her prayers. The words made no sense, she had muddled them, no doubt, but the sounds themselves were like a blessing:

> The light of evening, Lissadell,
> Great windows open to the south.

After the words came, she would doze a little, murmuring, comforted like a child.

Then everything changed. New people came, a lot of them. They had come after dark and there was screaming in the house.

Michael had called down to Kerim, who was guarding her door.

'People on the shore –'

Bridey's heart had leapt – police? But she had soon been

undeceived. The voices upstairs quieted. A signal must have
been given. The intruders were friends. Bridey heard the
noise of the boat as it grated up against the gravelled
landing-place. She tried to count how many from their
footsteps, but six or a dozen, she couldn't tell. She had wept,
from weakness only, she told herself. They kept a sharp
look-out at night, then. The edge of the lake had been
overgrown with bushes, as well as studded with trees – but
the water itself would be bright. These young people were
efficient, despite their quarrelling. It's hopeless, a voice beat
in her mind, but she turned her thoughts resolutely and tried
to hear what was going on upstairs.

Some of it was loud enough. Natasha was having something like hysterics.

'Dead ...?'

The question that didn't sound like a question could have
been heard half-way across the water. The new people were
quiet-spoken. Natasha shrieked, a great wailing sound like
any peasant woman. Afterwards, her voice came clear.

'Then we'll have the execution now –'

Bridey could not have been quite certain that she had no
hope of rescue, because terror struck her, worse than it ever
had before. She rolled off her mat and crouched in the
corner, hiding, shivering.

But Natasha didn't come. Something got in the way of her
running feet. She must have opened the door upstairs, for
Bridey heard the new voices. Men's voices.

'... MAYDAY is not just for one man.'

They spoke English like Englishmen.

'We made the list only to get the Colonel,' Natasha said.
She sounded sullen.

'That is what you may have believed.' The voice was
schoolmasterish. 'In fact, we would like to have most of
those prisoners. And the money. The publicity that stretches
out while we negotiate is the best thing for the cause.'

'Now the Colonel is dead I'm the one who says what will
be done here.'

Natasha was claiming leadership. From what Bridey heard
in snatches here and there, Natasha didn't stand a chance.

Bridey felt a certain relief, but what difference would it make in the end? There were bits of talk she couldn't make out. The 'schoolmaster' thought the others should have waited for the Prime Minister's daughter to come back from Washington. More arguing. '... knew about him and the girl ...'

Did they mean her? Or Cynthia? What him and what girl? Whatever Natasha was talking about, the new people didn't think much of that either.

'Childish tricks ... no purpose ...'

For once Kerim spoke up.

'... very necessary. The Colonel agreed ...'

The door banged shut, and she heard no more that night.

In the morning Kerim came down with Michael. Suddenly these two were allies. Bridey gathered they were not happy – the invasion was unexpected. But one thing pleased them.

'... her nose out of joint. She thinks the whole organization could be run by a woman. Because she slept with the Colonel –' her brother was spiteful. 'Gave her too much rope ...'

Michael's thoughts were on the new people.

'... bossy lot altogether. Thought the Colonel was the boss ...'

Kerim's voice was unsure.

'... started the Saviours of the Workers of the World ... Our branch ... MAYDAY ... this special job ... I thought the Colonel was ...'

Whatever the boys had thought, the new people stayed. And had their way, it seemed. She was fed regularly again and Natasha and her brother had to take their turn on guard. Some of the new people left by night, Bridey heard the tread on the gravel and the boat going off. But not before another row with Natasha. One of the new people took Michael's place once, bringing Bridey's food – but she could not make much of him. His stocking mask was drawn to hide every inch of his head, and his clothing muffled his body.

Bridey heard Natasha's step following his, and her laugh that had no amusement in it. 'You don't need to stifle yourself,' Natasha called after him. She lingered at the door.

Didn't care for the stench, Bridey thought. Only Michael would take the pail out, and he not often.

'You'll have to kill her anyway,' Natasha cried. 'She's seen us all without our masks.'

The man's hands – white, smooth hands – tensed as he put the inevitable bread and cheese beside her. His gaze passed over Bridey incuriously; she might have been a piece of furniture – of small value. But she could feel his anger and she saw the expression change in his eyes. She guessed that his mouth tightened. Whatever his original plan had been, now he had to agree.

He joined Natasha outside and firmly locked the door behind him. His step was not as quick as the others. Bridey had the idea that the new people were older, and more methodical than the three original gaolers. Whatever he thought, his tone to Natasha was cool.

'It's been decided you must take leave,' he said. 'You are too well known to disappear. Questions have been asked ...'

As the two of them walked further away, Bridey could hear little. But it was enough.

'... kill her before I go.'

'Of course not. If negotiations start up, we'll need ...'

If negotiations start up. Then the government wasn't negotiating. Bridey had not expected that they would, yet it was still a blow. But why? she thought, tired of her own hopes and despairs. She already knew her captors intended her death no matter what happened.

Need, the man had said. What did they need? Perhaps they meant to chop off bits of her and send them to Charlie, to start the bargaining. It had been done before. And they would need fresh meat. She tried to think of something else. She tried very hard. That girl was well known. Bridey had never seen nor heard of her but that meant nothing to them. And she had seen three of them plain ... yes, they would make sure. She had to die.

Because of Natasha. Natasha, who had been alert, even in the warmth of the sun. Natasha, who had a famous face and had not cared from the beginning if Bridey saw it, knowing it would mean her death. Natasha, who had struck her so that the blood ran. Despite her weakness, Bridey felt a devouring hatred – she had never known such a feeling, or anything like it. It was as though another woman had sprung to life, but it was herself all right, she could feel the new energy of it as she wished she could have grabbed the gun, turned it on the girl and escaped in the boat over her dead brown body. The rage lashed about so that she could not lie still, but pulled without regard of pain against her bonds. At last, when it subsided, it left her bleeding, feeling dried up and spent, and only a sullen loathing remained; and then the fear came.

Fear, a new kind, with her arms covered in goosepimples and her insides a lump of ice. She didn't want to die, to be finished, nothing. Her eyes were wide; she had never known she was afraid to die. Sorrow at leaving Charlie, her friends, her girls, yes – but crass, animal-like fear – Or was it animal? She didn't know. She had been taught, and she believed – she *did* believe, she tried to tell herself – that the soul lived on.

But as she looked round at the cellar, stinking as it was – the stone-flagged floor, the green-streaked walls, and the little window, her Lissadell – even this was better than being dead. The soul – the soul might live on, but what was that to her, Bridey Lawdon? She had always listened to the priest; she had done what she could to save her soul, but now it seemed to her she had tried to save it as something with its own value, apart from herself, like a child or even a dog or cat. What *was* a soul? What had it to do with Bridey? For now she knew what Bridey Lawdon was. Bridey was the new curtains and the kitchen with the tap that dripped and she never remembered to get mended, Alma and St Anne's, a chat on the phone with friends, a glass of whisky in the Public Bar, and cuddling next to Charlie on a cold night – even, though she didn't like to think it, this cellar and the young people, the ropes, the breadcrumbs scattered on the mat. And without any of these things, whatever strange ghost might wait for the Resurrection, it would be none of her.

You atheist, she told herself, and was ashamed. She had

gone with Charlie to his church once when they had gone for a holiday at Lawdon Court. People there would like it, Gervase had said. The vicar had preached a sermon on faith ... the substance of things hoped for, the evidence of things unseen. She remembered, and the congregation, so tidy and well dressed and so – polite to God, she had thought, laughing at them a bit, in her way. Now everything she hoped for was lost and gone ... there was no evidence of things unseen. She had seen too much of other things, Natasha's face, and for that she would die.

She must be feverish; she couldn't think, and her thoughts jumbled in her mind. The same things over and over. Die because of a face she had never seen before and, if she had been set free, probably would never have seen anyway. What a strange joke. If she wasn't crying she would have laughed. A woman brought up in the Church, and at the last, just when she needed it, she found she had no faith at all.

That night was long and bitter. She thought she heard the sound of a mouse in the wall, and she had a sudden envy of that mouse who would live when she was dead. Natasha hadn't left yet, because some time before dawn she came to relieve whoever was at the door. In her usual happy mood.

'... tonight,' Bridey heard her say. 'But I'll be back. In time for the execution.' And she laughed.

THIRTEEN

8 MAY

It was a strange meeting in the small house between the Irish terrorist and the English policeman. It was only later that Capricorn had time to wonder how he had recognized him – he had seen Collins's photograph on file, but it had been a bad likeness. The man himself had an odd resemblance to Field Marshal Montgomery during the war years, without his military stiffness, but with all his authority. Collins was, after all, a Field Marshal in his own army.

Yet he had known him at once, almost as though he had been expecting him, which was absurd. Again, it was only afterwards that Capricorn really took in the enormous risks that Collins had run to come to him. All the British police, the army, not to speak of his own men who could give him a bullet in the knee for trafficking with the CID. Collins had been wearing a shoulder-holster but his gun had not been drawn. He seemed to know all about Capricorn, and for the moment trusted him. Just as he, in this matter, trusted Collins. Why him, Capricorn wondered, and not Lawdon?

Collins explained that soon enough. He would not endanger any of his men by responding to Manning's overtures. He might have risked contacting Lawdon, not really a Special Branch man, but he believed Manning had Lawdon under surveillance. Capricorn was sure he was wrong. Of course, he was not privy to all the mysteries of Special Branch. Collins naturally gave no hint as to whether he had received Lawdon's message through Bridey's sister Eileen.

Capricorn had asked him to come inside, but Collins refused with a shake of his head. He felt safer, no doubt, in the shadowy corner of the balcony, with the handy tree beside him – Capricorn had been warned to cut that down, after a little trouble once before, but he couldn't bring himself to do it – the garden before them and then the lonely park stretching out into the night.

A breeze lifted and shook the branches of the chestnut tree. Intermittent patches of moonlight fell on Collins's face. Capricorn wondered afresh why he had not sent one of his men – a sense of urgency? And perhaps he did not trust them entirely. 'Sinn Fein' – Ourselves Alone – that had been true of the Irish rebels once, perhaps no longer true for all of them. The world had changed. Manning believed that the wild men of the Provos could never have created and continued so much havoc in the North unaided.

Collins's remarks were brief and very much to the point.

'I hear you're her friend. But you'll not find them. Your government, I understand, is not giving in to their demands.'

He paused, and saw the question on Capricorn's face.

'We don't know who they are. But I have a notion –'

Capricorn was very quiet, very still.

'There's a lad called Liam Doherty. A merchant seaman, one of us. But he dropped out of sight over a year ago in Singapore. I'd had word he'd been seen with an Arab group – the ones who tried to blow up the El Al plane at Orly. He's an easy one to notice, there's grey in his hair. It's only a chance, now' – his face, upturned to Capricorn, glimmered against the shadows – 'but someone who looked like our Liam bought a second-hand van for five hundred pounds cash from a garage in Holloway three weeks ago. Gave his name as Michael Reilly. He wasn't seen again in the neighbourhood, and no record of any change in registration.'

He knew a lot, this Collins, Capricorn the policeman couldn't help thinking. As though London were Dublin in the 1920s. But Bridey Lawdon's friend felt a leap of the heart – a name, a face, something to go on, something tangible. He believed Collins was more certain of this Liam's involvement than he confessed – he would have to be to take such a chance. Giving information on one of his own men, even one absent without leave, could mean worse for him than a bullet in the knee.

Collins went on, his voice cool enough, but the tension

underneath was plain.

'Stay out of it,' he said. 'One whiff of police and all the lines will be cut.'

He was tracking this Liam in his own way. If he found him, he would not come again but he would get a message to Capricorn. At this time, he would not say how. 'It's for you to act,' he ended. 'I have to be off before long.'

'We don't have long.' Grim, Capricorn told him about the execution date and Issa Rashid.

'I know all about Rashid,' Collins said. 'When I heard he was dead I had to come. That's bad, very bad for Bridey.'

He and Manning agreed on that.

'Shooting his way out,' Collins added, 'he was too clever for that. Like the fingerprints he obliged you with. For sure, someone else started the shooting and planted the gun.'

'We didn't,' Capricorn said.

Collins smiled. It was merely a stretching of the lips.

'For once I believe the English police. Too ambitious a man can be a problem. All the money now, so easy for these young fellows to get their hands on. It can turn a strong head as much as the weaker ones, like our Liam's. The thirteenth, you say. Five days, if they stick to it.'

In the darkness Capricorn could voice his worst fear.

'If she's still alive.'

'Probably she is,' Collins said. 'If they still want an exchange. They might need her to write a letter, record her voice –'

The other possibilities they did not discuss.

Capricorn watched as the dark figure skimmed down the tree, moving like a shadow among other shadows across his garden, and soon was out of sight.

He could have telephoned, Capricorn thought, there was no need for him to come. But he understood why Collins had come. Collins wanted to see, face to face, the man he was about to trust. To trust with his honour and his life. And perhaps for a moment to ease his sorrow with another man who shared it.

He had risked coming, though he could have been wrong

in his trust. Capricorn might have been armed, and risked a shot, though that wasn't likely. Certainly he could have raised an alarm. But he had not raised the alarm. Chief Superintendent Capricorn, CID, had stood on his balcony and watched Rory Collins go. Capricorn's work had been his life. For this night's business, were it known, he would be discharged from the Force. He could be open to criminal charges. His colleagues would call him traitor.

Manning, perhaps his best friend, in this case would be for prosecution. Manning was, as Capricorn had always been, a man governed by his mind, of clear decisions, a strong sense of right and wrong. The capture of Rory Collins was of vital importance to the nation and would be his first concern. The rescue of one innocent woman had to be secondary to that. If he were there he would say, with perfect logic, that to let Rory escape meant the slaughter of many innocents.

Yet Capricorn could not put his hand out to pick up the telephone. Even now Manning could have the area surrounded with a good chance of closing in on Collins by morning, and the best hope for Bridey would be gone. Capricorn could not deceive himself. Good as Manning's men were, armed with the description of this Doherty, there was far less chance of them tracking him in time than there was for Collins with his network of spies and informers who reported to him but never to the police. Yet if Capricorn did nothing and if Collins's inquiries proved fruitful, Manning would have to be told at last. His men would have to be at the scene of rescue. If he did call Manning, he thought, would it be for the sake of duty, or to save himself? Collins had had more courage than that. There was no need for him to have told Capricorn about Doherty. He had only gone that far knowing he might be killed, through Capricorn's action, or by chance capture, or by his own men. For him that was the ultimate step, and he had taken it.

For the first time in his life Capricorn's mind did not serve him. There was no use trying to sleep. His bedroom, so carefully arranged for his comfort and rest, looked hateful to him. He thought of that other man, dodging and hiding in the dark. Capricorn wandered into his library and picked up a book at random. Then, restless, he went downstairs. He poured himself a drink, still thinking of Collins: the two of them joined in a confusion of loyalties, not knowing what they did or where they were, and only the strange love they had for a woman the one clear light in the dark.

Though not, he knew sombrely, the same kind of love. Rory's love for Bridey had been romantic, a love which often, even when it fades, leaves behind it a sense of chivalry. Capricorn knew all about such loves. He looked up at the portrait which had graced his drawing-room wall almost as long as he had been in this house. His friend Rose, now Lady Theale, for whom he had a lifelong affection. And there had been others, all elegant, swan-like creatures. But his feeling for Bridey, that plain brown sparrow, was quite different. Absurdly, he found he wished he could explain to Manning, as though it were something very important that Manning must understand.

Their job, their chosen work in life, was to preserve order. But if Bridey could not be saved there was no order, nothing would make sense. He could get up in the morning and try to go about his business, but he would have no business. Bridey was not only her own dear self – somehow the special quality that she made manifest was the heart and centre, the meaning, of all he had ever tried to do.

But he knew he could not explain to Manning. There were no words. He looked at the book he had brought downstairs, in hopes of quieting his mind. *Coriolanus* ... he had no interest now in the factions of ancient Rome. The drink had not soothed. It was almost morning. He went into the kitchen and made coffee. Outside the birds were already stirring.

As he sipped the coffee, black and strong, he turned the pages of the volume absently. Certainly no comfort there. His eyes were caught by the lines:

Lest that their wives with spits and boys with stones
In puny battle slay me.

Boys with stones in puny battle. Manning had told him of the children of Northern Ireland, from eight to fourteen years, given seventy-five pence a week to throw stones at British soldiers. The boy of twelve who had set a bomb in a large and crowded shop ... Had Collins been responsible for those children, or was it his new allies, the thought of whom had made the Irishman uneasy on this night?

Capricorn felt a sensation close to helplessness. He was doing what he felt must be done, but his own mind was against him, the mind which had been his ruler all his days. 'You're cold, Merle,' had been his aunts' perpetual cry. Between duty and inclination he had never had too hard a struggle, but now he had abandoned that cool judgement to follow an older wisdom, or, he saw plainly, to err. Perhaps, he had to recognize, to do both. Outside the realm of his guiding intelligence the paths were not distinct.

The book had slipped from his hand. He bent to pick it up as it lay open, with fluttering leaves, upon the floor. Coriolanus and his troubles, Act One, Scene One.

> The kingly crowned head, the vigilant eye,
> The counsellor heart, the arm our soldier,

The counsellor heart. He had forgotten. There had been a belief, once, that the heart itself was the place of counsel, the truest guide.

The coffee had warmed him. Dawn was breaking. The air was sweet with the smell of chestnut flowers. From the garden came the song of a blackbird rising joyfully. Another day of spring. Capricorn rose, the night behind him, and readied himself for the work of the day.

FOURTEEN

8 MAY

Once the sun came up the violence of the fear subsided, but her spirit did not lighten. Even the repeated words of 'Lissadell' brought no relief. Then, obstinately, hope flared again. Perhaps Michael would pity her after all. If he came in, she would smile at him. Perhaps he would think of his own mother ... But no. She knew enough about those lads, they would kill their own mothers if they thought it would help their cause. Later, she was flooded with grief. With so many people in the house, even if rescue came it would be useless. They could pick off the policemen as they crossed the lake, and anyway she would be shot at once. Certainly the look-out would be maintained.

Despite the food she had taken she felt weaker. Full daylight found her close to apathy. No one could find her here. No one knew of these people. MAYDAY – no one had ever heard of them – until now. Only Michael, whatever his real name was, he might be known. Rory might know of him. But Rory couldn't come to England. Nor would he want to. In the way of Irishmen, he hadn't wanted to marry, but for all that, he was angry she left. How he had despised her at the last – and he hadn't known the worst.

Now that she was so tired, almost numb, knowing she had no faith and had been a pious fraud all along, thoughts came that she had shut out so carefully all the years. All the lies were gone now, and she was left with nothing but the truth. Upstairs, people were walking over her head, talking away, no doubt, but it meant nothing. Whatever was said or done would make no difference to her. She was left here, for as long as she was left, just with herself, what there was of it plain to see. Bridey Lawdon, virtuous wife, help to fallen girls – how she had liked that. Respected. Perhaps the wife of the future Commissioner. Forgetting Bridey Collins, who had lingered, flirting and cuddling, on the hills with her cousin Rory, until her father sent her off. And then playing the same game with young Charlie in the soft green places round Lawdon Court. Charlie, who had asked her to marry him, and, as it turned out, none too soon.

Poor Charlie – she had led him on, as the old women used to say. If it hadn't been for her loose ways, he probably would have married his cousin Anne once he had settled down. He had always liked her; Lady Lacey she was now, and a widow. Well, they might make a match of it yet. Then Charlie would become a Commissioner at the last.

Ignorant as she had been, her pregnancy had taken her by surprise. And all she had thought of was the mortification. The Lawdons had been so kind about the marriage, no fuss at all, and when her father thought it best she didn't return to Ireland they had arranged a great wedding with their family and friends. And all she could think of was how she would walk down the aisle in her white satin, trying to hide her belly under her bouquet. That was what had shamed her, and hardly had she understood what had happened.

She had been used to teasing the Irish boys and leading them a dance, but it was only then she realized how careful they had been. Hugging and kissing away and out of sight was one thing, but no more. Englishmen without the fear of marriage in them had no such holding back – and that was why so many Irish girls she knew who came to England were in trouble in their first year. Well she knew it now.

But then – all her pride had seemed to be in ruins round her. Until – not that she had *thought* of wickedness. She hadn't had to think, it was in her. Like her not having faith – it was all one. Nor had she said anything, even to Charlie. And afterwards she told herself she had done nothing. Just running and jumping about as she had always done and taking the pony Charlie had given her for wild rides about the lanes and across the fields, jumping the old stone walls and over the ditches. Just over three and a half months it had been, and her purpose soon accomplished and no one, she thought, the wiser. Certainly not the Lawdons. The housekeeper had given her some old-fashioned looks when she took to her bed for a day or two. Of course, she hadn't seen a doctor, and that was probably why she had never been able to have a child after.

She had refused to think of it, blotting it out of her mind all these years, but it was there, just the same as if it had been today, sitting with her in the cellar and Sister Alphonsus saying, 'Be sure your sin will find you out,' as though time were all one moment. Now she would die with the murder of her child still on her conscience. For somehow, although her soul seemed not to belong to her, if it lived at all, her conscience was still hers. She knew, for she felt the whip of it. Never had she confessed, telling herself it was the merest accident and no one's business but her own. The night before her wedding she had remembered, but only because Rory had come and called her the bad names and she was glad he had not known that.

Rory. She could think now, when it didn't matter, what she had never admitted – she had loved him once. If it had been Rory's child, and the two of them in Ireland with no grand relations ... But that could never have been.

There would be no priest to shrive her, or her poor lost soul, but she could make an act of contrition. 'Holy Mary, Mother of God –' Outside she could hear the step of the girl, walking up and down. She couldn't finish. There was no contrition in her, only hatred for that girl burning away, smothering her with the greyness of ashes.

A step on the stairs. It was Natasha's relief. She would go off now, on her leave, and play with her friends. London, Paris, or perhaps they liked the Riviera in the spring. It sounded like Michael. They were quarrelling again.

'The Colonel's orders –' Natasha protested.

'Ah, you and your Colonel. Worms' meat, he is now.'

The door to Bridey's cellar burst open, and slammed behind the girl. Weak as Bridey was, rage gave her strength. Why should she go to her death like a sheep to the slaughter? She had a right to her life, and the right to fight for it. Her ankles were still tied tight but she lunged across the cellar floor, striking with her tight-bound hands across Natasha's face.

In a strange elation she felt the girl's bones under her hands, and wetness. She looked – Natasha had forgotten her mask again. But Bridey's blow had not drawn blood, except a thin scratch from the wire handcuffs. There was no strength in her. Yet she would have killed if she could. Natasha leaned back against the door, hardly noticing Bridey or anything else, rubbing her wrist across her eyes like a child. Bridey stared. She was startled at the difference in that face since she had last seen it. Without make-up the girl was sallow with dark bruises under her eyes and she looked old. She had run in to get away from Michael. Tears poured down her face.

The passion of Bridey's hatred slowly cooled. That girl could feel grief. She had loved her Colonel. Natasha caught her glance. The two women gazed at each other with no liking or understanding, but Bridey knew she had been wrong, stupidly wrong, again. The girl, though monstrous, was no monster. Even Natasha, Bridey thought without joy, was human after all.

FIFTEEN

8 MAY

The new New Scotland Yard was the same as ever. Inside its characterless corridors it could be any season, any day. As Capricorn entered his office his telephone was ringing. Bly was on the line, agitated. Capricorn had an odd sensation, like coming up from deep water, or sinking into it – a change of element.

Hoggett, whom Bly had suspected from the first to be the killer of Muffy Mirro, and whom Capricorn had released, was now very much back in the case. Bly's suspicions – quieted for a time by what appeared to be the facts, and by the young man's passionless demeanour – now seemed to have been well founded.

'The bike in the photo was his all right. The neighbours knew it well. We went round at five o'clock, but he's cleared out. I'd warned him not to leave the district, but he's scarpered.'

Bly's tone was that of a policeman disgusted at losing a suspect, yet there was a slight edge of satisfaction.

'Camper and the bike both gone. Dead lucky he was, there. You know, he never hid that bike. Turns out he always parked it round the corner. Muffy created long and loud, hanging out of the window cursing if he roared up to the house while she was having a lie-in. Not as silly as he looks.' Bly was grim. 'When we took it for granted he'd used the camper he twigged straight away that would let him off. Led us up the garden proper.'

Bly said a lot more. He didn't say, but of course Capricorn knew, that it was up to the Yard, specifically himself, to institute the long-drawn-out proceedings of a nationwide hunt. Wearily, Capricorn said he would begin at once. Bly thought a warrant should be issued for Hoggett's arrest, of course. He had no doubt now that he was the killer.

Capricorn didn't argue. Certainly Hoggett must be found. He had lied; he had run away. Fortunately, Copper was already at his desk. WPC Hardcastle was certainly not keeping him from his duties. He told him Bly's news, and for once left all the business in the Inspector's capable hands. Not that Copper had been struck with Bly's certainty of Hoggett's guilt.

'Silly young bugger might just have gone off on a job and forgotten to say. Probably busting somebody's eardrums in the Midlands or Southend. D'you think we need a warrant?'

'Well, start inquiring and use your judgement.'

Like Copper, he found it hard to see Hoggett as Muffy's killer. If Muffy had been punched in the head and died accidentally, then perhaps – but surely not this killing, that youth. Another picture came to Capricorn's mind, a youth with dark, sullen eyes. For no reason ...

Was he becoming xenophobic, he wondered, like old, mad Mrs Bullen? As a matter of routine he had had inquiries made about Tüssün Hamed, and now he took out the folder. He had looked over the entries before they were filed, and they had been of no interest. They added nothing to what his father had already told Capricorn. Old Hamed, so unusually, uncharacteristically helpful. An echo from the night came to Capricorn as he thought for a moment of the odd love between the ageing Levantine and the young English Fawn. For love it seemed to be. An unhappy love, with their marriage forbidden by young Tüssün, Moslem, Pan-Arab. There it was in the file. Tüssün had become a Pan-Arab at the university, like so many boys of his type. The American University at Beirut.

A thought chimed in Capricorn's head. Rashid – he had been a teacher once. He wondered where. Manning would know, of course, but he wouldn't trouble Manning just now. Abruptly, he called up an Aid and gave him the job of finding out. It was not for an Aid to wonder what it had to do with the case of Muffy Mirro. Only Capricorn was willing to conjecture a link between the kidnap of Bridey Lawdon and the murder of the Fawn. Manning believed his idea was fantasy – wishful fantasy, because Capricorn had wanted to be part of the search team. Perhaps Manning was glad Capricorn was not part of his team. Certainly he had no scrap of evidence. Only the strange coincidence that the two women had known each other rather intimately.

Capricorn went back to the file on Tüssün. Why had his mind jumped to that youth – merely because he had first seen him lying in a pool of blood, an image connecting itself with the bloody corpse of Muffy Mirro? There was something else. Several things – unusual, now that he considered. It struck him that Tüssün had shown little of the normal citizen's anger at the bombing of the office and his own injuries. He was silent by nature, perhaps. Capricorn had questioned him in the hospital and he remembered his replies, but he checked his own handwritten notes anyway. Then he saw what had been teasing his mind.

'I don't know anything about those girls. I never heard of Muffy Mirro, until it was all in the papers.'

That must be a lie. Marian, the Wendy Doe at Dean Street, was his father's mistress, and came to the office. She had brought them the wedding roses: Capricorn remembered seeing them in Tüssün's waste-basket. Muffy had been Marian's most important Fawn; she had caused trouble and had had to be sent on an unpaid holiday. Certainly Marian would have talked about this to Hamed while she was at Mouna; it was no secret. Tüssün must have known about it. A young man involved in a business with such young and pretty girls would surely have his gaze and hearing stretched.

Capricorn looked at the neat, handwritten report as though it held some secret. Why should Tüssün have lied? Merely to save himself the trouble of further inquiry? An older man might do that, but in Capricorn's experience young people were inclined to enjoy the limelight, to exaggerate their knowledge and importance. Was Tüssün hiding something? Muffy had always been mysterious about her real lovers. Copper had said she 'had a fancy for young stuff'. Though to a policeman Tüssün seemed merely a rather insolent,

disagreeable youth, he might have his charms to a highly-sex-
ed young woman.

But a fanatic Moslem? It was possible, Capricorn thought
slowly. Muffy's abundant charms, easily available, might
have proved overwhelming. Moral reluctance, turning to
disgust, could have been, at least in part, a motive for her
death and the manner of it. Capricorn's lips twitched in
distaste, but his mind leapt ahead.

There was the evidence of the mad Mrs Bullen – not always
so mad, perhaps. She had spoken of a Pakistani carrying the
mysterious plant – the plant that had never been mentioned
in any public announcement. A woman of her sort could
easily mistake a dark-skinned Arab for a Pakistani. Capricorn himself had asked Tüssün the routine question. On the
night of Muffy's death, he had said, he was at home. Home
was an address on Greek Street, next door to the business
office of Mouna Import-Export. Capricorn had forgotten to
ask Hamed exactly what Mouna imported. Very slack
indeed. The boy said he had dinner with his father. But old
Hamed, Capricorn remembered, had gone back to his office
on business with his accountant, and worked late. Capricorn
suspected that if asked he would say he had seen his son -
during the important two hours, but ...

It was an odd business about that plant. Bly, he remembered, had thought nothing of it. The old woman had
gossiped to the policemen at the scene; it had probably been
there for weeks without Hoggett's noticing; no murderer
would walk up to his victim's house bearing a potted plant
for any onlooker to remark. What had it been – a flowering
plant, delicate blossoms – white, like Muffy's make-believe
flat. Muffy, a romantic in her own way. Lilies of the valley,
he remembered, in an ugly plastic pot. Just such a pot as he
had seen on old Hamed's desk.

He was growing foolish, Capricorn decided. Manning was
right. Those pots were sold in every multiple shop and
florist's in the country now. But the foolish idea nagged in
his head until he looked for another file. It took a moment
to find it – the Wendy Doe of Dean Street, old Hamed's Miss
Marian, was Marian Slater. Her telephone number was not

the same as the Hameds'. Marian Slater lived at Wood Green, and it was Mrs Slater who answered the telephone and summoned her daughter at his request. Marian might be old Hamed's mistress, but she spent at least some of her nights at home. The appearance of respectability was kept. Capricorn saw why old Hamed had some honourable intentions to his Wendy Doe.

Marian's voice was sleepy; he had woken her from her rest after her night's labours. Capricorn explained to her that he was investigating the bombing. If Tüssün had been unusually calm about it, Marian was as vocal as any outraged British matron would be. She was more than anxious to help find the villain, though she was somewhat puzzled by Capricorn's questions. Yes, she had often taken plants and flowers over to her employer's offices. The rooms were so dreary, depressing. As there were two offices, Capricorn asked, did she usually take two plants or just one? Most often one, she said, because Mr Hamed looked after his, watered them well and they lasted longer. Tüssün would never bother. She had taken him some lovely lilies of the valley, she explained, but the next day they were gone. He said the charwoman had knocked them over and spoiled them, but he had probably done it himself.

'That charwoman wouldn't touch the desk tops. She hardly ever does the floors properly.'

And so Marian had taken some of the roses after the wedding.

'Lovely blooms, but hot-house, they didn't last long.'

Mr Hamed, she added sadly, really loved flowers, but he had nowhere to grow any, living on Greek Street. He had been looking at a cottage in Chipping Ongar, but Tüssün –

Capricorn, subduing the first professional excitement he had felt on this case, inquired when she had taken the lilies of the valley, and when they had disappeared. Marian remembered exactly when she had taken them, for she had bought some for her Fawn office as well, and, a tidy-minded, frugal girl, had kept the bill. She had taken one to Mouna on her way to work. It had been two days before the murder.

And had Miss Slater noticed when the plant had gone? 'I couldn't say for sure.' Marian, still puzzled, was trying hard.

A clank of metal on china. The kind mother had brought her sleepy daughter a cup of tea or coffee, no doubt. Marian gave a long gulp that exploded over the telephone.

'Was there a bomb in the pot?' she asked. 'It was very small.'

'We have to check everything,' Capricorn murmured. She had no reason to like Tüssün, but it was better to stay well away from the truth. He didn't know how far loyalty to the boy's father might take her.

'I was very busy – I was behind with my work – all the questions, you know, after Muffy – I didn't get to the Mouna offices for a day or so, but the morning of the wedding I looked in –' the words came faster now that she recalled – 'I know it was gone then, because I asked Tüssün about it. As usual, he was in a nasty temper. How Hakim – Mr Hamed – well,' she corrected herself hastily, 'that's why I took the roses. Mr Hamed says it cheers him up a lot to see a few flowers round the place, especially when he has business worries.'

Capricorn wondered what business worries old Hakim could have. The Fawn business raked in money as quickly as a gambling house. A certainty was forming in his mind. Not so fast, he counselled himself. London was full of flowers. A hunch was not evidence. There was nothing tangible to connect Tüssün with Muffy. Nothing that would stand up in court, or even distract Bly from his suspicions of Hoggett.

He wondered where Tüssün and Muffy could have gone to make love. Muffy had not been in the habit of taking her other lovers to the house she shared with Hoggett. Baker had his studio. Hotels were expensive and Tüssün would not have wanted to be seen. His father, conducting his discreet affair with his own Fawn, must spend many nights away from home. Tüssün would have taken Muffy home to Greek Street, so conveniently close ...

Capricorn's mind went back over the years to the days

when he was a young, struggling sergeant in the CID. He had caught an elusive murderer, who claimed no more than a nodding acquaintance with his victim, by a thorough search of his home. The man had made a clean sweep, or so he thought, of all the dead girl's effects, but Capricorn – no, not he, he remembered, but a rather lazy young constable – had poked behind a chest on which he had been resting himself and found there a garment, no more substantial than a square of muslin, but enough to have put a noose round the murderer's neck.

Unlikely that Capricorn would have that luck again, but he would like to look. He would not need a warrant; he had an easy excuse. The building containing Mouna's offices had been searched by the bomb squad after the explosion; as Hamed lived next door the same tale would serve. Capricorn would take some of the bomb squad with him ...

It took time to make his arrangements, and it was after lunch when he arrived at the house on Greek Street. Old Hamed was in his office next door; his son was absent. Capricorn and the squad made a careful search on all floors; they were somewhat amused, having been told they were searching not only for hidden explosives, but also for a lady's garments.

The Hameds, Capricorn found, lived simply. The furnishings were scant. Two small rooms on the ground floor served as bedrooms, and nothing there suggested even the occasional occupation of any woman. Drawers and wardrobes held only men's clothing. No cosmetics, facial tissues, hair-dryer. The sheets were coarse, the towels scanty. Two worn toothbrushes sat on the bathroom shelf; the one piece of soap was strong, and smelled of disinfectant. The floors upstairs were all used for storage: nuts, dates, figs – Mouna Imports actually was a business, after all. There was no attic. The small cellar was damp, disused, rat-infested. The electric light did not function. The squad found it harmless.

Capricorn had wasted not only his own time but that of the men of the squad, perhaps a worse sin. Not only was there no connection to be found with the dead girl but, even after all the men's hard work among the figs and dates, there was nothing that might connect the Hameds with the bomb on their premises next door. And why should there have been? Manning was right. He had let his imagination run away with him.

His head, where it had received the crack, ached anew. Before leaving Capricorn flashed his torch on the wall shared with the building next door, idly looking to see if it showed any crack after the bomb-blast. A piece of old plywood leaned against the wall and he moved it aside, expecting his hands to get dusty. They did not. There was no crack in the wall behind it – or was there?

Capricorn had been brought up as a magician. The piece of wood which should have been dusty, but wasn't, propped up against the wall for no apparent reason, caught his attention. The wall seemed solid. There was no plaster down here, the brick had been painted over at one time, but some of the paint was peeling from the damp. Although most of the wall was common bond, there was a fancy arch effect built into the wall near the floor, the kind of work usually only done round an opening. But there was no opening. The two buildings originally had been one property, no doubt, with access both upstairs and in the cellar. Later, this opening, like the others, had been bricked up.

There was a shuffling of feet behind him. The squad, finished, were ready to leave. He had a crick in his neck from stooping; this cellar had not been meant for a man of his height.

'Hold my torch,' he said.

His hands, magician's hands, almost of their own will, patted the wall. The men were forgotten, all his attention was in his fingertips. It did not need a magician, he decided. Simple enough for the average citizen if he thought to investigate. The paint inside the arch looked as old as that on the rest of the wall, but it had been darkened to match. Capricorn's probing fingers had found what he expected. A thin brick veneer covered a panel, carefully fitted. He tried it cautiously, but though it should have been movable it didn't budge.

Capricorn sent a man to the next building with orders not to disturb Hamed. In the cellar an ancient workbench was set up against the common wall. The demolition men had carefully examined the bench after the blast but no one had probed the wall itself. The engineers had merely looked for stresses and strains.

'The terrorists were lucky that the blast itself didn't loosen it,' Capricorn remarked, as he pushed the panel through. His remark was not acknowledged, however, for the man he had sent next door was too astonished to speak. A little poking round revealed that the cellar under Mouna Import-Export was filled with explosives, bomb-making equipment of several kinds, and a handy cache of guns, all well wrapped against the damp. Capricorn found the steel tubes and fulminate of mercury: the suitcase bomb had been made in the cellars and was waiting in the hall for someone to pick up and deliver, no doubt, when Capricorn had stumbled in. This was the cellar that the bomb squad had found innocent of a matchstick.

'They kept the stuff on the other side,' Capricorn suggested. 'But after this cellar was searched and found clean they decided it must be the safest haven in London for a time.'

Brisk now, less oppressed than he had felt since he was taken off the Lawdon case, he sent word to Manning. But he didn't wait. With his heart beating fast he went at once to confront the Hameds.

To his disappointment Tüssün was still out. The old man had not been unhappy when the police had descended upon him earlier, accepting the search as necessary business to do with the explosion. He had smiled his most ingratiating smile and inquired solicitously after the Superintendent's head injury.

He might be less solicitous now, Capricorn thought. Hamed received him in his home attire, shirt and trousers with, despite the pleasant temperature of the evening, a loosely-corded woollen dressing-gown over all. This heightened his look of a rather depraved monk, and indeed he had been at his devotions – account books were spread over the dining-room table. Capricorn told him at once of the cache in the cellar.

Hamed turned green. He clutched at Capricorn's arm and seemed undecided what he wanted to do first, then tried to do everything at once – explain his innocence, his ignorance, and also to remove himself from danger. He could have been acting, but it wasn't likely. Old Hamed was not the kind of man to sit calmly on top of a bomb factory – especially knowing that the bomb-makers were careless. His son, Hamed ventured, could not know of it either. To Capricorn's ear that last remark did not have the same ring of assurance. But the man was undoubtedly trembling, truly aghast.

'I – I suppose I must be arrested,' he said. There was an air of hopelessness about him that Capricorn found puzzling – surely it would be normal for Hamed to be demanding his counsel.

'I am not arresting you, Mr Hamed,' Capricorn replied. 'I want a few more answers, and there will be other detectives coming who doubtless will want a lot more.'

Hamed confessed, gulping, to actually owning the two buildings behind the veil of a limited liability company.

'But I have never even been in the cellars,' he claimed. 'I looked once, but they are too small, too damp to be of any use –'

Capricorn thought of the goods stored upstairs; that was certainly true.

'Yet someone was using them, Mr Hamed, whether you knew it or not,' Capricorn pointed out.

It could have been without his knowledge. Tüssün – if it was Tüssün – could have let his friends in through whichever building was empty at the time. Hamed, embarrassed, confirmed what Capricorn had already guessed. No one knew of it, not even his son, but ... He gave Capricorn another address. It was merely a small flat that he rented, quite agreeable, on Berwick Street, over a shop. Quite cosy. For such times ... Capricorn would understand. Capricorn did.

The father claimed he didn't know of his son's whereabouts. He often disappeared for days at a time. Young men nowadays ... Capricorn took the opportunity to ask if he had seen his son after dinner on the night of Muffy's murder. Hamed of course claimed that he had – twice he had called up to ask for books to be brought over to the office – books that he had been working on at home. He pointed, as if in explanation, to the books now on the table. His gesture was more dramatic than convincing. Capricorn asked if he remembered at what hour he had last seen his son that night. Hamed was all too pat. At midnight, he said, he had told his son he should go to bed, so that he would have no excuse to refrain from work in the morning.

Capricorn asked for, and received, the large cabinet photograph of Tüssün that decorated the chimneypiece. It was a very good likeness. Old Hamed looked lost when Capricorn took his departure, and followed him to the door.

'If no one except Miss Slater knows of the Berwick Street flat,' Capricorn suggested, 'you might be well advised to go there for a time. I don't have to tell you not to go off without letting us know your whereabouts –'

'Of course I would not go, Superintendent.'

Capricorn put a man to watch him just the same, but he didn't expect Hamed to run. Perhaps there wasn't anywhere for him to go. He had the air of a man for whom flight could be no escape.

SIXTEEN

8 MAY

At the Yard Capricorn was not received with the enthusiasm he had expected. His chief congratulated him, of course, on finding the cache of weapons, but with some reserve. He was about to dine with the new Deputy Assistant Commissioner, and spoke over the buzzing of his electric razor.

'He'll be asking about the Mirro case. There was a nasty bit in the *Evening Moon* saying that the Yard has dropped everything for Bridey Lawdon. No other crimes being investigated – a field day for every villain in London.'

Evidently the Commander believed Capricorn had found the arsenal while searching not on the Mirro case, but in the hunt for Bridey. Through the buzzing Capricorn pointed out that he had been looking for evidence in the killing of Muffy Mirro.

The Commander was stroking his cheeks.

'I don't know why I bother with this thing. Present from my wife. It takes twice as long and you don't feel shaven afterwards.'

He asked for, and got, Capricorn's reasons for making the search.

Putting the razor down the Commander stared at Capricorn, much as Bly would have done.

'Plant pots? Mad women? You'd better bring him in on the weapons matter. Though there's no *proof* he knew about them. Counsel will say it's not likely he'd want to blow himself up. Still, questions have to be asked.'

Capricorn knew he had no real evidence yet that pinned Tüssün to Muffy's killing. Yet his feeling now was even stronger. He was quickly dismissed – his chief was short-tempered. There had been talk of his becoming the new Deputy AC, but he had been disappointed. Doubtless there was no pleasure for him in his dinner that night. Capricorn

himself was to have no dinner at all. As soon as he got the
warrant he found that Tüssün had returned home of his own
accord, all unaware of the happenings of the day. He flatly
denied all knowledge of the arsenal – anyone could get in and
out of the cellar, he pointed out, especially on the Mouna
side. There was public access to the different offices, and the
cellar door had always been left unlocked. There was no way
Capricorn could disprove it. His own man had used that
entry.

Irritated – the Commander had stared at the sticking
plaster still on Capricorn's scalp as though the blow to the
head had addled his brain – Capricorn ordered Tüssün taken
down to the station. Manning and others would have to have
their crack at him. If only someone had seen Tüssün and
Muffy together! In defiance of the doctors Capricorn pulled
the plaster from his head. The pain made him wince, but it
did nothing to sharpen his mind.

He sat at the wheel of his car, wondering where to go. As
for every night since Bridey's kidnap, the idea of going home
at the end of his official day was impossible. His home had
been his refuge, but he had no refuge now. Like old Hamed,
perhaps.

Reaching for a cigarette, he found a letter in his pocket,
unopened since that morning. He had been carrying it round
all day. It was from his solicitors – he gazed at it absently.
His inquiry had slipped from his mind, but they had been
unusually prompt. Of course, the papers were on file. Dolly
would be pleased. His thoughts went back to his last visit,
and Boohoo's talk that for him had opened up a whole new
view of the case of the dead Fawn. Boohoo – she had been
the one person in whom Muffy had confided. Perhaps – he
wasn't hungry anyway. Soon he was on the road to Paddington.

His aunts had occupied the same house for about thirty
years. There was no chance Capricorn could have missed it
even in the dark. But that evening no one could have missed
it. The famous sound of a Merlino row greeted him as he
turned the corner and neared what the neighbours called the

Merlino madhouse. Dolly should still have been at the Palladrome; he had hoped to find Boohoo alone. All at once it seemed as though it had been a long day.

Capricorn was not the only one to be annoyed by the commotion. Ivan himself opened the door, disconsolate. His appearance had changed: his hair was cut in a modern style and dyed brown; he wore a new and expensive suit, wide at the shoulders and narrow at the waist, a tie that came from the Burlington Arcade, knotted too low and slightly askew, a cream-coloured silk shirt, grubby – Dolly had never been one to bother with the laundry – and a gold ring with a cluster of diamonds that might be real looked too bright on his work-gnarled hand. Ivan had given up the profession a long time ago.

He was relieved to see Capricorn.

''E's 'ere again,' he said, his head jerking unnecessarily in the direction of the parlour. Tod's shrill voice was plainly to be heard denouncing Dolly and all her works. 'Bloody cheek,' he grumbled. 'Busting in on man and wife at 'ome.'

His voice carried no conviction.

Capricorn's arrival was unmarked by the rest. Boohoo, arrayed in her Fawn costume, was watching from the comparative safety of a fat armchair. Dolly and Tod were both arrayed for battle. Dolly wore her new all-sequined dress and looked like a sausage with scales. Despite the mild weather, she had added an ancient comfort, her purple velvet cloak with ermine tails, somewhat moth-eaten now. Tod was quivering inside a cavalry officer's uniform from the First World War, complete with breeches plus a row of medals, though he stuck to his usual sandals and had added a slouch hat. If he had aimed to dominate by this martial effect, he had failed. Dolly was very much in the ascendant, and although her face was scarlet and her green eyes out on stalks, Capricorn had the instant impression that his aunt was enjoying herself. Even Tod, Capricorn fancied, was not as distressed as he appeared. Having lived so long with the Merlinos, perhaps he found life dull without them.

Emboldened by Capricorn's presence, Ivan spoke up.

'Since we have visitors, Tod Parks, perhaps you'd like to sling your 'ook.'

Dolly grinned malevolently. 'Yes, why don't you 's off,' she said. 'A family gathering, this is.'

'We don't want no old geezers playing soldier,' Ivan went on heavily. ''Specially seeing as you was never in no uniform as far as I've ever 'eard.'

Tod started. 'Listen to who's talking,' he said. 'Ran off when the war started and never was 'eard of again.'

'Lies, all lies,' Dolly snapped.

'You know I was stranded in Australia. Couldn't get back. Nor well enough for the Army, I wasn't.' Ivan sounded sulky. Perhaps he had had to explain many times before.

He gazed at Dolly with an attempt at romance. 'I would have come back after to my Doll, but I'd been told she was killed in the Blitz. Terrible shock it was. My stomach's never been the same since. But as soon as I found out different I took the first boat home.'

It was no worse than the tales the Merlinos told habitually, but Ivan didn't have their swagger.

'Well, this ain't your 'ome,' Tod said shortly. 'Call me what you like, Doll, I don't care. I've found a buyer and I'm selling. It's no good you going on about what Nelly will say, she can get her own 'ouse if she wants one. Or your rich 'usband from Australia can sell 'is diamonds and buy you one.'

He glared at Ivan. Tod had been stirred to jealousy.

'And since you never paid me no rent,' he went on, 'I don't have to give you any notice.'

He was gazing at Dolly now from under his pale, half-closed lids – he was also a little frightened, Capricorn thought.

'But I'll give you to the end of the month to get out,' Tod added, and then looked smug. 'I see you've got a lot of junk collected.'

Capricorn caught Dolly's arm firmly as the first instalment of the junk, a brass candlestick, was about to fly in Tod's direction.

'Good evening,' Capricorn said, 'glad I caught you at home, Dolly. I should have telephoned earlier, but I've been busy. I remembered the other day that Carter and Winthrop had handled the matter of this house shortly after they took care of my first lease. They looked it up, and I have this document from them.'

He handed Dolly the solicitor's letter and turned to Tod.

'You perhaps had forgotten, Tod, quite natural, as it was so long ago.'

His explanation was drowned in the whoops and cries of Dolly who was dancing round the room. Tod had been a squatter in the house when the aunts first moved in. It had come under the ownership of the local council who then, in some scheme of civic improvement, had offered it to Tod for a low price on very easy terms. Tod, whose career had been intermittent at best, had been unable to meet the terms and had sold his interest to the aunts for a modest sum. Over the years the legal papers had been forgotten, as the aunts had always had to pay the bills. But Carter and Winthrop had not forgotten. Tod had no rights in the house at all. Capricorn could almost feel sorry for him; Dolly gloating was a horrid sight and sound. Her hoots could wake the dead.

Ivan, who, it seemed, had risen from the dead, felt his new importance and clutched Tod by his collar, jangling his medals, in preparation to throwing him out. Tod had always looked like a man made of straw, and now the straw was rather damp. He wept. For a man rumoured to have earned a quarter of a million pounds – even if he had lost most of it – his attachment to the house was remarkable. But fortune, in her ill mood, wasn't finished with him yet.

'Just the same, now everything's settled, perhaps I'll do you a good turn,' Dolly said, very smug. 'Without us you don't know what's going on.'

She fished in a jumble of letters and cards, buttons and wrapped toffees on the chimneypiece and came out with a blue airmail letter which she brandished triumphantly.

'Just heard from our Nell today. On the Coast, they are now.'

Capricorn had to adjust his thinking quickly. His aunts Nelly and Tilly were not suddenly restored to an English seaside town, but were playing on the West Coast of the United States, probably in Los Angeles.

'The Clattering Bones have just cabled an offer to 'uman Sadness – a package of four albums and appearances round the country for a year.'

She grinned, showing her full set of porcelain teeth, uppers and lowers.

'No word of any offer coming for you.'

Tod looked totally crushed. Dolly's prediction had come true, all too soon. Human Sadness, with his electrified *banshri*, had taken over his act and left its originator behind. Tod departed without need of Ivan's thrusting hand, clutching feebly for his cape, the emblem of his successful post-Merlino self, which he had forgotten to put on that morning.

The door closed behind him. Ivan returned, rubbing his hands in glee.

'Well,' he said heartily, 'now I've got you to myself, Doll.'

Dolly's dance of triumph halted abruptly.

'Yes,' she said. Her enthusiasm quickly flagged. 'Do us a favour, Ivan. Go and knock up the Off Licence and get a bottle of brandy and a bottle of port.' She took some notes from her handbag and thrust them upon him.

Ivan looked at his nephew by marriage doubtfully.

'Don't mind 'im. Nothing to do with the licensing. Too posh for that.'

Dolly's ideas of the different duties of the members of the Metropolitan Police were all her own.

''Sides, Merle and I have got some family business to discuss.'

Ivan leered, though uncertainly.

'You'll have to get used to talking your business over with me, Doll.'

But he went, crackling the five-pound notes in his hand quite happily.

The room was suddenly quiet. Even the forgotten Boohoo

did not stir, but something made her sad, for two shiny tears rolled from those amazing eyes. For once Dolly noticed.

'We could all use a drink,' she said. 'Tell you the truth, Merle, it gave me a bit of a turn, seeing Tod crawl out like that. Silly sod. Could've done something for hisself if he'd let us look after him.'

Capricorn, though impatient to get to his questioning of Boohoo, had to reply. 'Well, it would be awkward now in any case, wouldn't it, now that Ivan is back?'

'Oh, 'im.' Dolly leaned her elbow on the chimney and looked gloomily into the glass, fiddling with her curls. 'Never do anything with him. Look at those 'ands. He was no success in Australia, all a lot of cobblers, that is. D'you think we don't know what goes on in the business, even down there? A layabout, that's all he is,' she said. 'Dead skint. Come 'ome and he's on the ear'ole all the time. Saw us on the telly and twigged we was doing good. Remembered all of a sudden he was my 'usband.'

Her face darkened. The idea did not please.

She gave her nephew a cunning glance.

'Wouldn't have let him in the house but I wanted to do Tod a spite, see. Now I'll have to get rid of 'im. Wish the girls would come home, and no mistake. Our Till would drive a man out in half an hour. All these new laws,' she went on, grumbling. 'Can he get our money, Merle? Rather Tod had it than him.'

Capricorn couldn't answer at once, but he had some ideas of his own about Ivan. When he had a minute he would make some inquiries. The Off Licence had been obliging, he saw; Ivan was already staggering back under a load of bottles.

'Really, Dolly, I had come round because I wanted a word with Boohoo here. Are you going to work tonight?' he asked the girl. Her costume suggested it. She wriggled her little Fawn boots but said nothing.

Dolly grinned.

'No, she was expecting someone, see, and he likes her rigged up like that. But he must have heard the row and buggered off. Looks a treat, don't she? Clever kid, managed to pinch that from Dean Street and that Marian there is a right

Tartar. Watches everything like it was 'ers.'

'Well,' she added, as Ivan entered, clinking, 'I'll let you two 'ave your talk.' She poured generous portions of port and brandy. 'I'm going upstairs, I want to watch my show on the telly. Think I've got to get rid of that singer of ours, turn the milk sour, he would.'

It struck Capricorn that Tod could have taken his place – but it was no time to mention that.

'Why weren't you at the Palladrome tonight?' he asked rather absently, watching Boohoo's bell-shaped head drooping like a long-stemmed flower to the glass, the rosebud mouth sucking the drink far too speedily. He had a momentary discomfort when he became aware that that dazzling white, beautiful body, in the dress more erotic than nakedness, was having its customary effect on the male, though his mind was far from sexual adventure.

Dolly, gathering her habiliments and bottles and glasses, paused and looked back at him with disgust and disdain.

'We closed,' she said shortly. 'Don't you ever read the papers?'

But Capricorn did not reply. With Boohoo's tear-drenched gleaming eyes upon him, before her mind was fuzzed with more alcohol, he was going to produce his good, clear photograph of Tüssün.

Half an hour later he had a signed statement. Boohoo had seen Tüssün more than once, she said, after she finished work. He was waiting in a doorway near Kettner's. The first time she had been nervous, but the second time he was joined by Muffy Mirro, who had slipped out of the club before her – Muffy hadn't cleared her tables. Muffy and Tüssün had gone off together.

The day that had begun for Capricorn with such strange anguish was ending with hope. It was dark when he made for his car to head home. He would call Manning's office from there, he thought, but he was certain there would be no news. No one was going to find the terrorists without the help of Rory Collins – or himself.

With Boohoo's statement he hoped he had enough evidence now to charge Tüssün with Muffy's murder. And

Capricorn was certain that, proof or no proof, Tüssün was connected with some group of terrorists. Whatever might or might not be provable in court, Capricorn couldn't believe that a sharp-eyed young man, who definitely did not have his mind on his father's business, could fail to be aware of the comings and goings that must be part of the business of an arms dump and bomb factory. Tüssün would have to answer questions now. His own counsel would so advise him. With all his weariness, Capricorn felt more at ease than he had for days.

The road was so familiar that he didn't look about him, but strode along deep in thought. The street lamp was out, but there was moonlight. He should not have been taken unawares, but he was. Luckily, as he approached the car he paused to fumble for his keys. A shot rang out, splintering the side glass of the car. He ducked, another shot hit the car, there was a moment or two of silence, followed by a scrabbling sound from across the road, like something heavy falling into the privet hedge.

A car came round the corner fast but slowed down at the kerb. Two men appeared suddenly from behind the bushes across the road and pushed Capricorn towards the open door of the car. Both of them carried razors. Capricorn had no fancy to be kidnapped. He was a tall, powerful man, and he had flung one of the men from him with a quick judo throw before he heard a familiar voice.

'Get in the car, Super, don't be a fool. There might be more of 'em. Cocky there just saved your life. Come on.'

Capricorn went reluctantly. The voice matched the pale profile next to him in the back of the saloon car. The man ultimately responsible for saving his life, it seemed, was Pete Moletta.

SEVENTEEN

8 - 9 MAY

Capricorn's annoyance at being saved by Moletta was not quickly soothed. He insisted on stopping at the nearest telephone booth to call the Yard, and Cocky and his companion faded away into the night. Moletta stayed until the police cars arrived. His men had done their work too well; Capricorn's attacker was dead from the razor wounds. Later, Special Branch were to identify him as an Arab student from London University, not previously known to have any political or criminal proclivities. And to make it worse Special Branch recommended that if Capricorn *would* return to his own house he must accept protection.

A plain clothes man watching the front of his house, and one in the garden seemed to Capricorn an absurd waste of a small force. But Manning had been worried, and there was Mrs Dermott to consider. Tiredly, Capricorn wondered if he should send her away. Manning's voice on the telephone had been grave.

'The terror campaign is being stepped up. This is the first time a London policeman has been targeted merely for coming across one of their caches. It didn't take them long to organize it, either.'

Capricorn pointed out that he had also arrested Tüssün Hamed, and Manning told him that Tüssün had refused to answer any questions on the weapons matter, after declaring that he knew nothing about them at all. 'Whoever handled that stuff in the cellar was careful,' Manning went on. 'We didn't get a single useful mark off the lot. We might have to let him go.' He sounded very tired.

It was past four already. The clock in Capricorn's bedroom was striking the half-hour. Manning was still at his desk; he must be sleeping in the office. No one could charge him with lack of diligence. But there were still no leads in the search for Bridey.

Manning had continued with his own concerns. 'A pretty pass we've come to. A Chief Superintendent rescued by the worst villains in London. What the papers will make of this – I can imagine. If you tell them it was Moletta's men who did the killing, they're likely to think you're bent. "Chief Superintendent involved in underworld murder."'

Capricorn knew that Manning was right. It was a mess, and not much could be done about it.

'I don't know what kind of job we're doing,' Manning went on. 'The country's being taken over by common criminals and assassins.'

Moletta had said something similar. 'You lot aren't doing your jobs, Super. Country's being run by a lot of foreign mobs.'

Moletta had shown much more interest in the Hameds than Special Branch had so far.

'Thought the old man might be taking an interest in you after you pinched his son. But it was just luck we spotted you being followed on the way to Paddington. The car that followed you dropped off that geezer by your car when you went into the house. So I set Cocky and Sam to cover you when you came out. He was too quick off the mark – nearly got you anyway.'

Moletta had to be thanked, and Cocky and Sam deserved thanks also – though there was trouble ahead. They would have to make statements and appear before the Coroner, and questions would be asked about the carrying of illegal weapons.

'Don't worry,' Moletta said, with his narrow smile. 'Forget about Cocky – you never saw him. It wouldn't do. Sam's all right – he'll be back. The only thing he'll be carrying will be a nice little penknife, with a thing for taking stones out of horses' hooves. He's employed, you know. Assistant in the catering.'

He seemed to be laughing, soundlessly. His chest moved, but his facial muscles were still. 'A regular hero – attacking an armed assassin like that. Our Sam will come out in a blaze of glory.'

He might, Capricorn thought. Unfortunately, as a Chief Superintendent, he himself would not. But he could not care about that now. His mind was caught by Moletta's statement about Hamed.

'You said *old* Hamed ...?'

In the few moments after the attack Capricorn was more forthcoming with Moletta than he might have been later.

'I don't think the old man is involved in this. A quiet type. A sort of superior clerk.'

Moletta laughed.

'Don't tell me he took you in with that tale. He's the owner of Fawn. It was a group of Arabs got up the money; Hamed put the deal together and runs the whole thing behind FCC and Inter-Konto. Not rich Arabs, small business types. Harper didn't get all that much, believe me. But he was glad to get out. Just a little grafter who got on to a good idea. It was June Halliday made it work for him – a good head on her, June.'

His tone suggested a certain regret of his cavalier treatment of that lady.

'Part of the deal was that June stayed on.'

There was no reason for Moletta to lie. So Hamed had been less than honest – but that was hardly surprising. It didn't mean that he had anything to do with the terrorists. He said as much to Moletta, who wasn't impressed. Moletta wouldn't like a rival in Soho; it had been his territory since the death of his former chief.

Of course, Moletta thought that Mouna Import-Export was merely a cover. 'He would lie in his teeth anyway. Taxes – and the Immigration. Don't know how he got here. He was in a few other businesses before he came. Porno stuff. Knocking shops. Came from Smyrna, and they say he was in a bit of trouble there.'

From houses of prostitution to the Fawn Clubs – it was an imaginable leap. Probably a report was on its way from Interpol.

'Yet Marian seems really fond of him,' Capricorn said.

'Women,' Moletta had replied scornfully, 'no accounting for women, Super.'

When they parted, Capricorn had seen the satisfied smile on his face: a wide smile, for Moletta. The Yard really owed him now.

First thing in the morning Capricorn was called to the Commander's office. He had perhaps been struck with the same thought as Moletta, and was not smiling. Probably he hadn't enjoyed his dinner the night before – the new Deputy AC was the son of a former senior officer in the Indian Police and was rumoured to be a hard task-master. A file was open on his desk next to two folded newspapers.

'What's all this about now?' he said, markedly irritable.

'Someone took a potshot at me in the dark,' Capricorn said, wondering why he should feel faintly apologetic. 'Moletta and his cohorts had been following the man and came to my defence – too enthusiastically, I'm afraid, but the attacker was in the act of shooting.'

'You weren't hurt, I see.' It seemed a bow to sympathy, but it wasn't. As Moletta had predicted, Sam had left the station the night before in a blaze of glory, but the Commander was not as easily impressed as the men who had been at the scene. 'This is very embarrassing, Capricorn, very embarrassing. What are we going to put before the Coroner? Your chief defender –' the Commander was openly sarcastic now – 'has come forward with a most unlikely tale. I understand your friend Moletta has been very evasive, referring all questions to you. It looks as though you two are very thick.

'The young man who was killed,' he went on heavily, 'happens to be the nephew of a Saudi diplomat here in London. His father is one of the more important oil sheiks. They are raising Cain this morning. The boy was killed on a dark street by a member of Moletta's gang. Caterer's assistant!' The Commander snorted. 'A likely story. There's no proof the boy attacked you – his uncle says he was on his way home from a coffee bar. How do you know it wasn't Moletta's man shooting at you? It's a question which will certainly be asked.'

Mainly, Capricorn thought, because Moletta had no reason to want him out of the way at the moment. But that didn't sound flattering to the police, either.

'The bullets were found in my car,' Capricorn pointed out. 'The gun was lying next to the attacker.'

'Planted, the lawyers are hinting.'

'Fingerprints?'

'The gun was wiped of course, and then the boy's marks pressed on after death. Certainly there would have been time before the local men got there.'

'But I was with Moletta and Sam,' Capricorn protested, then remembered how Sam – and Cocky – had slipped away when he made the phone call.

'You'll have your chance to explain in court.' The Commander was gloomy. 'You might have been had, you know, by Moletta. A sly rogue. I don't know why you've never managed to put him away. Now his men have killed this apple of a Saudi family's eye and got you mixed up in it.'

He threw the newspapers to Capricorn.

The *Daily Comet* had a headline: YOUTH SLASHED TO DEATH: POLICE INVOLVED.

The *Wire* was more restrained, but perhaps more painful.

The death last night on a street in Paddington of Abdul al-Muhanna, son of the Sheik al-Muhanna of el Hasa, raises some serious questions. According to police, this killing took place during an attempt on the part of the youth to murder a CID Superintendent. They claim he was thwarted in this attempt by two men who came to the Superintendent's assistance. One of the men is a well-known Soho figure, a Turf Accountant and nightclub owner, the other one of his kitchen workers ...

The *Wire* did not give Capricorn's name; the *Comet* had not been so bashful.

'A totally innocent youth, by all accounts,' the Commander said. 'Good student. Never been in any trouble.'

'But why would Moletta want to set up this model youth? Besides, he had no way of knowing that I was going to Paddington last night. I didn't know myself until I actually went.'

'*I* don't suppose he was a model youth.' The Commander

ignored the last, difficult statement. 'That's his family and the lawyers. Perhaps he was selling drugs, like a lot of these youngsters. Not that he needed the money, but he might have enjoyed it anyway – got his own supply. Very likely from your friend Moletta – he's the main supplier now, isn't he? Then ran foul of him somehow – who knows?'

Capricorn did have a prick of doubt. His mind had been full of terrorists – and there was the coincidence of Moletta's seeing him followed. But he dismissed that idea. The whole thing was far too elaborate. The fancy might pique the newspapers, and it would certainly be a bugbear at the inquest, but it simply was not Moletta's way. If he had wanted to get rid of one of his runners it would be a quiet affair with him a long way from the scene where it took place.

'This happened right after I found the terrorists' weapons and arrested the son of the house where they were stored. As you know, I was investigating Tüssün Hamed for the Mirro murder, but I think he's involved with the terrorists as well.'

'Yes, I've heard,' the Commander said, not appeased. ' *His* solicitors have been buzzing. Another persecuted student –'

'A drop-out,' Capricorn remarked.

'Yes, well, it makes no difference. Have you noticed how the description "student" protects any young law-breaker like a halo? Time was, a young man with a bomb or a gun was an anarchist or a felon. Now he's just another student persecuted by the police.

'I don't think we can hold young Hamed.' He and Manning were like-minded. 'It's very suspicious, that weapons business – more than suspicious. Either he, his father, or both are involved, but there's no proof. And we don't have enough on the Mirro case. I read your report. Those witnesses are too unreliable. A madwoman and a prostitute – your Miss Krapp is known to the police in Paddington. I got her former employer on the phone this morning – a Miss Halliday. She thinks the girl's tale is a taradiddle, made up to embarrass the Fawn organization. She had been dismissed for soliciting

customers, and was very resentful. Miss Halliday says she's
the sort of girl who cries a lot and changes her stories day by
day. If that's true, counsel would make nonsense of her on
the stand. I can see that Bly still thinks Hoggett's the killer.
Have you found him yet?'

Capricorn, who now did feel remiss, hadn't even inquired
of Copper how the hunt was going. He had presumed, as he
had heard nothing, that Hoggett was still missing. He replied
in the negative.

'On the evidence it looks like he should have been held and
charged,' the Commander said. 'A very slapdash inquiry, it
seems to me. I've heard the *Sunday Wire* is going to run an
article "Can our present police and security forces cope with
modern conditions?" They've always been friendly to us,
you know. And the *Evening Moon* is beginning a series with
eminent persons giving their views on our abolition and
replacement by something more modern. Well, I'll see you
later at the conference.'

Capricorn wished he could skip the routine conference. He
feared he would hear more of the same, and he did. One or
two other senior officers seemed to believe he had become
involved with an underworld killing. One even mentioned
Copper's working with Moletta on a previous case. Special
Branch knew better, but they remained grim and silent.

Back in his office the date glared up at him from his desk
in red letters: 9 May. Four days – three and a half, now.
Tüssün was the only possible connection with the terrorists,
and the Commander was talking of releasing him. If only,
Capricorn thought, he hadn't arrested him. As a policeman,
his mind hadn't been functioning. Tüssün should have been
under surveillance, but how he was warned. His trail might
have led somewhere ... If only al-Muhanna hadn't died ...

Too late now. He was as bad as the rest, blind, obtuse.
Capricorn agreed with the trepidations of the *Sunday Wire.*
The Yard was *not* coping ...

Only with Lawdon and Burke did he have fellow-feeling
now. Sallow, looking shrivelled, Burke responded to the
personal tragedy without Manning's cool detachment. Burke
came to tell him quietly that Special Branch was checking

very thoroughly into the background of young al-Muhanna. Manning was almost certain he was a soldier of MAY-DAY.

'We've found out more about them,' Burke told him. 'Though so far it hasn't led us any closer. SWW – The Saviours of the Workers of the World – was a splinter group off the PFLP formed by Issa Rashid. MAYDAY is the action outfit – perhaps intended to be one of many. MAYDAY themselves probably don't know – and we won't, now we've lost Rashid. Manning thinks he had employers who wanted to get rid of him. Stopped taking orders, perhaps. Or it might have been part of the usual warfare – Department 5 up to tricks.'

Burke was referring to the subversion department of the KGB. At one time the thought of foreign powers fighting out their differences inside an English prison would have seemed strange, if not fantastic. Now Capricorn heard Burke with no reaction at all.

'One of the prisoners, who has refused to testify,' Burke went on 'did tell Manning that Rashid went over the wall because he was threatened from inside. We can't get out of him who did the threatening – perhaps he really doesn't know.'

'It lines up,' Capricorn said slowly. 'The same people who lifted his marks and planted them. But if MAYDAY is just a group of soldiers cut off from their command ...'

His voice trailed away. In those conditions it would be almost impossible to trace them. Except for Collins. He hadn't even told Lawdon about Collins, much as he wanted to give him some hope. Lawdon was a policeman who went by the book. His mind would be torn between his duty to report to his superior and his longing for his wife. Capricorn kept the hope and the guilt in his own heart.

As if reading his mind, Burke told him soberly that Lawdon's endurance had cracked. He looked at the calendar with the bold figures. Lawdon had gone to the Home Secretary to ask if some of the terrorists' demands could be met – anything to open negotiations. Capricorn found himself hoping that the government would agree – though in principle he was utterly opposed to such a thing.

Burke shuffled off. For the emergency he was indulging in the small comfort of slippers. Capricorn found he simply could not sit at his desk to try to track down Hoggett, whom he still believed to be innocent. He went instead to Charing Cross Road Station to try again with Tüssün. For the rest of the day and into the evening he used all his art to get some sort of statement from the youth, knowing that he was going further than was permitted by the Judge's Rules, but his feeling of urgency drove him on. Tüssün looked in turn arrogant and sullen, but he knew his rights and remained silent.

Leaving Charing Cross, Capricorn drove around, trying Tüssün's photograph on all the other Fawns and the anxious Wendy Doe, who begged him to think well of Tüssün's father. He spent hours scouring Soho and questioning residents and habitués, but no one other than Boohoo had ever seen Tüssün with Muffy Mirro – nor did he find a connection with al-Muhanna.

Capricorn went home at last, exhausted. He was not cheered by a call from Burke. The one lead they had, Bridey's scarf, had not proved fruitful. And Lawdon's appeal was being denied. The government, though sympathetic, were firm. In any event, there was little that could have been done on the prisoner exchange with Issa Rashid dead. The Commander had tried to insist that Lawdon take a leave, but no one seriously supposed that he would do so. The conversation ended without one ray of hope.

EIGHTEEN

10 MAY

At dawn, Bridey's skin was damp, her mouth was dry, and the few objects in the cellar seemed far away. Light-headed, she stared at the grating in the wall, watching the light come in, saying to herself, as she had been repeating for hours, 'Great windows open to the south.'

Sometimes the words brought a kind of happiness as they had done at first. Sometimes she thought of the girl whose face she had struck, the face swollen with tears. The wire handcuff had scratched Natasha's mouth, drawing blood, as Natasha's blow had caused her own mouth to bleed that first day.

She had wanted to kill Natasha then, but that was gone. Now it seemed strange that when they had stood together, no words had come. In honesty she could not have said she was sorry to the girl who would be her executioner – a new flicker of rage spurted up – yet she wished she could have talked to her. That girl, she was no older than Alma, younger than the daughter that she, Bridey, might have had. In all her hard ideas, no different from Rory; in her weakness, no different from any other woman.

There was something she would like to have told the girl, but it was not to be put in words. How she thought the girl was wrong, though not in her own seeing ... perhaps it didn't matter after all.

Bridey had stopped fretting herself that help would come. She knew that she would die. If they didn't kill her first, she would die from the choking in her lungs. She had had the 'flu before, but not like this, and then it was with doctors, and medicines, and staying in bed, and friends coming by to look after her with Charlie gone. Even the Merlinos had come, singing their songs to make her laugh until her chest had hurt more from laughing than coughing and Dolly had tried to stop her laughing by sitting down on Bridey's feet.

It had been a long time since she thought of it, but her own Mam had died of the influenza – no penicillin in Ireland then. The others neither knew nor cared, what was happening, but Michael knew. She saw it in his eyes. But Michael had seen death many times and had learned to bear it; he was troubled, but not tormented. It was the girl who had been tormented, though not for Bridey's sake – it was the girl who seemed possessed.

NINETEEN

10 MAY

When Capricorn arrived next morning, Copper was in his office, a brisk, smiling reminder of the everyday world. He was waiting to make his report on Hoggett.

'No luck yet, guv,' he said. 'If he's playing anywhere, it's in some hole nobody knows. Not exactly a *Melody Maker* headline, our Hoggett.'

While they discussed the possibilities, Copper was taking in his chief's haggard looks.

'Cheer up,' he said, as he was leaving. 'I've got a game on, might do some good. Tell you if anything comes of it. Bit dicey, so you don't have to know.'

There was nothing hidebound about Copper. As usual, Capricorn felt a little better after seeing that cheerful red-head. He wondered briefly what his game was, but his mind soon went back to the events of the night before last. The inquest on al-Muhanna was to be held the morning of the fourteenth – the day after the deadline set by MAYDAY. Al-Muhanna – MAYDAY – Tüssün. The connection was so obvious to him, but ... He took the photograph from his desk, the photograph that Boohoo had so quickly identified. She had had no doubts. But of course the cool, well-bred Miss June would impress the Commander far more than silly little Boohoo.

The photograph itself gave him a new idea – there was one person he hadn't shown it to the day before who might perhaps – He was soon at Baker's studio, lucky to find him in, somewhat startled on a glorious spring morning to find the studio full of beautiful girls wrapped in long-haired furs.

'We work a few months ahead,' Baker explained. 'I'm taking these for *La Belle* in October.'

Capricorn had to wait until the session was over before he could get Baker's attention, and then he was disappointed.

Baker looked at the portrait of Tüssün and said instantly that he had never seen him before. Vague as he was, Baker would not forget a face. Doubtless Muffy had kept her lovers strictly apart.

'An Arab, isn't he?' Baker asked. 'Don't come across too many Arabs in my work. Some of the society ones ...'

He remembered one young man who somewhat resembled this portrait. He went through his files – amazingly neat for such a woolly-minded young man – and pulled out a shot of a youth in flying overalls standing beside a Cessna.

'Never got a chance to use this,' Baker said. 'He flew in the Madrid-Marseilles Derby, but he came in fourth. He never wins. Always has a new 'plane to try.' Baker grinned. 'There's always a chance he'll crack up, so I'm keeping this for his obit. But he's not your man.'

He wasn't. His name was Kerim Khalifah, brother of the society beauty Tima, and the resemblance between the two young men was superficial. Baker could give Capricorn no information on Muffy and Tüssün. The only thing left was to try again with Tüssün himself – or see if Special Branch had done any better. But Baker, who was waiting for some Fawns who were late, tried to keep him a few moments, bringing out his favourite shots.

They were clever, but Capricorn didn't care for them: disco shots, showing celebrities caught off-guard, probably drugged, cavorting in ways ranging from the unseemly to the disgusting. The wife of a great national leader, with her skirt up to her ears, was being tossed half-naked from one man to another as in a scene of havoc and rape. Baker had superimposed these pictures on shots of rubbish heaps on city streets, and some on images of atomic blasts. But Baker, he thought, belonged to a generation which accepted the end of greatness along with the chance of a world destroyed, preferring drugged oblivion to hope, revering depravity. The older man found nothing to say.

It was a relief to see a more conventional piece of work done for *La Belle*: a picture of Lady Lawdon at a charity drive – Palestinian refugees – with a few society beauties, including Tima Khalifah, whose austere, blazing beauty was even more remarkable in her Arab dress. Capricorn was pleased to be able to praise something and depart, but Baker wanted him to wait.

'I could show you a lot more interesting shots of her,' he said, following Capricorn's glance. 'A coke-sniffer – she does some wild stuff.'

He tossed another disco shot at the reluctant Capricorn. The girl with the pure lines to her face had been dancing in jeans and boots and nothing else except some glitter in her hair. One booted foot rested on her supine partner, her head was tossed back in a wild laugh, while she held a stick pointed at the man's head as though it were a rifle.

'Fancies herself as Leila Khaled or Patty Hearst when she's stoned,' Baker said reflectively, 'a lot of them do. When they're not the Queen of the Harem. I could show you –'

Capricorn was spared by an irruption of Fawns, giggling and yawning. But Baker still followed him down the stairs.

'You wouldn't want to put that bandage on again and let me take a shot?'

Capricorn declined quickly.

'Heard you were in another dust-up,' Baker said, in no hurry to get on with his work. 'And Pete Moletta helped you out.'

From the doorway Capricorn could see a bit of the river, and barges chugging downstream. He wondered if the terrorists had taken Bridey out of London by barge – down to the coast, perhaps, and out of the country, where they could rest secure on friendly soil. The ports were watched, but it could have been done ...

'I wouldn't have thought you'd come across Moletta in your line of work,' he said shortly.

'That's where you're wrong.' Baker was still amiable. Nothing annoyed him or moved him to more than a snigger. 'Where d'you suppose people like Tima get the stuff when they're in London?'

The Fawns called shrilly after Baker, and Capricorn

escaped. He might as well have stayed where he was for all the good it did. Tüssün, against the advice of his own counsel, Capricorn believed, remained silent. Manning himself had been to the station earlier, and had had no better luck. A visit to Manning's office left Capricorn with two clear impressions: first, that Manning's men were no closer to finding Bridey Lawdon than they had been at the beginning; second, that he was in the way. The activity was frantic: there were only two days left to go, if MAYDAY kept their word.

Only Burke had a word for him. Burke, who was completely haggard now.

'If only they would send a communiqué – something,' he said. 'They nearly always do. This silence, it's terrifying.'

Capricorn had thought the same thing. But it wasn't a useful thought, and he pushed it away. There was no word from Collins either. He was distracted briefly by a call from the Commander – annoyed, it seemed, with Copper. Copper had been seen strolling about with Meg Hardcastle – who had taken a short leave.

'When we're so short-handed,' the Commander said bitterly, 'you would think Inspector Copper could keep his mind on his work.'

Capricorn made what he hoped were soothing sounds. He didn't believe Copper to be derelict in his duty; it wasn't his way. Certainly not for Meg Hardcastle, with whom he had an amorous friendliness and little passion.

The Commander went on to complain about Moletta and the scandal of the al-Muhanna case. Capricorn listened with only half an ear, while he himself began to wonder. He didn't believe the Commander's thesis that Moletta had set him up as an excuse for a gang killing, but he might know more about the dead would-be assassin than he had admitted.

Moletta was not to be found in any of his own establishments, but Capricorn tracked him down. He was having a late lunch with a woman in a Soho restaurant; the pair were easily visible from the street. He also saw Capricorn and, on a new easy note of friendship that Capricorn noted with distaste, Moletta beckoned him.

'Join us, Super?' he asked. 'I think you've met Miss Halliday.'

Capricorn could have eaten, but he would not eat with Moletta. He had a cup of coffee and reflected that that would probably cause another scandal if he were seen, especially by a reporter from the *Evening Moon.* The woman was indeed June Halliday. He had not recognized her at first glance – she looked different. She had cast off her shabby fur, the suit she wore was well cut but also very much that season's, her hair was done in a fuller, loose style, the pinched look was gone. In fact, probably as much as the sedate Miss Halliday ever did, she glowed. The troubles of her employer and his family had not affected her; fortune apparently was smiling.

Moletta also was pleased with himself. He answered Capricorn's questions without a lot of prevarication and sarcasm for once, and Capricorn was left with the impression that most of the story Moletta had told the night before was true. Except, of course, his desire to preserve a policeman merely as a public-spirited citizen would.

While he devoured his portion of chicken with orange and lemon sauce, which looked very appetizing, he told Capricorn frankly that, as long as he was trying to lock up the Hameds, they were on the same side.

'We don't need this foreign talent over here,' he said thoughtfully. 'They let too many of 'em in, if you ask me.'

Capricorn knew that Moletta would prefer to avoid violence if he could. Certainly he was eager to let the Yard do his work for him. He guessed that Moletta's new attentions to June Halliday were in the hope that he might get control of the Fawn organization, and that she would run it for him.

The room was small, the waiter running about quickly with a clatter of dishes. The smell of the good food was suddenly nauseating. Capricorn felt acutely that he was wasting time – a feeling which had become chronic. He was getting no further on his own case; he seemed to have bungled it utterly, and Bridey Lawdon was still waiting for help that had never come.

Miss June was eating a crème caramel; Moletta had reached the coffee.

'Was there anything else I could do for you, Super?'

He was nudging Capricorn: very likely he had a few matters to discuss with Miss June alone. Capricorn looked at him blankly. For the moment he could not even remember what he had come to see him for, or what questions Moletta had already answered.

'Do you know Tima Khalifah?' he said abruptly. It was the only thing that came to his mind.

Moletta raised an eyebrow. This, he indicated, was hardly the time for the Superintendent to be looking into his illegal activities. Besides, surely that was a matter for Drug Squad.

'I see her about sometimes,' he said.

'Not lately,' Miss June observed, 'she's quite dropped out of sight.'

She hesitated, but Moletta, apparently, gave no signal that she should be quiet and she continued.

'That's unusual in her set. They tend to run together. And they habitually make sure they're being photographed, even if they're just going to get their toenails cut.'

Moletta, having decided that frankness could do no harm, made his contribution.

'She's back in London. Saw her picture in the early edition of the *Evening Moon*. Breakfast with some Yank disco star at the Cavendish.'

'Swooney Loon?' Miss June suggested. 'He's staying there.'

'Said she might go with him to the States. She can do what she likes; old Khalifah is as rich as Croesus. As rich as that bastard whose son tried to do you in – sorry I can't tell you anything on him.'

He grinned, pleased to remember his new role as saviour. Capricorn felt like a man who had been raised from the dead, only to find he'd been raised by the Devil.

But the Devil and his lady had put an idea in his head. It

wasn't much of an idea, but the only other plan he had conceived had already been turned down by the Commander – to book Tüssün on the bomb factory charge, and then offer him in exchange. In fact, the Commander had said they would have to release Tüssün: lack of evidence. Capricorn thought he might as well follow his hunch – if his notion could be dignified by that description.

A call to the *Evening Moon* provided him with the Khalifah girl's London address, a big, popular hotel. On the way he thought of Baker's photograph, Lady Lawdon and Tima – the occasion was the raising of extra money for the Lawdon Fund. The Lawdon Fund, Capricorn knew, provided help to Palestinian refugees who wished to re-settle in other countries. It was a natural interest for Lord Lawdon, whose father had loved the Arab people. But of course, the Lawdon Fund was controversial in the Arab world, the radical groups wanting no part of this scattering of the Palestinians. Most Arabs discreetly boycotted the fundraising, but Miss Khalifah had not. It was only a week after that picture had been taken that Bridey was kidnapped, almost certainly in mistake for Cynthia Lawdon ...

When he arrived at the hotel he was disappointed. Miss Khalifah had arrived yesterday, but she was out. The manager was an old acquaintance, a smooth, perfect hotelier, and perhaps only Capricorn knew that under his urbane exterior he had always longed for a life on the stage, and cherished his signed photographs of the Magic Merlinos.

In answer to Capricorn's questions he told him that Miss Khalifah kept her suite on a permanent basis, and so he was not informed of all her comings and goings, but he believed that she had been away for about a week.

'Her father is here,' he added, 'perhaps he could help you. He isn't one of our permanent residents, but he usually stays here when he is in London. He arrived yesterday from Switzerland.'

Capricorn sent up his card, and soon found himself in one of the hotel's most palatial suites, overlooking the river. A servant showed Capricorn in immediately. The man who greeted him was handsome and urbane. Any surprise he may

have felt at a sudden visit from the CID was not apparent.
He had left a sheaf of papers on a desk, but seemed, if not
at leisure, courteously willing to give his visitor all the time
he needed. His English was faultless – Capricorn guessed
that he had been to school in England.

'I'm sorry to trouble you – merely a routine matter,'
Capricorn said. 'I really came to see Miss Khalifah, but I was
told she is out.'

'If you hope I can inform you of my daughter's whereabouts, Superintendent, I am afraid I will disappoint you,'
Mr Khalifah said. 'I have been waiting for her myself. She
does not inform me of her plans.'

Capricorn noticed a copy of last night's *Evening Moon*
open on Khalifah's desk. The father had been reduced
to the same source of knowledge that he himself had
used.

'*Not* a driving offence this time, I take it,' Khalifah added.
'I did see CID on your card.'

Capricorn smiled. 'No, nothing like that. I am investigating
the murder of a young girl, a nightclub employee who
called herself Muffy Mirro. We have very little to go on, but
both she and your daughter have been photographed quite
frequently by a young man called Baker in his studio. It is
just a chance, but I was hoping Miss Khalifah might remember her – she was quite striking to look at – and if so might
be able to inform us of any male company Miss Mirro might
have had. The photographer himself was not helpful.'

Even the Commander could not object to that, Capricorn
thought. And there was some truth in it. He had provided
himself with a photograph of Mirro in her Fawn costume, and
showed it to the politely attentive Khalifah.

'This is the dead girl.'

Khalifah looked at it for a moment.

'Ah. Most unfortunate. But this girl doesn't appear to be
someone my daughter would be likely to know. She has her
own set. Of course, I can't be sure. If I find her before you
do, Superintendent, I will inquire.'

He smiled. It was a charming smile.

'I have to warn you though, that if she is not one of Tima's set, then very likely she will not have noticed much about her, although it would seem impossible to miss this – was she really called Muffy Mirro? My daughter is interested only in herself and her friends. Quite selfish,' he added – he was a very detached parent, Capricorn thought – 'though of course she is a radical, like so many young people. I wish I had never sent her to a university,' he went on, 'but her brother went, so she had to go. Now she likes to talk of returning to Moslem life.' His mouth twisted. 'Nonsense, but such noisy nonsense.'

Capricorn could well believe that her thinking was muddled, but knew it could not be easily dismissed as nonsense. Khalifah, with his resigned manner and his will-ingness to talk to a stranger, reminded him of someone. It was with a slight sense of shock he realized it was old Hamed, in his enforced single state, bemoaning the destiny that gave him a son like Tüssün.

'My daughter is supposed to be leaving with me in two days, Superintendent. Will your business require her pre-sence longer?'

Capricorn said he thought not, aware that he was hardly being frank. He remembered that the Khalifahs came from Bahrein.

'You are returning to Bahrein?'

'I make my home in Switzerland, Superintendent,' Khalifah told him as he showed him to the door. 'Reasons of health ...'

He smiled again. If he thought himself safer outside the Arab countries, Capricorn could hardly blame him for that. Then he remembered that this man's father was rumoured to have killed his own brother, the head of the family, and wondered what went on behind the smooth countenance of the man beside him.

Khalifah watched as he put the photograph of Muffy Mirro back in his pocket.

'So many killings,' Khalifah said with a sigh. 'One won-ders where it will all end. I see that Issa Rashid, that troublemaker, was himself killed. He was one of my daught-er's instructors at the University. Perhaps we were better off in Bahrein in the days of dates and pearl fishing ... with the woman behind the veil. So many changes, so fast – they confuse us all.'

At any other time Capricorn would have been interested in this cultivated and perhaps lonely man, but now his mind closed tight on the name of Issa Rashid. His interest in Tima Khalifah increased tenfold. After thanking her father for his assistance Capricorn hastened off to the manager again and made a request. This time the manager was hesitant, but Capricorn was persuasive, and was soon going up to Tima's rooms with the key.

The girl's suite was every bit as spacious as her father's. In one way a policeman's life was easier now, he reflected as he entered. At one time such a suite might be guarded by a maid while her mistress travelled. But few women, even of the super-rich, kept ladies' maids any more.

He didn't know what he'd hoped to see. Stacks of terrorist literature, guns in the wardrobe? There were no books in the rooms at all, let alone guns. Miss Khalifah had left, it seemed, before the chambermaid had been in – everything was in perfect order, except there were far too many red roses. Tribute from the disco star, no doubt. The wardrobe was filled with clothes, mostly Western, with one outfit of Arab dress.

Then he found his first conclusion had been wrong. She had been in after the room was tidied. In the bathroom she had left scattered underclothes, a shirt and a pair of jeans. Soft leather shoes had been tossed into the waste-basket. Capricorn examined them curiously. They were hand-made, not much worn, but sopped with water, and the soles were caked in mud. He had an impulse to take those shoes. Miss Khalifah had thrown them away and would not miss them. He wrapped them in his copy of the *Evening Moon* and decided to deliver them himself to the police lab at Lambeth.

He walked out of the hotel into the Strand. The entrance was busy, and nobody noticed him and his parcel. A bus drew up at the kerb; there was a press of passengers getting on and off. A man stumbled against Capricorn; clutched his hand

and was gone, unrecognizable in the throng. Capricorn looked at the slip of paper in his hand – a dirty bit of ruled paper bearing the typewritten words:

Seen shoplifting female necessaries in the town of Epping.

Taped to the message was a small photograph, probably a passport picture, somewhat faded but still clear enough. Liam/Michael stared up at Capricorn blankly.

TWENTY

10 - 11 - 12 MAY

After all, Manning asked very few questions about Capricorn's source of information. If he guessed the truth, he was heroically silent. Liam Doherty had not been known to Special Branch, but now they had a name and a face men were sent to saturate the area. The Special Patrol Group was called in. And as so often happened in a case, once a lead was found, others followed rapidly. Lambeth worked quickly for Capricorn and soon reported the soil on Tima Khalifah's shoes was clay and sand. A tiny pebble of gravel had been lodged under the tongue of the shoe. One of the areas the soil could have come from was the beach and hornbeam thickets of Epping Forest – perhaps near the old gravel pits.

That night no one slept. Manning had Tima put under surveillance, while he and Capricorn studied maps of the area.

'We'll find the place all right,' Manning said, 'if they haven't moved on – that's always a possibility. The real job will be getting Bridey out alive.'

At four in the morning they had their first disappointment. Tima Khalifah, perhaps deliberately, perhaps by routine care, had eluded the Special Branch men. She had gone into a well-known discotheque brilliantly outfitted and noisy and had left with a crowd, in a quiet dress, wearing a blonde wig, taking a car different from the one she had arrived in.

Capricorn cursed himself for not having kept her under his personal surveillance. Only Copper was cheerful – Copper, who came in grinning, triumphant. His plan that had been 'a little dicey' had been simply to dress Meg Hardcastle, herself a tall, good-looking blonde, in Muffy's clothing and have her walk about the streets near Muffy's home, with himself a discreet distance away. With a little padding and a lot of make-up the resemblance had been striking. Copper had hoped this apparition might provoke some action – an attempt to follow and attack, or merely a useful recollection on the part of a witness.

He and Meg had tried this for three nights without success, but that night he had an idea. Muffy, according to Hoggett, had regularly taken a taxi home. But taxis were notoriously reluctant to go so far away from the heart of London. Copper had already checked all the minicabs serving the Soho area without any luck, but it had occurred to him that it would be just as cheap and simple for her to use a service close to where she lived. One of them, near the Tube station, was open all night. None of the drivers had admitted to knowing Muffy, but Meg Hardcastle, suddenly appearing at three in the morning, had brought on something like panic in a young dispatcher.

Copper already had a full statement. The young man had only recently been promoted to night dispatcher. He had been a regular driver for Muffy Mirro – and, a good-looking man, an occasional lover, though their only place of love had been the back seat of his car. He could not have been Muffy's killer – he had been dispatching cars at the time of her death – but he identified the murderer. One night after he had been called to Dean Street to take Muffy home, she had changed her mind and told him she was staying with a friend. She had paid him anyway, but, slightly jealous, he had watched to see whom she met.

On the night of the murder, he had seen her lover again. The young man had come up from the Tube station in a crowd and walked by the dispatcher's hut.

'He looked a right silly date,' the dispatcher had said, 'marching along with a bunch of bleedin' flowers.'

Later the Commander would puzzle why the murderer had made himself so conspicuous. There was no answer, except that he did not realize how conspicuous he was. English people liked flowers; they thrust flowers upon him. Muffy had been estranged – they had quarrelled about her abortion. He had to take his chance while Hoggett was at Clapham Common. The idea of taking her flowers to secure his entry was perhaps the thought of the moment. The dispatcher identified Tüssün's photograph at once.

Now that it no longer mattered, Hoggett himself was found. He had moved in with another cocktail waitress who had a flat of her own in Brixton. She somewhat resembled Muffy Mirro.

With Tüssün formally charged with murder, Capricorn was released at last to devote himself to the hunt for Bridey, with Copper assisting.

'I know a bit about your Tüssün,' Manning had remarked, but they had no time for that now. Manning had charts of the town, the forest and its environs, laid out before him and was pinpointing likely areas.

'They wouldn't be holding her out of doors,' he said. 'It's simply too difficult. They'd be running into picnickers in this weather. They must have taken a house in the locality.'

'The Khalifah girl's shoes were soaked,' Capricorn pointed out.

'Yes, but that could have happened anywhere,' Manning said. 'Possibly she travelled part-way by water – a good way of dodging surveillance. North up the River Lea, perhaps, and then picking up a car to drive eastward. Certainly they wouldn't choose a place near the Hollow Ponds, nor Connaught Water,' he said. 'Much too public. Khalifah – and her brother if he's in it – are noticeably foreign, they'd want to be out of the way. But we'll make the search. We can't afford to miss anything.'

In a few hours they'd shifted their headquarters to the local police station. The tiny town, principally one wide street, lying on a ridge of hill, retained something of an old-world look and yet sparkled fresh and clean in the sun – so different from London and its grime and rubbish that to the tired Capricorn it looked unreal, a Never-Never land.

Some shopkeepers recognized the photograph of Liam Doherty. He had been in town once or twice, buying supplies of food, cooked meats, cheese, milk and bread. One man thought he'd seen him get into an old van, but couldn't tell its make or licence number. But Liam wasn't seen that day. Every man at their disposal was scouring the area, no small task with urban districts hemming the forest on all sides. Men were sent to tramp through the forest itself, with strict orders to attract as little attention to themselves as possible. But, when dark fell, Manning ordered the forest prowlers withdrawn.

'Simply too dangerous,' he told Lawdon. 'If they *should* stumble into MAYDAY accidentally – Bridey would be too much at risk.'

The calendar on the desk said 11 May.

Very early next morning a call came in – a local matter. A woman was complaining – for the second time, she pointed out – about a noisy van using the path that ran by her property at all hours. 'Youngsters – only going down there for no good. Carrying on. Disgusting.'

A sergeant brought the complaint to his superiors. The old woman's house was the last one in the lane. There was nothing beyond it, the local Super told them, except Badger's Pond and the old Ralston place.

'But they couldn't be there,' he said, frowning. 'The grounds were submerged and it's practically a ruin ...' his voice faded away.

The Town Hall was very helpful about the old Ralston place. Built on the shore of Badger's Pond, actually a small lake, it had once been a forester's house, and was later sold to the Ralston family. After the famous Chancery decision of 1874 on forest land, the title was called into question. Litigation went on for decades, and eventually the Ralston descendants moved away. Gravel pits had been worked at the lake's edge and caused the bank to collapse, and eventually the house was surrounded by water. Already in bad condition, it had been abandoned while various civic bodies were in contention as to which was responsible for taking action. The area surrounding Badger's Pond was thickly wooded, with bushes down to the water's edge.

Manning sent in a team, ostensibly picnickers, with field glasses and cameras with telephoto lenses. The house was definitely occupied – figures were made out, but not clearly. A helicopter reported a row-boat drawn up behind a hedge. Excitement rose at headquarters – a painful excitement that became more acute when a policeman reported having seen a girl the night before driving very fast down the New Epping Road, a girl who resembled Tima Khalifah, except that she was blonde. The car the girl had been driving was found hidden in a copse near the lake, next to a battered Ford van. Almost certainly they had found MAYDAY's hideout.

Only Copper was dubious.

'Might as well have gone to Brighton Pier,' he said.

'The warm weather came early,' Manning pointed out. 'Last month it would have looked desolate enough. And nobody did notice them. If Doherty hadn't been spotted –'

He avoided Capricorn's eye. Both of them knew that without Capricorn's mystery informant they would never have found the place.

'Not such a bad choice from their point of view,' the Commander said. 'It's impossible to take them by surprise. We'll have to let them know they're surrounded and negotiate for Bridey.'

Manning glanced up.

'What can we offer?'

'Their lives,' the Commander said shortly.

'They're fanatics,' Capricorn said. 'Young Hamed kept a bomb factory in his own house. At best they would keep Bridey as a hostage while they try an escape, more likely they'll kill her as soon as they know they're trapped. They have announced her execution for tomorrow.'

'There's no way we can launch a boat without being seen,' the Commander argued. 'Even with the trees and heavy bushes, the minute we're in the water we're plainly in view.'

'We could wait until dark,' Lawdon said.

Suddenly they were all talking at once. The room, the largest in the station, was too small for so many men and their voices bounced off the wall with a sound like Bedlam. Chairs scraped, the table was pushed, Copper, impatient, kicked at a waste-basket until it overturned. Only the photograph of the Queen by the window smiled through it all with an eternal calm.

Manning's quiet voice stopped the hubbub.

'Moonlight tonight. And no chance of cloud.'

Burke muttered a curse.

'I don't know,' Manning said. 'Dark would bring other problems. We have to be able to see what we're doing when we get to the house.'

'A helicopter –' an SPG man suggested, but Lawdon shook his head.

'Too noisy, too dangerous.'

Manning agreed, and went on.

'Even if there were cloud over the moon – and the weather people say no chance – MAYDAY could be using snooperscopes.'

'Snooperscopes?' The local Super was puzzled.

'Infra-red devices for spotting a target in the dark. Used by troops in Vietnam,' Capricorn explained. 'I suppose there's a lot still about.'

'They won't be short of money or fancy equipment,' Manning said. 'Our only chance for any surprise is to have the first team go in under water. Dusk would be best. If we send them down from this promontory here –' he pointed to a place on the chart – 'where the gravel pit was, they might pass unnoticed.'

Burke, who had been one of the picnickers, agreed. 'The bushes hang right over the water there.'

The local Super nodded. 'And there's a steep incline, I know. A child fell in and nearly drowned two years ago.'

'The men could come up in the shelter of the hedge,' the Commander said. 'The worst problem would be crossing the few yards to the house ...'

The Clerk of the Works had come up with a plan of the house, dating back half a century. 'I don't think it was changed much after that,' he said. 'Electricity was put in once, but of course there's been no service there for years. Squatters moved in about ten years ago, but it was so uncomfortable they moved out. There must be holes in the roof –'

There were cellars.

'There were no curtains or shades, so that's probably

where they've kept her,' Burke said.

'Damp, if not full of water,' Copper, the country house-holder said, and, looking at Lawdon, was sorry.

'There's good draining into the lake,' the Clerk replied. 'This was the wine cellar, there's a barred window at ground level.'

'Wherever she is, the problem is getting the men across the lawn,' the Commander repeated. 'Almost certainly they'll keep a watch on the doors and the windows.'

'If they get that far,' Copper muttered.

Capricorn caught his glance. Both of them had worked with an underwater team before. They were as good as they could be, but half a dozen men with weapons were never really silent. And very likely they would be noticed as they got into the water, and as they swam across the lake their air bubbles would be seen, and the terrorists would be waiting for them.

'We'll have to lure them out,' Lawdon said suddenly, but the other men were silent.

There was no way to lure MAYDAY out. In the Los Angeles case, Capricorn remembered, the house had caught fire: two of the terrorists had crawled out, but they had come out shooting. Only a tenant of the house had managed to escape. All the rest had died.

'You can't do it unobserved,' Capricorn said slowly. 'The only way is to do it in full view – and have them think it's something else. Now you see it, now you don't.'

Even as he was speaking, he knew already what had to be done. It was quite clear, and it was the only chance. Even then it could fail easily, but it was a chance. That it involved doing the one thing he had dreaded all his life made no difference: that was by the way, a difficulty that someone would have to face. He was the someone, that was the throw of the die.

Manning gazed at him steadily. There were no jokes now about the conjuror's assistant.

'A group of men in waders, in daylight,' Capricorn said. 'Cutting and tidying up bushes on the promontory. Dredging down into the gravel, scooping the stones, setting up bulwarks, sinking earth – getting the lake ready for summer bathers.'

'MAYDAY might start shooting,' Manning said.

'Not if the men don't go any further than the promontory. We could take in equipment; benches, a diving board – a new one in bright colours. It's an obvious spot.'

'But what –' Lawdon, though ready to grasp at anything, looked puzzled.

'In all that activity you can sink a wooden box, a large wooden box. Then you stop, pack up and leave for the day. They might keep watching for a while, but when nothing happens they'll get slack. At dusk I'll get out – there'll be bubbles, but they won't spot them under those bushes. I'll carry my equipment with an octopus rig for Bridey. One man, quietly in and quietly out.'

All the sound in the room at the country station had ceased. The men were staring at Capricorn, those who knew his history and those who didn't.

'The box and some other things I'll need are at my aunts' house in Paddington,' Capricorn ended. 'I'll need a wet suit, webbing and waterproof pouches for a gun, and a good set of burglar's tools. Two snorkel masks with compressed air tanks, and one large tank to hold air for two hours. Some stuff from the lab – I'll give you the formula. It must be in a glass-lined flask with a special spout – my Aunt Dolly will show you, but the webbing must hold that tight.'

While other minds lagged behind, Manning comprehended at once.

'It would be good, very good,' he said, 'but – you're assuming Bridey will be in fit state to swim – if you can get her out. There might be a guard right in the cellar.' He didn't look at Lawdon. 'She could get wounded.'

'Whatever the situation,' Capricorn answered, 'her danger will be less with one man than a party. There's that much less chance of being seen. Even if there's a guard in there I'll have the advantage of surprise. They won't expect anyone to try to get through the bars. With a silencer on the gun we might still do it. If I can get her out I can get her through the water.'

Manning was still doubtful.

'I'm agreed to your getting her out,' he said, 'but then you might need help. If she's unconscious or drugged she'll be a dead weight; you won't be able to use your gun if you're seen – I think the frogteam should go in, but after you, leaving you time to get her out of the house. Once they're there they can hold off MAYDAY. We'll bring up a boat once they land – oars, but with a motor so that we can make speed on the getaway. With Bridey out of danger we can do what the situation requires.'

A senior officer intervened. 'We might be able to avoid any shooting. If they don't open fire we can sit tight. Let them cool off. They might give up – it's happened before.'

Manning's face was expressionless, but Capricorn knew that Manning had no more faith in MAYDAY's willingness to surrender than he had. Capricorn stuck to his point.

'I think that any help would increase the danger,' he protested. 'Much better I go it alone.'

But he lost on that. The decision was taken. His plan would be used, but the underwater team would follow. A timetable was worked out, allowing for Capricorn's entrance and escape. Only he knew many of the variables, but it had to be settled, and the men were to follow him within half an hour of his leaving the box. Capricorn got on the telephone, his voice sounding quite natural as he made his arrangements.

TWENTY-ONE

12 MAY

It was black dark in the box. The slight hiss of the oxygen was a roar – a comforting roar. He hadn't known a blackness like this since he had been six years old – it seemed that night was dark, but it was never a complete blackness, there was always a glimmer somewhere. There was a glimmer now, he knew; the face of his watch; but tight-packed as he was in the box it was hard for him to wriggle his hand up far enough to be seen – and he mustn't start looking so soon. Two hours – it had to be two hours. Dusk would not come until nine o'clock, and he had insisted the team 'knock off' at seven.

'No one will believe the British workman is still at it after that – we're pushing it as it is.'

No use thinking about where he was. They had stripped one of his father's coffins – the aunts had kept them in the attic all these years; they saved all the old equipment. The brass knobs and rails had been removed, the polish sanded off and smeared with earth, it looked utilitarian enough. The smell of the earth had sickened him, but that hadn't mattered either.

Manning's men had made convincing enough foresters and park-workers. They had not moved too fast, stopped to smoke, and occasionally leaned against the trees and chatted. In one of these interludes Manning had mentioned, to Capricorn's surprise, that he also had been investigating Tüssün Hamed, before the discovery of the bomb factory. Capricorn's conclusion that Manning was not interested in the Hameds had been entirely mistaken. Manning had even begun to keep them under surveillance – too late. Manning believed that Tüssün was the actual organizer of the blackmail – he had inherited his father's business brain after all, Manning told Capricorn, though Tüssün put it to a rather different use. Manning had been put off the scent at first because Tüssün had included his own father – Moletta had been right; Fawn was in financial trouble. It was contributing to MAYDAY – no wonder old Hamed was in terror.

Capricorn would have been interested, were not all his senses informing him that he was in a tight-fitting box, with a tank of compressed air, under ten feet of water. He had no great fear of death. As a policeman he had had to face it before – and any policeman knew how to face fear and not succumb to it. But this –

He had recognized years before that his fear of being closed in, buried, was not the fear of the situation itself. He could know intellectually there was no danger in his situation, travelling in a Tube train or squashed in an airport ante-room. But the fear was of the fear itself, the fear that came suddenly, as if from nowhere, striking with a terror that could freeze the heart. He wondered, still, about his father's death – a heart attack, the doctors had said, probably it had happened when he first was lowered in his coffin into the lake where he was entertaining a crowd of fairgoers. The Great Capricornus had had no heart trouble until then. Had the fear struck him at last, as it had done his son so many years before? Had he lain there in the dark, hearing the movement of the water, the faint hissing of the air, his heart seizing in the sudden, inexplicable rush of panic?

It was the Merlino aunts who had saved him, young Merlin, after all. Looking back, he could see what a nuisance a child had been to those hard-working women. When he had run off from his father they had allowed him to trail around the provinces with them, though certainly his father, quietly rich, had never sent them a penny for his support.

He tried to concentrate on his new feeling of gratitude to those Gorgon females, filling his mind with pictures – lodging-houses, third-rate halls – to keep from thinking of where he was. To keep from thinking of panic. He tried to ignore a pervasive smell – could it be real? The coffin had been clean – the smell of corruption itself. All in his mind, he knew that. Panic. He knew all about that too, the terror of terror.

How long had he been there? Manning and the rest were not too far away. Copper, a fine underwater swimmer, was going in with the frogmen – it was good to have Copper. He could be counted on to keep his head. What time was it now? He felt the prickles of fear rising. His heart shook – perhaps the air flow was too meagre, the valve of the tank faulty. He was hot, sweating, his muscles jerked. His hands rose to the lever. He must get out – he MUST get out – He was going up –

As his hand lifted, his watch scraped against his cheek. It was too early. He might be seen, and Bridey's last chance could be gone. With the panic still clutching his guts, he knew he was observing it, letting it happen, consenting to it as he refused to turn the lever, open the lid and float up to light and air. His panic was real, it was present, but he was living through it, and, with the knowledge of his own acceptance, the demons slowly retreated to the place from where they came.

It was a long two hours. The spells of panic came again; he was soaked with sweat under his wet suit; but they retreated sooner. He knew, if he lived through this night, he had overcome his old bugbear at last. His mind was already busy, planning his approach. When the time came, he was prepared.

As he opened the lever, he had changed to the mouthpiece of his octopus rig. The water pouring in was cool against his wet suit. His tools and pistol, fitted into the waterproof pouch on the web about his body, provided enough weight so that he wasn't forced to the surface, and he struck out in the direction of the island.

It was dark, and for a time he feared that something might have happened to slow his watch – an unfamiliar diver's watch – and that he had released himself too late. By moonlight he would be as conspicuous as a traffic policeman at a crossing. Cautiously he surfaced, and blinked to clear his vision. After all, it was twilight, dimmed by an evening mist. The elements were not so hostile after all.

He landed as he had planned, coming up under an overhang of straggling hedge, coiling himself horizontally on the mud. If there was a look-out above, almost certainly the glasses or the snooperscopes would be trained on the opposite shore. He hoped that the frogmen wouldn't be inspired by the mist to approach the water early – Copper would manage to hold them back. Capricorn's heart thumped, less from fear than the idea that Bridey might be there, a few yards away.

Just a few yards away. As silently as his skilled hands could, he drew his pistol from his pouch and stuck it in the holster in his webbing. The second pouch he left as it was. This, then, was the moment. Before him he could make out the dim shape of the house. Dead ahead, according to the plans, should be the wall with the iron grate at ground level.

A shriek broke into the quiet from behind him; instinctively he turned, gun in hand; a gull flapped off over the water. He caught his breath and brushed the sweat from his forehead. Pushing his way through the gap in the hedge, he inched forward on his belly over the grass. No light came from the windows, but he thought he heard the sound of voices coming from somewhere inside – muffled – they used an inner room, perhaps, an old dressing-room or pantry.

As he came within five yards of the house, he froze. In the upstairs window a dark shape loomed – a man's head and torso. He was scanning the woods across the lake. Capricorn lay perfectly still. After a few moments the man withdrew – making his rounds, no doubt. Capricorn moved swiftly the last few yards – the look-out would be back. His hands found the rusty bars almost before he saw them.

Time had passed, but Bridey had no idea of the hours or the days. Her mind was a chaos, with the girl looking at her with accusing eyes, Rory's eyes, a child's eyes, and then it was Charlie and then the girl again. In the intervals when her mind was more clear she did her best to pray, even though she no longer knew to whom she prayed, or why, a strange new game of hide-and-seek when she, who was nothing, searched for something that might be.

She floated into a limbo that knew evil but not hope, where

despair was the breath of every day. But she would not float on, passive, with the ease that was no freedom; she thrashed violently, frantically, if not for hope then for some certainty, a truth to clutch and hold, and in her frenzied reaching it came to her again; despair itself was not of the natural order, it was a deadly sin. A sin – the word was the warning light in limbo – the steadiness in the flux.

A sin – she had wanted to try to tell Natasha – it was mistake, error, a seeing of reality all askew. The despair receded as its unreality was perceived, and Bridey was touched with a sense of awe at the power of the spirit in her that, when called upon, could drive back demons to the gates of hell.

During the night the bouts of delirium returned, but less often than before, and her new certainty was not lost. She slept for a time and woke to see the light at the window. Lissadell ... The fever had broken. She had thrown it off. She still felt weak as a baby, and the stiffness and soreness was there – she saw that she had rolled off the mat, and she pulled at it with hands that were new-born kitten weak. The comfort was a blessing. Silly to care, a woman who was to die soon, and yet the feeling of health was a joy.

She lay, watching the sun grow stronger, beaming into her prison through her 'great window' like the evidence of things unseen. The words came back and now she understood. No longer could she say 'it's all too deep for me' in her old lazy way. She had thought her faith was lost as though it were a button or an old shoe. Bridey Lawdon – she had been like a woman who sat in her kitchen and cried she had no bread with the ingredients all round her and the fire close to hand. But just as bread must be made every day, her faith must be made to live every moment. She felt awe again as she realized it was the very breathing of the soul. Faith – it sounded like a paean in her ears – it *was* the substance of things hoped for, the evidence of things unseen. The substance itself, the evidence now which was eternity.

Her new understanding had brought a peace that was not rest, for understanding itself was a work to do, and one that was just beginning. But her mind was clear, and many old mysteries rose before her clear and bright. Just as in her strange life down here, bounded by the damp walls, beside the broken dish, in the mouldy smell and bucket-stink with her strange new companions, she was and was not the same Bridey as the Bridey Lawdon of the house in Kensington, in all the glory of her household with the piled-up stuff of the new curtains under her eye, waiting confidently for her man – so again would she be in faith when this had vanished, too. Like her, all of this would be gone and yet not gone, and Charlie and these children would be then as well as now.

With the clarity her rage had blown away, dispersed, no longer merely crushed by weakness and despair. She wished she could talk to the fiery Natasha, her brother who perhaps only followed where she led, and Michael – there must be something she could say to him. But no one came.

As the day wore on and approached its close, she heard the footsteps overhead. They were there, but no one came to feed her. Perhaps this was to be her last day on earth. She wanted to tell them what she herself had seen – but how could she find the words? – all God's promise there, bright about them, and faith was joining themselves to the promise to become a part of it –

She saw them all, herself as well as the others, following their way like the stars in their courses. Just as the heavens turned, and one smooth pattern fitted into the next, so they were in the eternal firmament, endless, fixed, damned, unless they reached out to God's good grace and the order changed. Natasha, Kerim, Michael – they were young yet, there was time. She could pray now, and she closed her eyes, and, with the old familiar words, instinct with new feeling, she prayed for Michael who could have been her son, and for Natasha who could have been her daughter – for them all.

For hours she was deep in prayer, forgetting where she was and what was to be. When she opened her eyes at last there was no light coming from the grating above, only a grey blanketing haze. The day was done. She would hear only night sounds now – the boat if it was taken out, perhaps the wind slapping the water, the hoot of an owl, the soft scratching of a mouse. Her ears, trained to the little sounds of quiet, picked out the faintest of noises coming from outside: the slightest shuffle, the faintest tapping at the bars. She caught her breath; the sound ceased. But a moment later she heard a voice, a familiar voice, though it was the merest whisper. Her new knowledge had brought hope and even before she made out the words she felt delight but not surprise. It was her good friend Merle, and he had come for her.

The most acute danger was while he waited for Capricorn's custard to do its work on the bars. First he peered through. The cellar was dim, but Capricorn could make out a figure stretched on the floor. It looked as though its hands and feet were tied. His heart skipped a beat as the figure stirred. Bridey, it must be Bridey, and she was alive. Deliberately he forced himself to wait a moment to adjust his vision and to stare into the corners. There was no one else in the room.

The bars were rough, pitted with rust. They were cemented into the brickwork, but the concrete was crumbling under his hands. He tried them cautiously, with all his strength, but they held. He took the glass-lined vial from his pouch and poured the acid mixture around the base of four bars. The smell was sharp, but he hoped it would be smothered by the stinks of the house, old dirt and human waste, mingling with those of the stagnant waters of the pond. There was nothing to do but wait. Thirty minutes was probably the minimum he could expect, the bars were holding more strongly than he had hoped. God knows how long he had. Certainly he could not wait a half-hour; the frogteam would be coming, and Bridey must be out by then. Perhaps she heard him breathing; her face lifted towards him, but she had the blessed sense not to cry out. He whispered very softly, and she was still.

There was jagged glass on the sill; he would have to warn her. His watch showed minutes and seconds in figures, far slower, it seemed, than any pair of moving hands. He heard a window open above – and then close again. The back door opened, a few yards off, a foot came down on the path. It was over – he must be seen.

·Where do you think you're going?'

A voice, subdued, cold.

'We need bread and milk.' An Irish voice. 'I can hardly take the boat in the morning.'

'There's plenty of milk and enough bread for two days. We won't need more. Get back inside, you take over the door at midnight.'

There was more argument, but the footsteps went back inside. The door banged. Capricorn's hands were trembling, and for the moment he was weak. Incredible – but they'd missed him. From upstairs he heard a woman's voice, cursing.

At last his watch showed twenty minutes had gone. He'd have to try it, but he daren't use metal – the sound would ring all over the lake. He tugged at one of the bars, but it still held, immovable. He tried the next, pulling hard but bracing himself so that he could control it if it gave, no sudden scrape or wrenching noise to alert the household. The second bar began to give, and as he pulled with the slow, careful motion his father had taught him, he felt it moving. The top had been less firmly set, and with a circling movement he loosened the bar and went on to the next.

With three bars loose he could get in and Bridey out. The space was small, the glass ripped the suit from his right shoulder and he felt the acid burn, but that burn was nothing to the rage he felt when he saw the infamous heavy-wire butterfly manacles digging deep into Bridey's crossed wrists. He cut them as swiftly as he could and loosed her feet, but she was very weak, and he carried her to the window.

'Once you're out, stay flat against the wall. Do you know how many there are?'

'Perhaps six, maybe more,' Bridey whispered.

Her voice was clear but her body shook, and her right arm seemed partly paralysed. Capricorn tore off her skirt and padded the sill and then pushed her through to the grass. He followed her out. It was much darker but still misty. They might do it, alone –

Creeping with hardly a sound, they were almost at the water's edge when a shout came from the house.

'Men in the water!'

A rattle of gunfire came from above. Bullets spattered the gravel, and Capricorn pushed Bridey behind the hedge and turned to fire at the gunner in the window.

'She's gone!' The cry rang from the cellar. The man above gave a last burst of fire across the water and tumbled headlong to the ground below. Another man rushed from the house with a repeater rifle, firing at dark figures coming from the lake, and a third stood in the shadow of the doorway, shooting an automatic pistol. Capricorn, hidden behind the hedge, brought them both down, while the frogteam formed a line and passed Bridey safely behind them.

A boat was already on the water and a voice roared through a megaphone: 'Drop your guns and come out! You will not be harmed.'

A machine-gun answered: half the frogteam rushed the house. A man jumped from an upper window; he doubled up on reaching the ground, but a second later his gun was firing. A blaze of fire came from the men on the water's edge; his body jerked, and then lay still. A grenade whistled by Capricorn's ear to fall into the lake. A glow came from the windows – the men inside had lit torches. Capricorn was exposed, and a shot grazed his shoulder: someone was shooting from below.

'Get Bridey in the boat,' he shouted.

Another shot spat at his feet. The glow reached the cellar – Copper was at his side and picked off the marksmen. Capricorn could see him grinning through the mist.

The gunfire from the house was subsiding. More men were landing; the searchers were going from room to room and had reached the topmost floors.

Voices came from the windows.

'In here –'

'Watch that –'

'Petrol –'

'Looks like that's the lot –'

A boat bumped against the muddy gravel.

'Bridey!' Lawdon was with his wife. It was his miracle; she was alive and she was safe.

Capricorn turned, smiling, to see Lawdon's face by torch-light – transfigured – as he helped his wife into the boat.

A high scream ripped through the dusk. It could have been an animal sound, but it was followed by a scuffling noise, a crash, yelling – a gun roared, and a volley of fire answered. A woman's voice howled curses and shrieked, 'Die, pigs – die –'

A window smashed, and the air was full of gunsmoke and the smell of petrol. An explosion roared and the crashing of brick came from the front of the house. The men on the ground jumped back and flames spurted from the upper floors. For a moment a girl stood, a black figure against the window, a machine-gun cradled in her arms. She jumped like an athlete, in a shower of sparks, and charged forward, screaming as her gun raked the line of men, her hair flaming. A frogman fell, an SPG man clutched his arm as his gun dropped in the water, the others aimed their weapons.

'Natasha!' Bridey called. Before anyone could move or think, she slipped from Lawdon and ran towards the girl, her left arm outstretched, into the line of fire coming from both sides.

She didn't die at once. Capricorn was stupefied, but Lawdon took her hand, and she smiled at him. She murmured something, but Capricorn, kneeling beside her in the mist of the lake touched now by the rising moon, could make nothing of her words. It seemed as though she said 'Great windows ...' The sound lost itself over the water.

TWENTY-TWO

13 MAY

The official inquiry would come later, but after the first hours of clear-up and investigation it was decided that none of the rescuers was to blame; Special Branch, CID, Special Patrol Group. Every care had been taken. Bridey Lawdon had been rescued, but for some reason she had given her life to try to save one of her captors. One SPG man had been killed, another badly wounded, several men had been burned in the flash-fire. By chance, there were few injuries from the explosion; the men had been crowding at the back of the house when the front wall blew, and the rest of the old house stood.

'Lucky,' the Fire Brigade had said. The one petrol drum had been fired by an accidental shot. Several others had been rigged to burn if the house were forced, with long fuses to give MAYDAY a chance to escape. The fuses were very simple, wicks that were ignited by burning cigarettes. 'Natasha' had been setting them as the team crashed in. They were still alive because someone in MAYDAY had bought the wrong wicks, the waterproofed kind used in fireworks which required more heat than the burning cigarettes had supplied. The inferno she had intended to create had been put out fairly easily by the Fire Brigade, who had been standing by.

The girl herself would live, but she was badly burned, especially on her face. It caused something of a sensation when 'Natasha' proved to be Tima Khalifah, the international society beauty. Her brother, the well-known young sportsman, was dead – he was the first member of MAYDAY whom Capricorn had killed. Liam Doherty was dead also. One of the older men survived, and it was another shock to discover that he was a respectable British businessman who had returned two years before from Hong Kong.

Most of the weapons and records of MAYDAY were found – some to be used at the inquest, others swept up and hidden away by Manning and his men for their own purposes. MAYDAY, Manning said authoritatively, was finished. Issa Rashid's action group, the Khalifahs, Tüssün Hamed, Doherty, al-Muhanna had apparently been subsumed by the larger SWW after Rashid's death. Not that MAYDAY had liked it; that was apparent from the notes and papers found in the house. They had thought of themselves as an autonomous group of rebels and had not relished being put under discipline.

The businessman – apparently not a 'soldier' but an organizer – had used the code name Cicero, and in the room used by Tima she had written obscenities in lipstick on the wall about the hated newcomer. The rooms were piled with weapons and ammunition, cases of tinned foods, bottled water, milk gone sour, newspapers, magazines and paperbound books, all in the dust and dirt of the years of neglect. The WC was not functioning, but had been used – the house smelled almost as bad as the cellar. Tima's room was splashed with scent, and her suntan lotion and cosmetics lay in a fashionable case on the bare mattress. The packing were littered with drafts of communiqués and manifestos – MAYDAY's puzzling silences, at least in part, had been because they could not agree, apparently, on what to write.

With his comrades dead or captured, Tüssün had broken silence. He, Comrade Ali, was proud to be a soldier of MAYDAY, and wished he had died with his comrades-in-arms. He was to be tried, however, on the simple charge of the murder of Muffy Mirro. Tima Khalifah would have to stand trial for forcible abduction and murder – it was her bullets which had killed Bridey as well as the frogman.

Manning had shown Capricorn her diary, a fine leather affair from the most expensive shop in London. It had been stuffed into her jeans. Her notes, and the corrections, were in an elegant French hand.

18 MARCH
>People's prison selected. Move arms.

29 APRIL
>Fulminate of mercury. Greek Street.

30 APRIL
>Alexandre – Solita.
>>Bridget – wife of member British Secret
>Police.

1 MAY
>ACTION — arrest of ~~Cynthia~~ Lawdon, ~~friend
>to Zionists,~~ enemy of the people

'She had to squeeze that in,' Manning pointed out, 'so some of the diary was written in advance – these jottings are reminders.'

2 MAY
>ACTION — On Colonel's orders, Mirro to be
>executed by Comrade Ali. Thus Comrade
>Ali will make amends for endangering group
>with unauthorized female.

Bly had a comment to make later. 'A formal execution. So all that carving up, diabolical stuff, was just to fox us.'
It certainly had.

3 MAY
>INTELLIGENCE — Comrade Ali reports that
>this prisoner probably has knowledge of this
>fathering child on executed female. The
>prisoner must be executed after Colonel's
>release.

There were no more regular entries until
10 MAY
>Breakfast Swooney Loon.

But across the intervening days were scrawled the words:

'Issa dead! Kill! Kill!'

The hand in which she had written this was markedly different from the rest, large and childish, jagged as though she were trembling.

'Up to that last it looks like children playing games,' Manning had said. 'Though she had trained in South Yemen – paid about five thousand pounds for the privilege, I understand. The weapons cost extra ...' He peered down. 'I wonder who Alexandre-Solita are.'

'Blameless, no doubt,' Capricorn said. He felt as though he were talking from another planet. 'A hairdresser, and the newest designer favourite with her set. See-through plastic jeans made to measure.'

'She won't be wanting see-through anything,' Manning remarked, 'according to the doctors. She'll be badly scarred.'

Manning had been very busy, trying to clean up the ramifications of SWW, his usual Herculean tasks. But unlike Hercules, Capricorn believed, he would come to no successful conclusion. In a world gone sour there were no triumphs.

Lawdon had gone to spend a few days with his brother and sister-in-law at Lawdon Court. Burke, who looked green and was complaining of indigestion, had wrung Capricorn's hand, but the two men had not spoken. Copper, to his embarrassment, was ordered to the Commander's office to reap praise for his work on the Mirro case.

'Well,' he had said, shrugging, 'they'll stop needling me about Meg for a bit.'

His words jarred on Capricorn. Even Copper seemed tainted. Certainly he would never marry the adoring Meg. Perhaps she was, simply, too good. Goodness was cumbersome, out of date, a blemish at the approach of the twenty-first century.

Capricorn had seen Hakim el Hamed for a moment after he had made another statement. He told Capricorn he had obtained counsel for Tüssün and would do what could be done, but he himself was leaving the country.

'I return to Smyrna,' he said, regretfully. 'Trouble with my papers ...' His brown eyes were large and sad. 'Miss Marian's parents, they will not let her join me now. And she is a dutiful daughter ...'

He looked like a very old man.

The Fawns were finished – under his ownership. Moletta would be pleased. Scotland Yard had laboured mightily – to benefit Moletta and Miss June.

Today was the thirteenth, the day they had all dreaded. Now merely an empty day. The skies were not sympathetic; hard blue, glaring. The sun shone efficiently. There was nothing left to do, so Capricorn went home. When he arrived on his doorstep, he wanted at once to leave. His home seemed like no home at all. Every object in it had been carefully chosen – it was the work of many years – each for its intrinsic beauty. Or so he had thought. Now he wondered. He looked upon his possessions with an enemy's eye. So much expensive elegance for a policeman, the son of a mountebank. Collected, perhaps, only to assuage the longings of a snobbish youth who had aspired to the ways of a world he had never really known. And failing absurdly. No family house, filled with the accretion of generations, ever exhibited such consistent perfections. At best it resembled a small museum, at worst perhaps a Bond Street shop window. His dream had no more substance than poor Hamed's for his Paradise Lost at Chipping Ongar.

Mrs Dermott looked at him and understood, perhaps. Silently, she handed him a cup of coffee, but it was only a black, bitter drink that his stomach rejected.

'Your aunt's in a state,' she said, over her shoulder. 'That detective you put on her husband, he found out Ivan divorced her in 1951. Has another wife and grown children.'

Capricorn had totally forgotten his aunt.

'Tod's going to see her tonight. I think perhaps he's no' so bad. A lot of his carry-on was just to get her to take notice.'

Mrs Dermott's voice faded as he let himself out again.
There was a park in the middle of the square with benches.
He went and sat on a bench. In all the years he had lived in
this house, he had never sat in the square. There was no
reason to do so now, nor was there any reason to do anything
else. As he sat he remembered, after all, he had some small
jobs – but he couldn't do them. His friend Rose had left
messages – condolences, no doubt. Delaney had sent a cable.
He would answer them later. Or not.

'Beautiful day, sir.' A young constable, who did not know
him, nodded courteously.

Capricorn gazed, dumb. Perhaps it was, for some people.
But not for him. His universe was dingy yellow, a jaundiced
mass of energy that was he himself and everything he saw.
He was spent, finished, yet there was no rest in him.

He saw Mrs Dermott rushing out of his house, a shopping
basket on her arm. She had got rid of the girl, the house was
empty. It looked lifeless. He noticed a window broken. No
doubt damp had already crept inside. The windows needed
cleaning.

What had Bridey said? He had leaned down, hoping for at
least a word, some last phrase for their old friendship's
sake.

'Great windows ...'

He could make nothing of it.

He looked up. A breeze stirred the young leaves, a bold
sparrow chattered. Mrs Dermott, at the corner, had seen him
and came back.

'I forgot to ask you ... my niece Jean MacDiarmid is in
London. A good girl, but her husband left her and her with
a child in school. She'd like to work a few hours a day. It was
poor Mrs Lawdon suggested I ask her, thoughtful lady she
was ...'

Capricorn's throat gripped. Pierced with grief, he found he
welcomed the onrush of pain, and the hateful yellow thing
that had seemed to be himself dispersed slightly.

'Whatever you wish, of course,' his voice was saying, 'I
would be very happy to have your niece ...'

Mrs Dermott thanked him. 'Have you had anything to eat,

sir?' She peered at him uncertainly. 'I was going shopping for dinner ...'

'Thank you, I'm going to Paddington,' he said.

'Oh, that's good.' Mrs Dermott was relieved at this return to normality, and Capricorn escaped from her thanks and comforting.

He let himself into his aunts' house and noticed that it had already been tidied up, though the charwoman was not in evidence. Dolly was up, dressing-gowned – though she had forgotten her wig – and was rushing aimlessly from spot to spot.

''Ello, Merle,' she said in surprise. 'Did old Scotchie tell you? Tod is coming back. Tonight, after his show. You wouldn't believe it,' she added, 'but I'm all in a fuss. The char didn't turn up. D'you think the place looks all right?'

Capricorn had never seen Dolly so a-twitter.

'Yes,' he said, 'very nice.' She seemed to have dusted some of the ornaments.

'Sorry about Bridey,' she said, 'a real shame. Just like her to get herself killed over some cow of an Arab.'

The pain went deep and it would last, but it was human pain. The evil apathy was gone.

'Want a Guinness?' Dolly said. 'What you doing here, Merle?'

He looked at her, Dolly the virago, trembling like a bride.

'Why, Dolly –' he hesitated, wondering himself for a moment what had brought him. 'Mrs Dermott said you were excited – I thought you might want company to steady your nerves.'

Dolly's mouth fell open. 'Gawd, whatever's happened to you?' she said, not disagreeably. 'Tell you the truth, I am glad you come over. I can use a bit of company. This is a dead 'ole without the girls.'

She came back with bottles and glasses, her voice floating before her.

'Boohoo left me, you know. Didn't like having p'lice about.'

She poured them both a drink, and after a glass of

Guinness she looked at him meditatively.

'You know what, Merle, you could strike me pink, but you're not 'alf so like an 'ead of frozen cod as you used to be.'

And for a moment it seemed to Capricorn that he could hear the sound of Bridey's laughter.